’Til Death Do Us Part

Samantha Baca

Haven Brook Series

Haven

HB

Brook

'Til Death Do Us Part

The Cradle Will Fall

The Ties That Bind

A Very Haven Christmas

Three Strikes, You're Gone

Cover Design: Richard Baca

Cover Image: Adobe Stock

Contents

One 1
Two 7
Three 15
Four 21
Five 29
Six 43
Seven 49
Eight 55
Nine 61
Ten 67
Eleven 79
Twelve 89
Thirteen 95
Fourteen 101
Fifteen 105
Sixteen 115
Seventeen 123
Eighteen 129
Nineteen 133
Twenty 141
Twenty One 145
Twenty Two 151
Twenty Three 163
Twenty Four 171
Twenty Five 177
Twenty Six 183
Twenty Seven 189
Twenty Eight 201
Twenty Nine 207
Thirty 211
Thirty One 217
Thirty Two 221
Epilogue 227
Other Books By Samantha 233
Acknowledgements 235
About the Author 237

One

Mia

The night sky was consumed by darkness as I continued to run, the loose gravel crunching beneath my bare feet. My lungs felt like they were on fire as I struggled to catch my breath, knowing that I didn't have time to stop. I paused for a second and looked over my shoulder to see if he was near. A car approached a few miles behind me, so I quickly darted behind a bush by the side of the road, hoping it was dark enough to camouflage me. My legs ached from running and had started to shake as I tried to hold my semi-crouched position behind the bush and catch my breath. I strained to listen for any signs of movement, hoping he hadn't caught up to me yet. I watched anxiously as the car passed by and waited for the perfect moment to cross the two-lane highway.

"If you walk out that door, it'll be the last thing you'll do. I'll find you and make you live to regret it!" His voice boomed inches above my head. The smell of whiskey was still fresh on his breath. I tried to move, but the weight of his body on top of me, combined with the numbness from the last few blows, had made it feel impossible.

I shook my head, trying to get rid of the image. Now was not the time to think about it, I reminded myself. I had to keep moving. I took a few deep breaths, filled my lungs with as much air as they could hold, and forced myself to push through the physical pain to stand up. Anxiety coursed through my veins as I checked my surroundings, one last time. Far off in the distance I saw the light on upstairs in the place that used to be my home. That reality was gone now. I can’t go home. A single tear trickled down my cheek as I used the back of my hand to brush it away. The immediate sting from the touch reminded me of why I left, why I ran, and why I would never be able to stop running.

The highway was deserted this time of night with very few cars passing by. I took one final deep breath as I quickly ran across the highway and into the tall grass on the other side. The wild grass was waist high and thick, which provided coverage as I moved through it. Exhaustion threatened to take over my body, but I kept pushing, the need to get further away my biggest priority. In the distance I saw the neon light of the gas station glowing against the pitch-black sky, and took comfort knowing that refuge was within reach.

Feeling lifeless, I laid on the floor and allowed the numbness to take over. I looked to the side and saw a pool of blood forming on the tile next to me from the open cut on my forehead. I closed my eyes, wishing the floor would open and take me away. Away from the pain. Away from the danger. Away from Damian. Away from this hell.

One last kick to my ribs, then I heard his footsteps fading down the hall as he went to his study. The door slammed shut and I let out a sigh of relief, praying that it was over. I struggled to roll onto my side as I tried to get up, but my body was in massive amounts of widespread pain. I knew he could come back at any minute, so I forced myself to my feet, taking a moment to catch my balance.

I don’t remember where my shoes ended up, they went flying across the room at some point during the attack. I had scanned the kitchen quickly, looking for them when I noticed my purse thrown on the kitchen table next to my cell phone. Without thinking, I grabbed both and opened the back door. I winced as I heard the chirp of the alarm confirming the door was opened, aware that Damian had heard it as well. I ignored the shakiness I felt as I pulled the strap of my purse over my head, across my shoulder, and took off running as fast as I could. I heard footsteps behind me, which forced me to run faster, making it to the wooded area next to the house before he could reach me. If I had any chance of surviving this, I had to run.

I quickened my pace as I approached the gas station, relieved that I was almost there. Off to my left I heard a vehicle headed toward me on the highway. I had almost made it to the end of the grassy area that merged into a paved sidewalk when I noticed a car slowing down as it pulled into the gas station. Not just any car. I squinted to try to get a better look at the vehicle and felt my heart stop when I saw that it was a black BMW with LAWMAN1 on the custom license plate. I pulled back into the grassy area immediately, taking a few more steps until my back was up against a tree.

Standing still, I hid in the shadows as I watched Damian park his car and get out. The gas station was quiet, only the store attendant and a few customers who were pumping gas. Damian walked over to the man at the closest pump and began talking to him as he pointed to something on his cell phone. The older man leaned in and looked at the phone before shaking his head no and turned his attention back to pumping his gas as Damian continued talking. I saw him glance in the direction where I was hiding and slide further back into the shadows of the trees. I peered around to try to get another glimpse of what was happening when I found the older man pointing in my direction and shrugging his shoulders. Damian looked to where the man had pointed, then back at the man who gave him another shrug which appeared to annoy Damian. For a moment I felt relieved that I was in such a dense wooded area which would make it hard for Damian to use his tracking app to find my cell phone. I debated whether to ditch it in the wooded area so he wouldn't be able to track me or keep it in case I needed to call for help.

Damian walked off and approached a group of guys who were busy loading a few cases of beer into the back of their lifted truck. He showed them his phone and I watched as they all shook their heads no as well. I continued to follow his every movement as he went inside the gas station and talked to the attendant while the group of guys finished loading the beer into the truck and took off. Damian's jaw was clenched as he passed the older man who entered the store while he walked out. The car door slammed shut as he fired up the engine and launched out of the parking lot, heading in the opposite direction. Either he had given up looking for me and planned to go home, or he went back to search the wooded area that I would have come from to find me. I didn't have time to wait and see. Damian's car passed by a few seconds later, the sound fading in the distance. With time so crucial, I pushed my way out of the grassy area and ran at full speed towards the store.

I was almost to the door when I saw the older man walk out, recognition on his face when he saw me. Fear flooded me as I tried to find a way out that didn't involve making a scene. I felt my body start to tremble as we stared at each other, concern etched on his face. My eyes stayed focused on his every move as he slowly opened the door, shielding me from the attendant's view, which wasn't hard given that he was consumed by something on his cell phone and wasn't looking up. I eyed the man cautiously as I backed away from the door, allowing him to open it.

"I saw you coming out of that wooded area, before the black car pulled up. At first, I thought maybe it was a bear or coyote, but then I noticed it was a person," he said as he nodded toward where I had been hiding. "When I saw you run back and hide, I knew something was wrong."

I stayed silent, unsure of what to say.

"He showed me a picture, asked if I had seen his wife. Said she's been missing, and he's worried about her." He paused for my reaction, which was met with continued silence as I took in what he was saying.

"I confirmed that I had seen something running along the side of the road. Might have been a person, it was too dark to see."

My heart sank. My only chance for help. My last lifeline. All were gone.

"Told him that whatever it was, was headed that direction, towards the motel at the other exit." He offered a warm smile as he pointed in the direction that Damian went when he left.

"Then my wife and I decided that we needed some water and snacks." He looked down and patted a brown paper bag that was resting against his hip.

"We're heading to Manchester, New Hampshire. It's about an hour and a half drive from here. You're welcome to come with us, though I reckon we better get a move on it if you don't want your husband coming back to find you.” Another smile crossed his face and he nodded towards a white Camry with lightly tinted windows.

“Thank you, anywhere away from here is perfect,” I said with a smile as I walked with him to the car. I waited for him to open his door before I opened the door and got in. I pulled the seatbelt and glided it across my sore body, fastening it as I looked out the window for any sign of Damian.

An older woman with rosy cheeks and gray hair turned around to look at me, her soft features instantly calmed me. I imagined these were two of the nicest people I had ever met.

“Not to worry dear, we’ll get you out of here,” the woman said softly as she passed the paper bag over the middle console that separated us, waiting for me to take it. I hesitated before reaching for the bag. The movement itself required me to lean forward which was painful. I forced a smile to hide the pain and try to show my gratitude as I pulled the bag into the back seat with me and opened the bottle of water that was inside. I took a long, slow drink, and allowed my body to take the break it needed. It occurred to me that I didn’t know where I was going and I had no idea how I was going to get there, but for now, I was free.

Two

Mia

The drive from Winchester to Manchester took almost two hours due to some traffic delays, however Mr. Bennett was pretty accurate with the original time frame he had given me before I got into the car. I had learned that he was retired law enforcement, and his wife Arlene, had recently retired from teaching for 35 years. Arlene bragged about Joe as much as he did about her. They were obviously a couple in love as they were headed to the airport for a 6:00 am flight to Ireland to celebrate their 50th wedding anniversary. As they continued to share stories with me, I learned that they lived in Colorado but had recently come to Boston to visit her mother who was starting hospice care. Part of me wanted to share personal stories of my own with them, like how I was also from Colorado, but I knew better. The less they knew, the better.

I listened as they told stories about how they met and fell desperately in love, despite their parents trying to separate them early on in their relationship. They had always wanted to have children and start a family; the cards were just never dealt that way for them. The trip to Ireland was the first of many to come, I was assured, as they saved their whole lives to spend their retirement years traveling the world.

My phone vibrated in my hand as a slew of text messages came through after we had reached an area with better cell service. The battery had dwindled down as my phone had been consistently searching for service. I touched the message button and stared at the screen of unread messages from Damian.

Damian: Your biggest mistake was leaving.

Damian: Did you really think I wouldn't come after you?

Damian: Like I said Mia- 'til death do us part.

Damian: It appears you have chosen to part. You know what comes next.

Damian: I will find you, and you will pay for this.

Damian: You can't just up and leave me.

Damian: Did you forget that I can track your cell phone?

Damian: How about a game of hide and seek? You TRY to hide, and I'll let you wait in fear before I come to find you.

I stared at my phone in terror. I knew that Damian was already tracking me and knew where I was. I discreetly shifted my position in the back seat to try to get a better view of the vehicles around us. While I had seen too many over the top movies where the crazy man comes flying up next to them on the side of the road and tries to force them off the road, I didn't necessarily put anything past Damian at this point.

A silence fell over the car when Arlene turned in her chair and looked back at me as she waited for a response. I felt bad, I had been so caught up in the text messages from Damian that I hadn't heard what she had asked. Her face had immediately turned beet red as she realized what she had asked might have offended me, given my silence in response to her question. Her eyes lowered in embarrassment and I watched her look at the scratches and cuts that covered my bare legs, covered in dirt and debris from trekking through the wooded terrain. I didn't want to be rude and ask her to repeat herself, especially when she already appeared to be beating herself up for asking whatever she had asked. Given where she was looking, I knew the question had to be about Damian. Self-consciously, I pulled at the bottom of my cutoff denim shorts, hoping they could shield her eyes from what had happened.

"You don't have to talk about your husband, unless you would like to, Robyn." Joe assured me as he caught my eye in the rearview mirror.

I had no intention of lying to the Bennett's. When asked my name, I froze, and Robyn was the first name that came into my mind, so I went with it. Instincts told me that I shouldn't give them my real name. It wasn't just for my own protection, but for theirs as well. They would never be able to say that they saw or spoke to Mia Stone if they never knew her name.

I watched as Joe reached across the console and took Arlene's hand in his, patting it in comfort as she turned her head to the window, avoiding eye contact.

"I was married for five years. We met my senior year in high school when I went to Boston for my senior trip. He was living there at the time while finishing law school and worked as a bell boy at the hotel that my class stayed at. We stayed in contact after I graduated and, on a whim, I decided to move to Boston. After I moved there, we started dating and eventually moved in together, getting married shortly after." I tried to be as personal as I could be, given that they were so open with me, but in the end, I kept it vague.

"What ended up happening after that, dear," Arlene asked with hope in her voice.

"He died."

Another awkward silence filled the car the last stretch of the drive and continued on as Joe went inside to check in. I knew that he had to be wondering why I would say that my husband had died when he had just talked to him at the gas station. As far as I was concerned, my husband died the day he first laid a hand on me. Someone else took over his body and my husband had never been back since then. A few minutes later, Joe came back with two key cards in his hand and I got out of the car, ready to say my goodbyes.

"This is your room key. Unfortunately, they only had two rooms left this late at night and they are on different sides of the parking lot, so we won't be close by. But we'll be in room 149 if you need anything." Joe extended his hand out to me as he waited for me to take the key card.

"Thank you. How much was the room? I have some cash." I had discreetly gone through my purse and the contents of my wallet while Joe was inside. To my surprise I found a stack of bills tucked inside of one of the inside pockets of my purse. On top of the bills was a torn off piece of napkin with a series of numbers written on it. I assumed this was Jade's doing, we met for lunch yesterday, which was disastrous to say the least.

"No need to pay for the room, it's the least we can do," Joe replied as he rocked back on his heels. I had a feeling that warm and fuzzy wasn't really his thing.

"Well, thank you, again." I clutched the key to my chest and felt relieved that I had a place to stay for the night. Deep inside I still felt anxious that Damian would pop up at any minute which made it impossible to relax or let my guard down.

"Get some rest. Oh, and we're leaving for the airport around 4:00 am tomorrow morning. We'd be happy to give you a ride as well."

"I appreciate the offer, Joe. I'll see you guys in the morning." I smiled and headed toward room 113, the key held tightly in my hand.

As I opened the door, I felt around for the light switch and immediately turned on the lights. I stepped inside, finding nothing to be suspicious, and closed the door behind me. I turned and locked the door, then secured the deadbolt. Anxiety continued to flow through me, so I moved the armchair that was next to the bed and forced it in underneath the doorknob.

There were two full sized beds in the room separated by a nightstand in the middle. I sat my purse down on the bed closest to the bathroom and pulled my phone out. The battery was down to 20% and there were another 7 missed calls and 8 text messages, all from Damian. His texts had turned from angry to sinister, taunting me in each message. There was one voicemail, my fingers trembling as I pressed the button to play the message.

Sleep well, Mia. Be sure to get some rest. You're going to need it. And don't forget to check under your bed, you never know where the boogeyman might show up.

I turned my phone off and put it down on the bed next to my purse. I laid back on the bed and closed my eyes as tight as I could, granted the swelling under my left eye made it painful, and tried to picture a happier time. The last two weeks had been a nightmare. From all of the scary movies I had ever seen, I knew it only really stopped once the bad guy was dead. So that must be my fate, I thought.

A knocking sound on the door interrupted my thoughts and I sprung up off the bed, ready to hide. I knew that he knew where I was, yet I was shocked that he was at my door. Panic filled me as I searched for a way out or a place to hide that he wouldn't find me. My hands began sweating while my mind continued to race.

"Robyn?" Arlene called through the door before knocking a second time.

My heart was beating a mile a minute. I walked to the door and pushed the chair out of the way so I could open it. With caution, I looked through the peephole to make sure she was by herself and that Damian wasn't standing outside with her.

"Yes?" I answered through the door without opening it.

"I'm sorry to disturb you honey. I thought you might need a change of clothes, and possibly some shoes?" She called through the closed door as she leaned closer to the door so I could hear her.

I looked down at my dirty bare feet and remembered that I didn't have shoes. I looked through the peephole once again before I stepped back and opened the door.

"I know it may be 'old lady' clothes but I thought it might come in handy since you don't have anything else with you," Arlene said as she handed me a pile of neatly folded clothes and a pair of tennis shoes piled on top.

"Not at all, this is very sweet and generous of you. Thank you, Arlene." I took the pile from her and smiled warmly at her, satisfaction on her face when I accepted her offer. My eyes darted around the parking lot, looking for a sign of Damian or his car.

"Well, good night." She waved as she walked off. Across the parking lot I noticed Joe standing in the open doorway of their room as he watched Arlene.

I closed the door and locked all of the locks once more, then pushed the chair back to its original spot. The pile of clothes looked to be more than one outfit, so I sat on the bed and unfolded each item Arlene had given me. There was a pair of denim jeans, a pair of black cotton elastic waist shorts, a pink tank top, a white button-down cardigan, and two pair of white ankle socks. The tennis shoes were solid white and appeared to be brand new. Sadness filled me when I thought about Arlene giving me clothes and shoes that she would need for her trip. I had already accepted the gift, it would be rude to turn around and give it back.

I left the clothes on the bed as I made my way to the bathroom and saw travel sized bottles of shampoo, conditioner, and body wash. I stripped off my dirty clothes in record time as I turned the hot water on in the shower. I didn't want to be in a vulnerable position in case Damian found his way in, but I needed a shower to wash away the life I had left behind. I covered myself with a towel as I walked the small distance of the room and made sure each lock was still secure.

The shower was quick and the water was hot enough to be soothing to my sore muscles, yet too hot for the open cuts and scratches that covered the majority of my body from running through the thick brush and trees. I finished my shower and had turned off the water when I heard a knocking sound. I stood still and waited, unsure of where it was coming from. The beating of my heart rang so loud in my ears it made it nearly impossible to hear anything else. My mind had to be playing tricks on me, I thought to myself as I heard another knock. This time it sounded closer. With a towel wrapped around my hair and another around my body, I slowly stepped out of the bathroom and into the open space of the room.

Nothing was out of the ordinary and looked exactly as I had left it. I tip toed to the door and leaned over the chair to look through the peephole. A knocking sound almost sent me flying before I could look through the peephole. I tried to steady myself and pushed forward again, this time making it to the peephole. I looked out the tiny hole and found no one by the door or close enough to knock on my door.

A few doors down I noticed a couple of girls walking out of their room, allowing the door to slam shut behind them. They were giggling and stumbling, apparently already intoxicated. A few seconds later, three guys walked out behind them. Two of them went to catch up with the girls while the other went to the next room and pounded loudly on the door. I immediately recognized the sound and took relief knowing that was what I had been hearing. I sighed and pushed off of the chair as I pulled the towel tighter around me.

I grabbed the black shorts and tank top from the bed and slid them on, thankful for clean clothes. I picked up my dirty clothes from the bathroom floor and hung the wet towels on the bar over the toilet. I made sure things were tidy and dirty clothes weren't left on the floor; old habits die hard. Here I was, fighting to survive my husband, and the one thing that I'm focused on is whether the dirty laundry is tidy. At that point, I wanted to kick my own ass.

One last check of the locks and I made my way over to the bed furthest away from the window and laid down. My dirty clothes were added to the clean clothes Arlene had given me, and all were crammed tightly into a small reusable tote. I always had a plan when I would go to the store for our weekly necessities, and it never failed that Damian would need something in addition while I was there. Our store no longer offered plastic bags, so I kept an extra tote bag in my purse for the times I needed it. And tonight, I had needed it more than ever.

The clock on the nightstand showed that it was almost one o'clock in the morning. My body was exhausted, but I felt uneasy about going to sleep, something just didn't feel right. I picked up my phone and remembered that I had turned it off shortly after I got here. It didn't matter at this point anyways, Damian confirmed he already knew where I was. Now it was a game of him fucking with my mind while he tormented me from the shadows.

I needed to rest if I was going to keep running. I forced myself to relax as I closed my eyes and tried to silence my mind. The room stayed bright with every light turned on and I was alerted by every little sound, so resting proved to be quite a challenge.

My mind was restless while images of the night haunted my sleep. I felt trapped as I struggled to get away from Damian. He was stronger than me and held me in a position that I couldn't get out of. Fight! I yelled at myself. Fight! He's going to kill you! His hands wrapped around my throat, my airway crushed as he closed them tighter.

I gasped for air and shot up off the bed. I stumbled in the dark, unsure of how the lights got turned off. I felt around the wall behind me as I tried to make contact with the light switch. Finally, I found it and flicked it up, fluorescent light filled the small room. I gasped when I looked at the open door, the chair moved out of the way. On the bed by the door sat Damian with his hands folded calmly in his lap.

"Found you."

Three

Mia

I've never had a nightmare that felt as real as the one I had last night of Damian in my room. In my dream I could physically feel him as he strangled the life out of my limp body. I felt the heat of his body as it overpowered mine. I smelt the whiskey that was always on his breath these days. I realized that at some point, my life itself had become a nightmare.

A few minutes after I had been jolted awake by the nightmare, Joe and Arlene had come by my room on their way to the airport and without thinking twice, I took them up on their offer for a ride. I had no idea where to go. The wildest thing I had done in my life was move from Haven Brook to Boston, and while that was scary, it was also thrilling and exhilarating to do something new with my life. Back then, I had a bevy of opportunities and was ready to embark upon my next adventure.

Now I was forced to make quick decisions, to constantly be one step ahead of Damian. I didn't have time to think about where to go or what to do, I had to keep moving. I was reluctant to purchase a plane ticket in case Damian found a way to track me with my credit card, but I also didn't want to spend all the cash that I had on a ticket either. Being the consistent hero that he was, Joe stepped in and purchased the ticket for me using his credit card, winking as he gave me an early birthday present.

I had never met anyone as sweet and genuine as the Bennett's. My heart was sad that they were never given the child that they so clearly wanted. Joe's eyes had saddened when he had asked about my father and I had told him that according to my mom, he never wanted to be in the picture and had left her before I was born. I imagined they would have been wonderful parents. Arlene asked if there would be a way to contact me after their trip, so she could make sure that I was okay. With a sad shake of my head, I declined the offer as I didn't want to risk them having any connection to something linked to Damian. The less they knew, the better off they would be in the long run.

It was bad enough that Joe now knew my real name, when I had to give my information to purchase the ticket. He seemed completely shocked when I gave my real name to the flight attendant, the color drained from his face as he looked at me in disbelief. I had felt bad for giving them a fake name, but I hadn't expected this reaction from Joe. It was as if I had personally insulted him. We said an uncomfortable goodbye with him embracing me in the tightest hug before pulling back as a tear slid down his cheek. Arlene looked as confused as I felt. I watched as they walked off towards their gate, Joe urgently whispering something in Arlene's ear before she turned around and looked at me with the same shocked face as Joe had.

I made my way to the waiting area by my gate and sat down. My purse and tote bag were light enough to continue to carry, however I felt like I might relax more if I took them off and sat them next to me. It was only a few minutes until they started boarding my flight, so I decided to turn on my phone and check if there were any new messages from Damian. I had hoped on the drive to the airport that he wouldn't be able to track my phone if it was turned off, which might give me some additional time to stay ahead of him. At the end of the day, I had no clue how the tracking app actually worked, but I did know that he would be able to find my exact location on it. He had done so many times before.

Damian: MHT is a busy airport this early in the morning, isn't it?

Bile rose in my throat as I tried to choke it down, along with the fear that threatened to take over again. I stared at the phone in my hand for what felt like minutes, before I was interrupted by the sound of the intercom, confirming they were boarding class B for my flight. I looked around, searching for a sign of him. Deep down I hoped he was bluffing, that he wasn't really at the airport, watching me. Maybe, if

I was lucky, he was sitting at home in his stupid recliner, tracking my phone and sending me text messages to make me think he was here. As subtly as I could, I sat my phone down on the arm of the chair and leaned over to grab my purse and tote bag. Without looking back, I walked away to board my flight, leaving my phone behind.

The early morning flight was almost sold out, with each seat filled and luggage bins overfilled. I had searched the passengers already onboard as I made my way to the back of the plane, taking a window seat in the very last row. I continued to watch the remaining passengers board, relieved when Damian wasn't one of them. A few hours later the pilot made an announcement over the intercom, letting the passengers know that we were about to land at Charlotte Douglas International Airport. The airport had been surprisingly busy at 8:30 in the morning on a Sunday with people whipping past me to get to their next gate. I pulled out my boarding pass, confirmed the gate that I needed, and found a place to sit for the hour layover before I boarded the next plane.

I had no phone and no idea where Damian was. For the first time, I was 100% on my own. My stomach grumbled as I smelt the breakfast sandwich a few rows behind me and I was reminded that I had yet to eat an actual meal since before the fight with Damian. There were a few food kiosks around me which allowed me to grab something without having to go far. Ten minutes later I had inhaled a bacon breakfast sandwich and finished the creamy caramel latte. My body hummed in approval as I allowed the food to settle in my stomach.

Time passed quickly as I waited to board the flight to Denver, thankful once we were in the air. I had made the decision to go back home when I couldn't think of anywhere else to go, which meant that I needed to make it to Denver first. Calling Haven Brook "home" felt odd as home should be filled with family members and warm childhood memories. But I didn't have an actual home to go back to, and the family that I did have, weren't really family.

I closed my eyes and tried to picture my childhood growing up as warm memories, unfortunately, there were very few. Images of Chase and Noah popped into my head, a smile brought along with them as I remembered our junior high and high school days together. They were the only good things that I remembered from my childhood. Two rough and rowdy boys who loved each other like brothers and treated me like their little sister. I had no siblings of my own, so I had clung to them as the only family that I did have.

A few moments later their faces were replaced with my mom's. She had a lit cigarette in one hand, and bottle of vodka in the other, as she sat on some guy's lap and laughed at me. I remembered this was one of the first times that I realized just how terrible of a person my mother was.

I was 11 years old and had been trying to get situated in middle school, but a few eighth-grade girls were bullying me. I had gone to my mom, crying, and explained what had happened. They had dumped my lunch tray in my lap in front of the entire cafeteria, then pointed and laughed as everyone else joined in. I was mortified. My mom had thrown her unruly, curly blonde hair up in a messy bun that bounced each time she threw her head back as she laughed at me. She was wearing a red silk robe that was loosely tied around her waist, pulled open to show off the black bra that barely contained her breasts.

I had wanted motherly compassion, for her to pull me into a hug and promise that it would be alright. Instead she had pointed at the stain on the front of my pants and said that it looked like I had peed myself. The harder she laughed, the more her body bounced, which forced her boobs into the creep's face that she was still sitting on.

Mortified again, I fought back the tears that threatened to spill over. My body trembled as it threatened to break down in front of my mom. I squared my shoulders and glared at her, not knowing what to say without risking her hitting me for talking back. It had been her newest thing, ever since the last guy had started trying it on her.

"Oh, you're such a God damn baby," she snarled when she noticed that I was upset. "Get over it and move on, Mia. Life isn't fair and it's time you learned that most people won't like you anyways."

My mouth hung open as I stared in disbelief at the words that my mother had spoken. Maybe it was all for show in front of her guy friend, but my mom had never spoken to me in such a degrading way before. Sure, she had been mean to me plenty of times and I couldn't remember ever hearing her say that she loved me, but this had been different. This had been intentional to create low self-esteem and to disregard how I had felt. She had it in her mind that she needed to control those around her so she could get what she wanted.
"In a few years, your boobs will finally come in and the guys won't have to question whether you're a boy a girl. I recommend you start padding that training bra now and take advantage of finding yourself

a guy to take care of you while you still have something to offer. It's not like they are going to want your *winning personality*." Bonnie continued, making air quotes as she shook her boobs in the guy's face. I watched on in horror as the guy wiggled his eyebrows at me before he leaned forward and nipped at my mom's boobs.

When Damian and I had first met, he wanted to know about my life and where I came from. I kept the details as vague as possible- I grew up in Colorado but didn't confirm which city; I was the only child of a single mother; I didn't have any connections to Colorado and therefore there was no reason to invite any one to our wedding. He pried, and I continued to keep everything locked inside.

Damian's mom had been curious about why my parents would not be attending the wedding, all the way up to the day of the wedding. I had been sad that I didn't have a father to walk me down the aisle or a loving mother who would weep from the front row as her baby got married. But I couldn't make something out of nothing, so I had asked everyone to let it go and we moved forward with the wedding. Damian's uncle, Ronnie, had walked me down the aisle which had made me feel special given the close relationship he had with him. Damian's father had died when he turned 13, and his uncle had stepped in to help raise him. The day had been a day to remember. Hundreds of people had filled the ballroom that overflowed with hundreds of white roses and white sheer fabric adorned across the ceilings, complimenting the crystal chandeliers. We stood under a beautiful handcrafted wooden arch that was covered in beautiful flowers of every color as we looked into each other's eyes and said our vows.

"Mia, I promise to love you always, through the good times and the bad. I promise to always protect you and to provide you a safe place to build our lives together. I'll always be your rock; someone you can lean on and who will stand up tall to defend you. I will weather any storms we encounter and help you to find dry land. I promise to give you the fairy tale ending, the happily ever after, that you've always dreamt of. 'Til death do us part." Damian beamed with pride as he held my hands and promised me a lifetime that I had always longed for.
Startled by violent shaking, I whipped my head up to see what was going on.

"Just a little turbulence." A flight attendant in the open space behind me assured me with a smile, calm and collected.

I let out a breath and focused my attention in front of me. As I had attempted to clear my mind before we landed in Denver, I had inadvertently done the opposite. According to the pilot, we had begun our descent and would be landing shortly. Whether I felt I was ready to go back home or not, I was more than half ways there. I had been so focused on getting away from Damian that I didn't think about what it meant to go home and have to face the life I had left behind.

Four

Damian - 2 Days Ago

"Doris! Is my coffee going to grow legs and walk itself into my office?" I growled at my secretary over the intercom.

I sighed and picked up the stack of paperwork that had been sitting on my desk all morning, apparently needing my attention. It would have been great if there was a note indicating what they needed instead of just being piled up on my desk, waiting for me to be some miraculous fucking mind reader.

The office door started to crack open and I glanced up without raising my head, seeing the meek frame of my worthless secretary approach my desk with my coffee in her unsteady, shaky hands. Doris had been my secretary for the past few weeks while my actual secretary was out of the country on her honeymoon. Why the fuck did I ever approve a 3-week vacation, I'll never know. Lisa promised me that I wouldn't notice a difference with the temp she picked from the agency we work with, but apparently Lisa was also delusional.

Doris quietly approached my desk with the coffee, watching me with terror on her face the closer she came. You'd think this girl had a job of feeding wild lions. Irritation quickly built and I shot her a look that told her to put the mug down already.

She quickly reached over and sat the mug on the coaster on my desk then popped back up and held her hands up like she had just been robbed. For fuck's sake. I let out a breath and tossed the pile of papers back onto my desk and turned to look directly at her while she waited for me to address her.

"Is there something I can do for you, Doris?" I asked sternly.

She reached up and pushed her glasses back up onto her nose and pulled at the hem of her shirt that was three sizes too big and hung over the loose skirt that flowed to the floor. I wasn't sure what fashion statement she was trying to make, but I would guess it was a cross between Amish and a nun. Hopefully for her sake, the outfit would soon swallow her up and be rid of the waste of space.

"Yes, Mr. Stone. Um, there's um a pile of papers that Mr. Ronnie Stone, your uncle, um left for you. They um, need your, um signature. Sir." She continued to pull at the bottom of her shirt as I contemplated humane ways to put this poor creature out of its misery.

"And where are these papers?" I asked sarcastically. "It would be helpful if you actually left notes on what you need, Doris." I felt the need to continue to address her by name. Not to be polite and show that I knew it, but because I liked to watch her squirm like a child who was being disciplined.

"There was, um, a note sir. It's right there." She pointed to a post it note that was sitting on top of the file beside the paperwork she was referring to that I just had in my hands.

I picked up the note and read it out loud.

"Mr. Stone, please sign the attached documents regarding the Heape case. Smiley face." I looked up at her with my eyebrows arched in disapproval of the handwritten smiley face.

"I'll sign these and take them to Ronnie when I'm done. Is there anything else?" I asked pointedly so she got the hint to leave.

"Yes, sir. Um, your wife called to let you know, that um, she was finished with her yoga class, and um, was meeting a friend for lunch."

I wondered why Mia didn't call or text me herself to tell me that she was done. That was our usual routine, she checked in with me everywhere she went, including lunch dates with so called friends. Mia didn't really have any friends and she never meets anyone for lunch.

"Who's the friend?"

"I'm sorry, who's who?" Doris asked confused, sliding her glasses up her nose. Again.

"You said that Mia said she was having lunch with a FRIEND. Who. Is. The. Friend?" I spelled it out for her, knowing that I was being a dick, but she had been irritating me long enough already.

"Oh, yeah, sorry. Um, I think she said Jake?" Doris replied, her eyebrows pulled together in an attempt to help her remember. "Yeah, it was definitely Jake."

Who the fuck was Jake? Mia better not be having lunch with that asshole waiter. My nostrils flared as I remembered his smug face from a few weeks ago and I pictured myself beating his ass into the pavement.

"Anything else?" Doris asked as she rolled forward to balance on the balls of her feet, desperate to leave.

"That's it," I said dismissively as she turned and walked out of my office, closing the door behind her.

I grabbed my cell phone and found 2 missed calls and 5 text messages. Three of the text messages were from Mia and two were from Claire. I opened Mia's first.

Mia: I'm at my Yoga class. I'll text when I'm done.

Mia: Yoga is over, we're going to grab lunch at the cafe next door if that's okay?

Mia: Haven't heard from you, called your cell twice. I left a message with Doris that I'll be at lunch. Call if you need me.

Maybe I was overreacting, but Mia never said in her texts who she was having lunch with. Was she really having lunch with some guy and acted so nonchalant about it?

I reached into my bottom desk drawer, pulled out the bottle of whiskey and added some to my coffee, to where it almost overflowed. I screwed the lid back on and put the bottle back in my drawer.

It was almost empty, again, which meant I needed to stop by the store on my way home.

I took a sip of my coffee to keep it from overflowing and gently stuck my pen in the cup to mix the whiskey in. As I waited for it to cool down, I opened the text messages from Claire.

Claire: Saturday night was fun, too bad we kept getting interrupted.

Claire: Maybe we should look into a conference or seminar out of town so we can get away together for the weekend. I can't wait to finish what we started.

A smile crossed my face as I read her text. She had been with the company as a new paralegal for a few months now and every day she wore tight skirts that hugged her ass and made me want to rip them off her. She was super curvy with big, plump tits that looked like they would bounce nicely in my face as she rode me. I had never been into redheads until she walked into my office to introduce herself and now, I've been walking around with a hard on ever since.

Damian: Sounds like you had something specific you were wanting to do Saturday night. Why don't you tell me about it.

I sat back in my high back leather chair and watched the dots bounce on the screen as she typed her response. I grabbed my cup of coffee and brought it to my lips to take a drink, spewing coffee across my desk as I choked when I read her response.

Claire: After sucking you dry, I'd let you fuck me from behind, letting you watch my sweet ass that you can't get enough of.

I had not been expecting that from her. We had only recently begun flirting and I was still trying to figure out what she was wanting from all of this. No need to wonder anymore.

Claire was so different than Mia. She was aggressive and powerful and took charge. Mia was passive and always let me walk all over her. Claire could walk into any room and men took notice of her. Mia could stumble into a room and few people would notice her. I used to find Mia attractive when we first started dating but she's changed over the last 5 years that I no longer felt like my needs were fulfilled by her.

Sure, she was the perfect wife. She cooked and cleaned constantly. She ran all of the errands. She attended all the bullshit events that I was expected to attend. She was the perfect fit for that life. But she was nothing more than that; hadn't been for a while and wouldn't ever be.

I never intended to start something with Claire, it just happened. There was this chemistry and I liked it. I liked the way she looked at me under her eyelashes as she showed me something in a report that I was reading. Or the way she leaned in close and allowed me to look down her shirt at her tits that were barely contained in her bra.

I debated on whether to text Claire back right away as I took another drink of coffee. Once it had completely cooled down, I finished what was in the mug in one big drink and wiped my mouth with the back of my hand. A few minutes later a loud burp that smelled like whiskey escaped and I was thankful that no one else was in the office with me. If any of the partners knew that I was day drinking, I would be terminated immediately.

I glanced up and saw Doris walk past my office and suddenly remembered that Mia was having lunch with someone and I needed to find out who. I opened the tracking app that I have on her phone and confirmed she was still at the cafe by the yoga studio. I grabbed my cell phone and car keys from the desk and walked out of the office, the door slammed shut behind me. Doris jumped at the sound as fear filled her face.

"Clear my schedule for the remainder of the day," I said as I walked out of the building.

The sun was brighter than I imagined it would be, so I quickened my pace to the car. My fingers felt around as they tried to get the key into the ignition, shaking in the process. Finally, I got the car started and began backing out of the parking spot when I heard a loud honking sound. I glanced in my rear-view mirror and saw a car passing by that I almost backed into. The driver gave me the bird while I impatiently waited for them to move so I could continue pulling out.

The drive was quick and didn't take long to get there when you ran red lights and didn't follow speed limits. I put the car in park and stumbled out, tripping on the curb in the process. I let out a slew of curse words under my breath and adjusted my tie as I tried to play it off to anyone who might have seen it.

I looked around the mini strip mall at the business names and spotted the yoga studio which was a few doors down from Jasmine's Cafe. Bingo. I walked over as I noticed a few tables outside on the patio with a few people sitting at them. I peered around the corner, into the cafe, and saw more people inside than out, and started searching for Mia. I saw her before she saw me. I watched as she threw her head back, laughing at whatever the person in front of her said. I tilted my head to the side, trying to make out who she was with, nothing to help me other than short black hair that was shaved in the back, like a guy's.

My nostrils flared as my blood pressure started to rise with my anger. I stormed over to where Mia was, surprise then fear crossed her face as I got closer to the table. In an instant, I reached out and grabbed her by the back of her head, lacing my fingers into her hair to maintain a better grip. If she thought she could have lunch with another man, she was seriously mistaken. People at the other tables jumped up in response and I heard the gasps as they took in what was happening. The guy across from Mia jumped up and backed away. Probably the smart thing to do, little coward. I watched out of the corner of my eye as he watched me. Part of me hoped that he would try to be the hero and step up to me so I could pound his ass into the ground where he belonged.

"Damian, stop! Let go of me!" Mia cried out as her hands tried to pry my hand out of her hair.

I ignored her as I tried to keep pulling her toward the door, her strength surprising me as she tried to fight back.

"Enough, Damian! What has gotten into you?!" She demanded as she finally got her elbow loose and jabbed me in the side, forcing me to let go of her. Everyone watched us with horror on their faces as I put a hand to my rib where she jabbed me.

"You think you can come have lunch with another man?!" I yelled accusingly at her.

"What man?!" She yelled back, throwing her hands up in the air in confusion, bewilderment on her face.

"Doris said that you called to say you were having lunch with Jake and here I find you with this asshole," I said as I jerked my head and pointed to the guy standing against the window, looking at us. Except it wasn't a guy. It was a very attractive female with short black hair that framed her face in the front, and apparently was shaved in the back. Someone who I would normally try to fuck. From the few times I had ever seen her, I now recognized that it was Jade.

"I told Doris that I was having lunch with Jade. Very clearly, I said Jade. I don't even know a Jake, Damian!"

I saw the anger and frustration on her face and knew that I'd embarrassed her. Instantly I wished that I would have added a little more whiskey to my coffee before coming here. It probably would have helped.

"I'm sorry," I mumbled as I looked back and forth between Mia and Jade.

"What did you say?" Mia asked with her arms crossed over her chest, still pissed.

"You heard me," I said with an assertive tone. While I didn't apologize to her often, it didn't mean that I wouldn't when I was in the wrong, but I also expected her to know her place. Women who thought they had power in a relationship was a dangerous thing.

Mia stayed quiet while she looked at Jade, then back to me. I let out a deep sigh and raked my hand through my hair. It was time to go and quit making a scene.

"I'm leaving, I'm assuming you'll be home shortly as well?" I asked even though we both know it wasn't a question.

"Yes. I will finish my lunch then go to the grocery store before I come home," Mia replied curtly with an edge to her tone.

"While at the store, pick up another bottle of-"

"Whiskey." Mia offered a smug smile as she finished my sentence.

I glared at her one last time before I looked at Jade and walked away. The room began to fill with quiet chatter as I left the cafe, everyone continued to stare as I made it to my car. I drove home in silence as I contemplated the ways that Mia would pay for her actions today when she got home. Disobedient wives needed to remember that even the best of husbands had breaking points, and I had reached mine.

Five

Mia

The speed limit dropped from 75 to 35 mph over the last 10 miles which confirmed I had made it to Haven Brook. I looked around and immediately recognized the small town that I had once called home. Off in the distance there was construction where they were building new homes. The car slowed to 30 mph as I made my way onto Main Street, careful to stay under the speed limit. I didn't want to draw attention to myself by getting a speeding ticket within the first five minutes of being back. Lord knew I needed more time to get settled in without anyone seeing me.

I pulled into the parking lot and found a spot close to the front of the store, which was helpful as it had started raining and I didn't want to get soaked. It had been a while since I'd been inside of a General Bob's store. Memories of my youth flooded my mind as I remembered coming here with my mom as we shopped the clearance racks when I would run out of clothes that fit me. That was the only time I ever got new clothes and was usually tied to a birthday or Christmas gift so she didn't have to get me anything later.

The store was still set up the same as I had remembered which allowed me to move through it quickly and get the things that I needed. The majority of my time was spent on the toiletries aisle, picking out shampoo, conditioner, and soap. I focused on finding the best deals to make what cash I had left go as far as it could. As I added a toothbrush and toothpaste to my cart I caught a glimpse of myself in the security mirror and decided I needed a few more things and went back to grab some hair color and make up.

A hundred and fifty dollars later I walked out of the store with bags loaded on my arms, filled with toiletries, some clothes, and basic food that I could store in the car like granola bars and meal replacement shakes. I pressed the button to unlock the rental car and popped the trunk open as I loaded it with the bags. My stomach growled and I contemplated whether to drink a meal replacement shake or sit down and have an actual meal while I figured out my next step. I didn’t have anywhere to go which made the decision an easy one.

I glanced up and saw the sign for SlowMo’s across the street from where I was parked and decided to treat myself to a home cooked meal. SlowMo’s had been around as long as I could remember. The owner, Moby, was an older man from the south who ended up in Colorado when the love of his life moved back to care for her parents. His love of cooking comfort food led him to open SlowMo’s which became an instant success in Haven Brook.

The restaurant was quiet with only a few patrons inside which was reassuring that I might be able to avoid running into anyone that I knew. When I left Haven Brook the town was steadily growing and had a population close to 50,000 people. I was curious to know what the current population was as I didn’t recognize a single face, luckily, which meant they didn’t recognize me either. I waited for the hostess, hoping I would be given a table in the back. Within a few minutes I had a table off to the side, away from everyone else, and had been looking over the menu when I heard a familiar voice in front of me.

“Well, well, well. Look at what the cat dragged in,” Noah said as he slid into the opposite side of the booth across from me.

My stomach sank. While I had missed Noah, I wasn’t ready to see him yet. I had hoped that I would have time to get myself together and not look like the train wrecked disaster who came running back home, only for him to say- I told you so. Noah and Chase had tried to warn me not to run off to be with some man I barely knew, but I was so desperate to escape my mother and the town that I felt trapped in, that I didn't listen.

I let out a shaky breath as I forced myself to lift my head and look at him. The hint of a smile that had been on his face when I first looked up quickly disappeared when he saw the bruises on my face. He no longer looked happy to run into a friend he hadn't seen in a while, he now looked worried and concerned. My eyes dropped to my menu and I tried to focus on the words that blurred across the laminated page as tears stung my eyes. It seemed it would have been a better decision to skip lunch and find a motel to hide in until my face cleared up.

I had been gone for almost seven years and had no idea if people would think that I had changed much while I was gone. But seeing Noah after seven years, I could see that he had changed for the better. Butterflies danced in my stomach as I wondered what Chase looked like after all of these years. Then dread filled me as I wondered if he was here with Noah, knowing that they had rarely gone anywhere without each other.

As much as I thought I wanted to see Chase, I wanted to give it some time so I wouldn't feel his judgement for not listening, though I was sure it was inevitable. Our last few years of high school brought the three of us closer together, and I inadvertently ended up with the biggest crush on Chase. Which of course meant that his opinion of what I did with my life mattered more to me than Noah's did.

Chase always had this easy-going charisma that made him easy to be around, which meant that he was also one of the most popular guys that I knew. Every girl wanted him. He was incredibly good looking with dark brown eyes that bordered on black, depending on his mood. Back in the day his jet-black hair was short enough to keep it from being too wild, but always slightly disheveled as the girls couldn't keep their fingers out of it.

"Mia," Noah called, breaking my focus on the menu and unnecessary thoughts about a crush I should be over after seven years. Butterflies still filled my belly as I thought about running into him. I let out a sigh when I realized how off course my life had gotten and reminded myself that I needed to live in the present and forget about the past.

"What's going on, Mia?" Noah asked in the brotherly tone he used to use when we were younger.

"Nothing. It's good to see you," I replied with a fake smile as I gave up and finally looked at him.

"Bullshit. Did that guy in Boston do this to you?" He pointed at the bruises on my face.

"Let it go, Noah." I didn't feel like getting into it with Noah nor did I want to pick up where we had left off seven years ago.
"You know Mia, I let things go seven years ago. And that was the biggest mistake of my life. I'm not about to keep making the same mistakes. So, either tell me what happened, or I'll get Chase involved and we'll find a way to figure out what happened," Noah said sternly as he leaned back and folded his arms across his chest. I had made the mistake of confessing my feelings for Chase to Noah one night after too many beers. One of the reasons I hardly ever drank since then.

"You're really going to go there? Really?" I asked with an eyebrow arched as I leaned forward in the booth to look at him. "I thought we were friends Noah." I laid the sarcasm on heavy with the last sentence, which he knew was a jab, not a question.

"Okay, fine. It was a low blow with the Chase comment. I'm sorry. One of us had to mention him." He let out a sigh and winked.

"But really Mia, you can't come back to Haven Brook, covered in bruises, and not tell me what's going on. People are going to ask because they are nosey. I'm asking because you're family, and I care. Let me help you, Mia."

"I don't need help." I lowered my eyes so he couldn't see the lie I tried desperately to hide as I bit my bottom lip to keep from crying.

"Really?" He said studying me, not buying a word I said.

"So, where are you staying? Are you going back to Bonnie's?" I felt his eyes on me as he watched for my reaction.

My head flew up, anger evident on my face. He knew my relationship with my mom had never been good and that I vowed to never see her again when I left for Boston.

"Okay, so that's a no. Then where are you staying? That Mazda you pulled up in?" He nodded outside to where I had parked.

"How do you know what I'm driving? What are you, some sort of secret spy since I left?" I taunted as I tried to loosen up. I adjusted my back against the worn-out leather of the booth and tried to make myself look more relaxed. If I was going to be back for a little bit, I would need at least a friend or two. It didn't do any good to burn every bridge along the way.

"I was finishing a phone call in my car when you came in. Nearly shit myself when I thought I saw the ghost of Mia Johnson walking into the same place I was about to have lunch." He smiled and I was thankful to see the playful side of Noah come back. He gave me a hard time like a big brother would, but at the end of the day, he was always Noah. The most kindhearted, genuine person I had ever known.

The waitress walked toward our table, confusion on her face when she saw Noah sitting opposite of me. I smiled at her as Noah turned to look at who I had been smiling at.

"Two today?" she asked when she reached our table.

"Yes, just the two of us." I felt a blush creep up my neck, assuming she must think we were here on a date.

"What can I get you to drink?" She looked back and forth between Noah and I, her pen hovered above her notepad, waiting to for our answer.

"Water is fine for me, please." I pushed my menu to the side of me. I had been here a million times and knew the menu better than their own staff probably did. In the few minutes that I had been back, I had already found that very few things changed around here.

"Same for me," Noah said as he reached into his front pocket and pulled out his cell phone. I watched as he swiped his phone a few times, silencing the vibration.

"Do you all need a few minutes to look over the menu?" She pointed her pen toward the menu laying in front of me.

"I think I'm ready, if the lady is." Noah winked at her before they both turned their attention to me. He was always such a womanizer, even when he wasn't trying to be. I hated being the center of attention, even in situations like this.

"I'll have the biscuits and gravy, with an extra sausage patty, please." I smiled before looking away and breaking eye contact, making sure she knew that I was done.

"I'll have the same."

"You got it. Be right back with those waters." She pushed the pen into the messy bun on top of her head and grabbed the menu off the table before heading towards the kitchen to put in our order.
I felt Noah looking at me and desperately wished I could get out from under his intense gaze. He was studying me, and I knew he was going to keep pushing until I talked about what had happened and why I was back. I didn't know if I was ready to talk about it yet. Every few minutes I was still searching around me, looking for a sign that Damian was there.

I had made it to Denver without any problems and knew that if he dug deep enough, Damian would be able to find my name when I rented a car. I went with one of the bigger car rental companies, hoping they were harder to hack and relying on them to maintain customer confidentiality. Granted it was usually fake in the movies, I still entertained the thought of him finding a connection to someone who could access their system and tell him what I was driving.

I had picked up a prepaid cell phone while in Denver in case I broke down somewhere or needed help. The cash that Jade had left me was dwindling quickly between the rental car, the cell phone, gas, and my visit to General Bob's. While Noah knew that I needed help, I don't think anyone, including myself, knew just how much help I needed. I had $250 left to my name to pay for this meal and hopefully find a cheap motel to stay in unless I wanted to live in the car for a few days. If I was going to stay in Haven Brook for a while then I needed to find a job ASAP.

We sat in silence for a few minutes, my thoughts scattered everywhere. Noah caught my eye and for a moment I remembered being a teenager and fearing my mother. Noah would always reassure me that he would protect me as he walked me to his house to stay for the night. Comfort embraced me and for a moment I wanted to sink into that feeling and allow Noah to help me again. To have that feeling of comfort again, knowing I was safe, but I knew better. If I told him what happened, I wouldn't be able to protect him if Damian ended up finding me.

"I remember when we were in junior high. You were constantly fighting with your mom and she kept threatening to kick you out of the house. One afternoon you had gone home after school and there was a torn-up suitcase on the front step with all of your stuff inside. You tried to get in, but she had changed all of the locks. When you knocked on the door, she looked out the window and laughed at you." Noah took a deep breath while he continued to look at me. "I found you a few blocks away, hiding in between the dumpsters, crying."

"I remember that day."

"You looked so defeated, Mia. The girl that I once knew, she was gone. I searched your eyes and I couldn't find her. But then you agreed to go home with me and my parents refused to let you leave. You fought us on trying to help you, but in the end, you stayed with us that summer and you were a tremendous help to my mother. After a few days of being with us, you felt safe again, and I saw the light come back to your eyes." His voice grew softer.

I wasn't sure why he was bringing this story up, but it brought a tear to my eye. I was so young and naive; I didn't know what to do when my mom kicked me out. Left to fend for myself, I was scared and had no idea where to go for help. I had decided that I would figure it out on my own. I would be strong. I would become a survivor. Noah's parents sat me down and told me that at 12 years old, I shouldn't have to survive my childhood. They explained to me what a parent should and shouldn't do as their eyes welled up with tears. I listened as they discussed their expectations for me and outlined the rules of their house. My mind was blown when things like going to school every day, doing my homework every night, and no drinking were on their list of requirements. These were things that I did on my own because I wanted to do well in school. It felt odd to feel like these adults cared about me, that they included me as part of their family.

"The light in your eye is gone again, Mia. Let me help you," Noah coaxed. "It's okay to trust me, I would never hurt you or let anyone else hurt you."

His words broke my heart and before I could stop myself the tears flowed down my cheeks as my body shook with every breath I tried to take. I had been holding everything inside since our first fight a few weeks ago and I knew that it would eventually consume me. It would eat away at the person that I had once been until there was nothing left. I desperately wanted to find the carefree, happy girl that I had been for a short period of time, before my life crumbled before me.

Noah quickly slid out of his side of the booth and into mine as he wrapped his arms around me and held me as I cried. I prayed that for just a moment, I could allow myself to have the comfort that he offered without having to fear Damian. I closed my eyes and allowed my breakdown to continue. A tear fell for every time Damian had called me a name or insulted me. Another tear for every time he hit me. More tears fell as I accepted that I had reached a point in my life where I once again needed help. I needed someone to save me because for so long I had been allowing myself to drown. For once, I wanted to live. I wanted to fight and I wanted to figure out my path in life. Footsteps approached and my eyes flew open, relieved when it was just the waitress bringing our glasses of water, and not Damian. She looked at me with concern and I struggled to smile, my face still buried in Noah's shoulder. I watched as she sat the glasses down on the table and pulled two straws out of her apron, setting them beside the glasses before she walked away.

I pulled away from Noah and reached behind me for a napkin to dry my face. My breathing was staggered as my body tried to recover from the breakdown. I tried to take a few slow, deep breathes as I blew my nose and wiped my eyes again before looking at Noah. I set the used napkins off to the side by the wall and slowly turned to look at Noah as I saw the waitress coming back with our food. Noah smiled up at her as he waited for her to set our plates down before getting up to take his seat on the other side of the booth.

"You all need anything else?" she asked while studying my face. My instincts told me that she was likely a mother with the way she eyed me with concern and stared Noah down for possibly making me cry. I shook my head no as I unwrapped the silverware from the napkin and set it to the side of my plate.

She walked away, throwing one more accusatory glance at Noah. I tried to hide my laughter, but I had already reached the point of hysteria and it found its way out. I tried to cover my face behind my napkin as I laughed harder than I had in years. The thought of this woman giving Noah dirty looks and judging him for making me cry sent me into a frenzy. I felt Noah pull my napkin down and laughed even harder when he had a full-blown smile across his face.

“Thanks for turning me into Ike Turner with the waitress,” he joked as he tossed his wadded-up straw wrapper at me.

I tried to stop laughing but it was impossible and turned into a snort laugh that sent me into even more hysterics. My sides hurt from laughing which reminded me of the recent trauma my ribs had suffered and put a damper on my fun. My laughing tapered off and I watched as Noah noticed the change as well.

“It was nice to see you laugh,” he commented softly.

“It was nice to have something to laugh at. It’s been a while.”

“I can see that.” Sadness laced his voice and I knew that he still wanted to know what had happened.

“I left Damian.” I blurted out. Whether I wanted to talk about it or not, I knew I needed to.

Noah stayed silent as he ate, waiting for me to continue.

“I left last night after we had a fight. We have been having a lot of fights lately, but each one feels like it gets worse than the one before. I didn’t plan to leave last night,” I chuckled as I remembered the events of the night and how chaotic everything had been since then. “But when he tried to kill me, I knew that I didn’t have a choice. He was no longer content with just hitting me a few times and yelling at me. He actually seemed to enjoy watching me in pain, and the more violent he became, the more I was afraid of him." I shuddered at the thought as memories made their way through my mind, reminding me of the violence I had endured.

I watched Noah struggle as I continued to talk to him about what had happened with Damian. I told him about the charity event that we went to a few weeks ago, that we were kicked out of, when he got drunk and loudly accused me of flirting with the waiter. That had been the first time he had hit me. I mentioned the hidden cameras around the house I had found that he was using to watch me on, including the one in the bathroom. There was the fight we had while I was out to lunch with Jade a few days ago, and his secretary had mistakenly told him that I was having lunch with another man. The fight we had last night after his company summer BBQ that we were forced to attend to appease his uncle. Damian was working hard to make partner, which meant we had a lot of social appearances we were expected to make. That got harder to do when my body was constantly wearing the evidence of what he had been doing to me.

"Last night he claimed that I was yet again, flirting with one of the partners at the BBQ. On the way home he had reprimanded me and lectured me on my behavior. Reminded me that I was his and that no one else would ever have me- *'til death do us part*. It was really creepy the way he said it," I shrugged as I felt as hopeless as I had felt last night when I left. What were you supposed to do when someone wanted you dead?

"We got home a little after nine and the second that we walked in the door, I felt him push me from behind. I tried to catch my balance but the force was too much and I fell forward and hit my head on the island." I absentmindedly touched the cut on my forehead as it replayed in my mind.

"He kept screaming at me, slurred words about me cheating on him. I couldn't focus on what he was saying. There was this ringing in my head that made it impossible and at that point I was just trying to stay conscious. I knew that he was drunk, but not drunk enough to really slow him down." I took the breath I needed and forced myself to continue moving on with the story. "I knew his habits and knew that within a few minutes he would go get another drink, and that would be my break from him. Once he made it to his study, he would pour his drink and down it. It didn't take him long, it wasn't like him to sit and enjoy it. He would down it and come find me. I knew that if I was going to leave, I had to go while he was in his study. So, without thinking twice, I grabbed what I could and I took off. I haven't stopped running from him since."

I took a deep breath, allowing my lungs to replace the oxygen I had expelled with the verbal vomit I had just unloaded on Noah. It felt good to have someone to talk to and to be able to tell someone what had happened. I had been living such an isolated life for so long that I missed having a friend to confide in.

Noah stayed quiet for a few minutes, his jaw clenched as he looked out the window. Anxiety started mounting as I waited for the lecture I was sure was coming. I didn't blame him for being disappointed in me. I wasn't able to get away from my abusive mother as a child, what made me think I could escape my abusive husband?

"Mia, that's a lot," he said as he took a deep breath and leaned forward. "Have you told anyone else what happened? Have you gone to the police?"

"No. No one knows but you. Jade was suspicious that he was hitting me when I missed the yoga class, but I didn't tell her what happened. She had tried asking about things at lunch, but it got interrupted." I gave a half shrug as we both knew what had happened after that.

"Did she know that you were going to leave?" he asked as he took a bit of his food and nodded to me to eat mine as well. I felt bad that both of our meals were now cold.

"I didn't tell her that I was going to. After I had left, I found some cash in my purse with a torn off piece of napkin with numbers on it. I think Jade stuffed it in my purse when I went to the bathroom at lunch. She was really shaken up about what had happened with Damian during lunch and begged me to leave. And I know she had cash on her, she had talked about making a down payment on a new car she was buying herself since hers was on its last leg. I feel horrible because I know how long she had been saving up for a car."

"Do you think that he knows that you're here?"

"I have no idea. I constantly pray that he doesn't, but at this point, anything is possible."

"I know that you don't want help, and I get it Mia. Really, I do. But you have no idea how helpless I am going to feel if you don't let me help you." His eyes met mine as he silently pleaded with me.

"I do need a job. Do you know anyone in town that's hiring? And maybe needs someone *on the side*?" I asked with hope in my voice that he might know someone that would let me do some side work for cash until I could get on my feet. I don't want anything tied to Mia Stone and make it easier for Damian to find me.

"Actually, I have a position open that is yours if you want it. You can start tomorrow." His smile stretched across his perfectly handsome face as he beamed with pride that I was going to allow him to help.

"Really? That's great, thank you!" Excitement quickly replaced the helpless feeling that had been eating away at me. One step at a time, that's all I had to get through.

"Don't you want to know what it is?" He laughed, knowing that I didn't care.

"Do I have to be employed as Mia Stone?" I questioned, hopeful that the answer would be no.

"No. But it does mean that Amelia Johnson would officially be back in Haven Brook." He grinned a wicked grin.

I groaned as he said my birth name out loud. I had gone by Mia since I was a little girl and very few people knew me as Amelia. But it was a compromise that I didn't mind making, especially since Damian never knew that my birth name was Amelia. I had legally changed my name to Mia as a teenager and manipulated my drunk mother to sign off on it when I threatened to tell the school about her drinking and recreational drug use. This had allowed me to sign our marriage certificate as Mia Johnson.

"Ugh. Alright. Fine. Amelia Johnson will start tomorrow. Just tell me what time and where to go." I sighed as dramatically as I could before picking up my fork to finish my food.

"Deal." Noah wrote the information down on the back of the receipt that the waitress had brought back sometime during my long rant. I hadn't even noticed that he had discreetly paid for my lunch until I saw him writing on his copy of the receipt.

"Thank you for lunch, you didn't have to pay." I smiled as he slid the receipt my way and put the pen down at the end of the table with the signed copy.

"You're welcome," he said with a wink. I could tell something was up with the way he was acting. He had this smirk he would get whenever he did something he wasn't supposed to, which had me worried about what he was up to now.

We finished our lunch and walked together to the parking lot, relieved that the rain had stopped. I gave Noah a hug, thanked him for lunch, and went to pull away when I felt him pull me back towards him.

"There is one other thing, Mia," he said with a crooked smile.

"What's that?" I narrowed my eyes at him, suspicious of what he was planning as I saw the wheels in his head turning.

"When we were younger, you stayed with me and my parents, so we could help you with your mom."

"Yeah. And?" I was confused at what he was trying to get at.

"You're going to stay with me again, at least until you get on your feet."

"Noah, no, I can't do that. I appreciate you offering me the job, that's more than helpful." I stammered through my sentences as I tried to process what he was offering. It would help me tremendously to stay with him and not have to pay for a hotel or live in a car, but I couldn't take advantage of him.

"It's not negotiable, Mia. So get in your car so you can follow me to my house and we can get you situated." He smiled as I started to speak and put his finger up to my mouth to cut me off. I knew I wasn't going to win this one. It felt nice being with Noah again, the family that I've always had and never let me down.

Six

Chase

“Alright, Liam, pull your shoulders back a tad, like this,” I coaxed as I helped adjust his posture into the correct position. “Now, take a deep breath, and keep your eye on the ball.”

I slowly took a few steps to the left, allowing him the space he needed to hit the ball as it came flying toward him. He had a stern look on his face as he focused on the ball, swung at the perfect moment, forcing the ball over the fence. He tossed the bat to the ground and made his way around the bases, a huge smile on his face as he ran toward me.

“I did it! I did it! I got a home run, Uncle Chase!” He launched himself into my open arms as I kneeled down to catch him. I hugged him tightly, thankful that he hadn’t reached the age where he would be embarrassed to let me hug him. I dreaded when that day would come.

“You did amazing! I’m so proud of you, Liam! One day, you’ll be even better than your daddy.” I winked as I heard heavy footsteps behind us, knowing they would hear me. I watched as his smile grew wider at the idea and lit up his face.

“Oh really?” A deep voice boomed behind me as Liam squirmed out of my arms and went running to his dad.

“Uncle Chase said that if I stayed focused, like really, really focused, that I could hit the ball. And guess what dad?! I did, I hit it really hard! And it went way far up over that fence!” Liam pointed excitedly in the direction the ball had landed. He was 7 years old and had recently decided to give sports another try.

“Way to go! I’m so proud of you, son!” They gave each other a high five followed by a secret handshake they had recently created and had been working on perfecting. “Sounds like you did a really good job. What do you say we celebrate by getting some ice cream on the way home?” Grant smiled at Liam and wiggled his eyebrows which got another giggle out of his son. “Just don’t tell nana.”

Liam got even more tickled with the thought of having ice cream before dinner, knowing that nana would have a hay day if she found out about it. But we all knew she would find out about it. She knew everything.

Grant was my younger brother, who was now a single parent to Liam after Liam’s mom recently lost her battle to cancer. Grant and Renee were high school sweethearts, nothing could tear them apart. Well, technically ovarian cancer did. Our lives were forever changed the day Renee passed. It was a loss felt by everyone who had the pleasure of knowing her.

It took a few weeks of everyone working to convince Grant to accept help. He was always such a proud man, and being the middle child, felt he had something to prove. I had helped my mom raise him after my dad passed away unexpectedly my senior year of high school. Grant was a year behind me, and Wyatt was starting his freshman year when we lost my dad. It was a hard position to be in because neither of them was old enough to be on their own and both of them resented me for trying to keep them in line.
My mom, also known as Nana to Liam, convinced Grant to move in with her six months ago, so she could help with Liam. Grant worked 50+ hours a week and nana couldn’t stand the thought of Liam being in daycare when she was all by herself in that big empty house. Those were her words, but they worked, and Grant moved them in without any more fuss about it.

“You wanna come with us to get ice cream?” Liam asked as he pulled at my shirt. I looked into his innocent brown eyes and knew that I would spend my life trying to give this kid anything he wanted. I knew what it felt like to lose a parent and I hated that he had to know that feeling at such a young age. He would never know what it was like to have his mom teach him how to dance or pick out a tuxedo for prom. There were so many memories that I had with my mom growing up, that I wished I could give to Liam. The aching in my heart accelerated when I thought of all of the things in life he had been robbed of.

“I wish I could, champ, but I have to get going. Maybe next time?” I felt horrible for saying no but I knew that Grant needed some bonding time with his son and I didn’t want to get in the way. Grant had worked overtime this week and it showed on his face. He was an exceptional dad and would spend every waking minute with his son, even if it meant he didn’t get any sleep or time for himself. I wasn’t going to stand in the way of the time they needed.

“Are you going to come to our house for dinner? Nana said that she’s making fried chicken with mashed potatoes and peach cobbler.” He looked up as if he was trying to remember his lines from a script. I waited for the line I that I knew was coming.

“Oh, and that you haven’t been by to see your mama in almost two weeks so she expects to see your behind at dinner.” I chuckled as he wagged his finger at me, apparently fulfilling his duty to guilt me into dinner by my mom. Grant laughed as he watched his son lecture me.

“Is that so?” I asked as I tussled his wavy brown hair before he could dart away. His friend, Luke, laughed and pointed at his messed-up hair. I smiled and watched the two boys, happy that I was able to take Liam every Sunday afternoon to get him out of the house. Luke had joined us today for some practice now that Liam wanted to try little league again.

“Well, you tell nana that I have some errands to run real quick but I’ll be there for dinner. You go enjoy your secret ice cream with your dad, and there better be some fried chicken left by the time I get there.” I pointed my finger back at him, mimicking him.

“Okay! See you in a little bit, uncle!” Liam took off running with Luke to the car as Grant and I walked behind them.

“So, what errands do you have to run?” His eyebrows arched as he waited out my response.

“Or is that the name you use for your sexcapades now? Don’t even bother to learn the girl’s name these days?” Grant joked and bumped my shoulder as we made it to his car. He was barely a few inches taller than me and always tried to use it to his advantage.

“Let’s see, that would be…… none of your business,” I shot back with a smirk as I climbed up into my lifted Tacoma and started the engine. I waved at the boys and Grant as I made my way over the 5 speed bumps that lead the way to the main road.

I hadn’t planned on doing dinner with my family tonight but my mom was right, I hadn’t been there in almost two weeks. After Renee died 8 months ago, I vowed to spend more time with family and to be the best uncle that I could be for Liam. It was time that I made my family a bigger priority.

My cell phone buzzed repeatedly in my pocket as the console on my dashboard alerted me of a phone call. I glanced at the screen and saw Nadia’s name. We had been talking for a few weeks after we bumped into each other, very literally, at the gym. Tonight I was supposed to take her out to dinner, and if things went right, drinks at my place after.

“Hey Nadia.” I pushed the button to accept the call.

“Hey, handsome.” Her voice played through the cabin of the truck laced with a flirty tone. I hated to cancel our date tonight which left me focused on trying to figure out what to say so she didn’t think I wasn’t interested.

“I can’t wait to see you tonight. I’ve been thinking about you all day.”

“There might be a slight change of plans, I’m sorry.” I wracked my brain, desperate to figure out a way to do dinner and still see Nadia.

“Does that mean that you’re cancelling on me?” If I had her on a video call, I would be willing to put money on her pouty face that I was positive she had on right now.

"I need to do dinner with my family, but I shouldn't be too long. I might be able to finish up around 9. Are you free then?"

"I have a 5:30 flight to New York in the morning. It will be an early night for me."

"When do you get back?"

"Next Sunday. I'm gone a full week."

Fuck. I had really wanted to see her tonight. There was so much flirting when we were at the gym, followed by explicit texts and some nude photos on her part, that my body was demanding that I see her. The constant teasing had me aching for a release. I blew out a breath as I fidgeted in my seat.

"But maybe we can do a few video calls while I'm gone? You know, late nights at the hotel can get so lonely," she purred into the phone.

"They sure do." I glanced at the screen as a new call alert came through and distracted me. Noah had the worst timing sometimes. I debated whether to answer the call or let it go to voicemail when I heard her sigh heavily.

"Well, you seem busy or distracted so I'll let you go and maybe we'll talk this week. That hotel room might not be so lonely after all." Nadia hung up, silence replaced the flirty tone from a few minutes before. I looked at the screen again and found a voicemail and missed call alert from Noah. "He can wait." I grumbled to no one as I turned onto the road that led to my mom's house. I guess I had it coming, but in all fairness, phone sex and continuing on with the teasing games weren't really my thing. I had more than my share of women and there was always a new prospect lining themselves up for me so I didn't really care too much if Nadia was pissed at me. While my body disagreed with that statement, I knew I only had to make a few phone calls after dinner tonight and I could have that problem taken care of.

Seven

Mia

It was a little after 10 when I heard the door open and saw Noah walk in with a petite blonde wrapped around his neck. He glanced at me sitting on the couch and pulled the girl's hands off of him as she grunted in protest. My guess was that she was barely legal and way past intoxicated. My eyes shot up in question as he shrugged his shoulders with a coy smile.

Growing up with Noah and Chase, I watched as they made their way through the pool of girls that were always throwing themselves at them. They were two of the hottest guys in school and every girl wanted to be the flavor of the week. Neither of them ever had an actual girlfriend that I could remember, and it didn't look like any of that had changed since I had been gone.

I knew that Noah had a date tonight, I should have assumed that he would bring her home. I had planned on hanging out in the spare bedroom so I could stay out of his hair, but my anxiety was already high from everything that had happened over the past few days that I decided to sit on the couch and veg out for a while. A warm blanket consumed me as I sank into the soft couch, reruns of Seinfeld on for distraction.

"I like the new hair," Noah commented as he tilted his head to the side, checking out what I had done while he was gone. I reached a hand up to my hair, my cheeks flushed at the compliment.
My hair was no longer long and blonde, a lifetime of the same look, gone. I had cut a little more than six inches off, leaving it to barely touch my shoulders. The color was a dark brown, and depending on the lighting in the bathroom, had looked almost black. Why I never colored my hair before, who knows. I immediately loved the new color and how it made my baby blue eyes stand out even more.

"Well, I'm off to bed." I folded the blanket and laid it on the back of the couch where I had found it. I didn't want to make it anymore awkward with Noah bringing a girl home so I made my way to the guest room and closed the door behind me.

The room was painted white with a few pictures hanging on the walls. There was a full-sized bed in the corner with a nightstand next to it and a dresser on the opposite wall. It was simple and yet felt cozy. I had taken the time earlier to take the tags off of the new clothes I had purchased, and with Noah's instructions before he left, had done a load of laundry while he was gone. The clothes were hung in the closet with a few things in the dresser.

I had rearranged my purse and was able to store the makeup that I had purchased in the cosmetic bag without it overflowing. While Noah knew that I would be with him for a few weeks until I could get on my feet again, I didn't want it to look like I had fully moved in or that I was invading his space.

There was a small tv sitting on top of the dresser with an antenna behind it. I curled up on the bed and turned it on, looking for something to watch. My mind was still busy, wondering where Damian was and trying to figure out my next steps. I flicked through the channels, not paying attention to what was on them, as I heard a thump against the wall.

Startled, I jumped off of the bed, my hand to my chest, as I tried to figure out where the sound was coming from.

Thump.

I quietly walked slowly around the room, tilting my head as I strained to listen.

Thump. Thump. Thump.

It was getting quicker and more rhythmic.

Thump. Thump. Thump. Thump. Thump.

"Ohhhh, Noah!" A muffled moan made its way through the wall into my room.

I palm smacked my forehead when I recognized the distinct sound. I should have known. The thumping continued as I turned the sound on the tv up some to drown it out, making sure it wasn't loud enough for Noah to hear.

I sat down on the bed, happy to know that I wasn't under attack, it was just Noah having sex. Granted, I didn't necessarily need to know about that either. Bored, I grabbed my cell phone from the nightstand and unlocked it. The home screen was bare, a generic stock photo as the background image. How depressing. I hadn't taken the time to play with the phone since I got it yesterday, not that there was much that I needed to do. ople always bragged about their new phones and how they customized their settings to make their lives easier, I never bothered.

Damian had always controlled my phone and set it up for me, that way he could control what I had access to, and what he wanted to have on it to monitor me. I opened the settings menu and scrolled through the options available.

Loneliness consumed me as I thought about the few people that I needed to add to my contacts. I didn't really have anyone, except for Jade, but I had no way of getting in touch with her unless I tried to find her on Facebook. Damian had the passwords to my social media accounts, as well as my email, so I didn't want it to alert him that I had logged into them from another device and him be able to track where that device was located.

It was better to start fresh if I was going to have any social media accounts. I found my way to the App Store and my finger hovered over the button to install the apps, uncertain of whether I should. I gave in and downloaded the Facebook and Instagram apps as I convinced myself that I didn't have to do anything with them.

I desperately wanted to talk to Jade to let her know that I was okay and to make sure that she was okay. Damian was crazy so I wouldn't put it past him to go after Jade, thinking that she had information about where I went. The look of concern on her face during lunch on Friday flashed through my mind as I remembered our last conversation.

"Mia, please, you have to leave him. Run, and don't ever come back," Jade pleaded as she reached across the table and held my hand. Tears filled her eyes as she continued to plead. "It won't stop, Mia. I know firsthand that it won't. I lost my sister because I was too late. I don't want to lose you too."

I blinked my eyes to force the tears away. Jade had looked so desperate when we said goodbye, it was like she held on a little bit longer, knowing it was our final goodbye. I thought back to the cash that she hid in my purse, knowing how selfless she had been to make sure that I had money if I decided to leave.

It wasn't like she could say anything about it, we both knew that Damian probably had a way of listening to us without being there, so we always talked as if he was there. When we said goodbye, she had whispered in my ear, *you'll be okay, just remember I'm always a call away*.

I hated that I didn't have my old cell phone, even though I was thankful that Damian could no longer track me on it. If I had it then I could call Jade and talk to her. Why would Jade say she would always be a call away if she knew that Damian was monitoring my phone? Why encourage me to leave then suggest that I call her when it could be tracked?

Clarity hit me and I sprung off the bed, grabbing my purse from the top of the dresser, and sat it down on the bed next to me. I quickly opened the pocket where I had found the cash and felt around until I found the piece of napkin with numbers on it. I had completely disregarded it when I first found it, unsure of what it was. It looked like a code or a password and I had assumed that she had accidentally left it with the cash.

I stared at the numbers 16175551782, waiting for something to make sense. It was too long to be a phone number. Or was it? I rolled my eyes when I separated each number and was able to make out a phone number. Jade had added in the 1 to make it less apparent. 1-617-555-1782.

A feeling of giddiness washed over me as I stared at the phone number. I wanted to immediately call her but fear took hold and I wondered if Damian was there and was waiting for me to call her. My fingers hovered over the keypad, unwilling to make a commitment.

I decided to avoid a phone call and test the waters with a text.

Mia: Hey

I sat the phone down and stared at it, waiting for something to happen. Apparently, I had turned an ordinary cell phone into some sort of magical device, expectations high that it would be Jade and that I would be free to talk to her. I watched as the new message alert showed on my screen.

My fingers trembled as they fumbled with unlocking the screen. I hoped it was Jade and that I hadn't text someone else thinking that it was supposed to be her phone number.

Then a terrifying thought occurred to me- what if the money was never from Jade? What if Damian was trying to test me, to see if I would leave? If he thought that there was a possibility that I would leave, then what if he was the one to put the money in my purse? He was the one who had been pissed at me for wanting to leave him, when I had never said that I wanted to leave. He put the idea out there, not me. What if he left the money, along with the phone number, so he could trick me into telling him where I was, knowing that I would think it was Jade.

The unread message stared at me as I struggled with whether to read it or not. If it was Damian, I just gave away my safety net of him not knowing where I was by being able to track my new phone number. I knew it didn't have the tracking app on it like my other phone, but I also knew that he had other resources and would find a way. I silently prayed that it was Jade and that there was no connection to Damian.

I realized there was nothing to lose by opening the message since I had already sent the first one. I pressed the button and read the message as a shiver ran through me.

Unknown: Where are you?

Eight
Mia

Those three words made me freeze as I stared at my phone. Had I been right? Was it all a test from Damian to see if I would actually leave him? Had I fallen for the ultimate trick?

The phone began vibrating in my hand, the number I had just sent a text message was displayed as the caller. I watched as it rang, unsure of what to do. I still held out a sliver of hope that it was Jade but my gut told me to stop the wishful thinking. The vibration stopped and a missed call alert replaced the image on the screen.

I took a deep breath as I tried to calm myself. There was no way of knowing who I had actually reached. Maybe it was Jade. Maybe it was Damian. Maybe it was some random person. The unknown was eating away at me.

A few seconds later a voicemail notification showed up on the screen. I hesitated as I pushed the button to play the message.

Hey Mia, it's me. Jade. Or at least I hope this is Mia and that you found the money and the number in your purse.

There was a pause and I could hear faint movement in the background before she came back to the phone.

If this is Mia, please call me back. I really need to know that you're okay. I've been worried sick about you after I called and texted you and you haven't responded. Then I got a call from Damian. So yeah, I'm worried about you. Call me?

Her voice sounded worried as I played the message again. I had no idea what I was trying to find in the voicemail but I kept searching for anything that would tell me that she was also okay and that Damian wasn't there, forcing her to play a role in his psychotic game. My breathing had started to return to normal as I tried to relax. I tried to think through all of the possible scenarios when I felt my phone vibrate again. Another call from Jade. Reluctantly, I answered the phone.

"Hi," I whispered into the phone.

"You have no idea how happy I am to hear your voice. Are you okay?"

"Yeah, I'm okay."

"Are you safe? What happened? Where are you?" Her questions came out in rapid fire, one after another.

"I'm fine." I kept my response vague, I still had no way of knowing whether Damian was with her. It could all still be a ruse.

"Mia, you don't sound fine." Her voice grew softer.

"Things are just, in the air right now." I didn't technically lie. While I had planned to stay in Haven Brook for a little while, I was more than prepared to run if this call took a turn for the worse. I had a feeling my life from here on out would constantly be up in the air.

"Are you sure you're okay? Is he there with you?" Jade lowered her voice and I could hear her cover the phone with her hand as she spoke again. "Use the word yoga if you're not okay and I'll find a way to get help to you."

I almost laughed as I realized that while I thought Damian was there with her, she thought that Damian was here with me. She was smart and I loved her quick thinking with a code word that was unique to us. Yoga wouldn't be anything out of the ordinary for me and Jade to talk about since Damian knew that we went to a weekly yoga class together in Boston. What he didn't know was that we rarely actually went to the class. While Jade was flexible and could easily do any pose, I could barely master corpse pose without injuring myself.

"I'm okay, really." I loosened up a bit as I felt more confident that she wasn't being coerced on the other side.

"You know, I would really just feel much better if I could see you. What kind of phone do you have? We can video chat."

I felt uneasy about doing video chat with her in case he was there but realized that he had better luck tracking the cell phone than finding where I was based on the bare white walls of Noah's guest room. After a few prompts from Jade I found the settings and answered as she called in again.

I answered the new call and watched the screen as it loaded, happy to see Jade's smile as she came onto the screen. She looked happy and didn't show any signs of being beaten by anyone recently so I assumed she had been safe from Damian.

"There you are," she said with a warmth in her voice, like a mother playing peekaboo with a baby. I watched as she took in my new look.

"Hi. It's nice to see you too."

As much as I was happy to see her, there was this unspoken tension as we looked at each other. It was like we were reading each other's minds, waiting for the other to say the obvious.

"He's not here with me," Jade said as she offered a sympathetic smile. "Watch." She took her cell phone and kept herself on the screen as she quickly walked around her apartment, opening doors and showing me behind the shower curtain. I smiled at the effort and was thankful that I didn't have to physically voice my concern.

"Your turn." She nodded to me and waited for me to show her that

Damian wasn't with me either. I showed her the small guest room, opened the closet door, and walked back over to the bed.

"What about the rest of the house?"

"Noah brought a date home and I don't want to be intrusive by walking through his house, taking some girl he doesn't know on a virtual tour of it."

Jade's eyebrows went up as she acknowledged that I said a man's name. I wanted to smack myself for what I had done. She needed to know that I was safe, not exactly where I was. I remembered a conversation I had with her when we first met, shortly after I had moved to Boston, when we were waiting tables together. We had a large party that night of drunken college guys, out for a bachelor party. The tips were scarce and the compliments unflattering. Jade had complained that there were no real men left in this world and that she was destined to either die alone or end up a crazy cat lady. I assured her there were still a few left, and that she would have to move to Colorado to find them. I warned her that Noah was one of the most desired men in Haven Brook and that she would have her work cut out for her if she wanted to try to tame him. Apparently she remembered the name.

"Are you back where you told me about early on in our friendship?" She looked at me with wide eyes as she made sure I got the hint she was trying to give. I appreciated that she respected me enough not to say the name. She knew how crazy Damian was and even though it appeared he would have no way to hear our conversation, we played it safe.

"Yes." A simple answer. That was all that was needed as I watched her sigh with relief and sink back into her chair. We had talked about my childhood before Damian and I had moved in together, and while I had kept it vague, I had eluded to my mom being abusive and that I had been lucky to have Chase and Noah to constantly protect me. At the time I had gone on and on about finding a man in Boston that would also protect me, little had I known.

"I'm really happy to hear that."

I smiled and for a moment we took in the silence as there wasn't anything more that needed to be said. I wished that I could bring Jade here, to have a friend in the place that I had decided to make my home again, but I couldn't ask that of her. I couldn't ask her to uproot her life and come join me as I constantly watched over my shoulder.

Involuntarily I yawned, the lack of sleep from the past few days had caught up to me.

"It's late and I'm sure you've barely slept. I should let you go."

"It's okay, I like talking to you." I blinked my eyes as they started to feel heavy. I was exhausted but I didn't know when I would get to talk to Jade again.

"Mia, get some sleep. You need it. We'll find a way to talk again soon, okay?" Her voice reassured me that we would find a way. We said goodbye and I heard the front door close as I sat my phone on the nightstand and plugged it into the charger.

A light tap at my door then it slowly opened as Noah peeked his head inside.

"I saw your light on and thought I heard talking, just thought I would make sure you were alright."

"I'm good, thanks." Another yawn. "That was my friend, Jade."

"Is she single? Is she cute?" He opened the door with his shoulder and watched me with a grin on his face as he waited for my answer.
"She lives in Boston. You're unlikely to ever meet her because I'm unlikely to ever see her again." I fought back another yawn. "But yes, she is single, and very cute." I winked just to torment him with the thought of there being a woman that he couldn't have. A frown formed on his face and I laughed.

"You're tired, you should get some rest." He nodded toward the bed that I was already sitting on.

"So I've been told."

“I’ll likely be gone by the time you get up in the morning so I left a key for you on the kitchen counter by the coffee pot. It’s programmed to come on at 8:30 before I leave, but I set it to stay warm until 10. You can come in around 11, when we open, if that gives you enough time to get up and ready?”

“I can go in whenever you go in if you need me to, I don’t mind.” Another big yawn. I was getting irritated and wished they would stop.

“Mia, you’re exhausted and I would rather that you sleep in some and rest. There’s food in the fridge, be sure to eat breakfast and pack a lunch before you go in.”

“Yes, sir.” I mockingly saluted him.

“Cute.” He rolled his eyes.

“I try.” I batted my eyes and tilted my head to play up the part.

“Alright, I’m off to bed. My room is next door, just come get me or bang on the wall if you need anything. The walls are pretty thin so I’ll be able to hear you.”

“Yeah, I know how thin they are.” I gave him a knowing look and watched as the blush crept up his neck.

“My bad.” He chuckled and smiled as he walked out and closed the door behind him.

I scooted over and pulled the blankets down as I slid under them, feeling cozy with the heaviness of the comforter. My head turned as it found the right position on the pillow, and before I knew it, I was fast asleep.

Nine

Damian

"Why the fuck do you call yourself an assistant if you don't actually assist anyone?" I yelled into the phone as I slammed it down and hung up. I had been in the office for 3 hours, yet the only work I had done focused on finding Mia.

I had turned the whiteboard in my office into an information database on what I had collected so far. Unfortunately there was very little on it at this point. I knew that she had made it to Manchester based on the tracking app I had installed on her cell phone, but by the time I had sobered up enough to make the drive, bought a random plane ticket and made it through security, she had just boarded the plane and I missed her. I had grabbed her cell phone from the abandoned armrest and tucked it in my pocket as I caught a glimpse of her as she faded out of sight. The flight information on the board showed she had one layover and was set to arrive in Denver around 11 am, their time. Mia had mentioned when we first met that she was from Colorado but I never bothered to listen when she told me where. Instincts told me that Denver was just another stopping point or a distraction in case I was able to track her that far. She was smart, I had to give her that.

With Mia leaving her cell phone behind, I had no way of physically tracking her anymore. I went home and went through her call logs and texts. I looked for anything that I might have missed when I had been checking on her after she first left. Given that she went back to Colorado, I focused on looking for recent contact with any of her old friends since she didn't have any family. It had surprised me when she left, I never thought she had it in her. On some level, I had hoped that she didn't have it in her. I wasn't looking forward to what would have to come next. If only she would have listened.

I spent the morning calling car rental companies in Denver, checking to see if anyone had rented a car to Mia Stone. There was one who was rather loose with their information but the kid was too stoned to know whether he should give me the information or not. By the end of the conversation he was convinced that I was trying to rent a car and that I go by the name Mia. He thought the secret was that he wasn't supposed to tell anyone that I was a man posing as a woman, dumb ass.

There were two rental car companies left that I hadn't called yet, though I had little hope that they would give me the information that I needed since I had hit so many dead ends. I picked up the phone and started to dial the number when I saw Doris's head bob outside my door before she cracked it open and peeked inside. I couldn't wait until my actual assistant was back from her fuck-fest, aka her honeymoon.

"Mr. Stone?" she asked meekly, her mousy voice made me want to put her head through the wall.

"What?" I snarled, annoyed as I put the phone down and glared at her.

"Mr. Ronnie Stone would like to, um confirm your reservation, um this weekend for the conference in D.C. Will you be bringing your wife?" she asked as she remained hidden behind my door. If I still had my dart board, I could use her head as target practice.

I was so focused on how much she annoyed me that I hadn't heard what she had asked. Or maybe it was the remainder of the bottle of whiskey that made its way into my coffee that kept me distracted. Either way I had no idea what this broad wanted but I was ready for her to go away.

"What?" I asked with annoyance, forcing her to come into the office and closer to my desk. Lovely.

"The conference in D.C. Will you, um, be attending with, um, your wife? Um. Sir?"

Shit! I had forgotten about the fucking conference. Ronnie had just talked about it this morning at the staff meeting and had rambled on for twenty minutes about how it was mandatory as he looked at me when he said it. I didn't have time to go out of town this weekend, nor did I have time to be stuck in D.C for an entire week. I needed to find Mia before I ran out of time and she was gone for good.

"Tell him neither of us will be attending." I shot her a look that told her not to question me about it and she turned and walked out of my office.

I took a few sips of coffee, using my pen to stir it. One big gulp and I felt ready to make the remaining calls. The phone was in my hand as I started to dial the phone number when my office door flung open. Startled, I jumped in my chair, dropping the phone on my desk. Ronnie stood in the doorway glaring at me as his eyes strained not to bulge out of his head. I had seen my uncle angry on numerous occasions, but I rarely saw him like this. He stared me down as he reached behind him and slammed my door shut. Fuck. "What is this that I hear that you're not going to the MANDATORY conference next week in D.C?" he asked as he approached my desk, leaning forward to slam his hands on the end of it.

"I have other things going on that need my attention," I replied as calmly as I could. Ronnie raised me after my dad died and had the unpleasant experience of getting me through my teenage years. He'd always been able to call me on my bullshit and the look on his face said he was about to do so now.

"What do you have going on that needs your attention? You haven't worked an actual case in weeks," he taunted, knowing that I hadn't taken a new case in almost a month. I glanced at the files sitting on my desk and grabbed the file on top of the pile.

"I'm working this case and it's going to need more attention. There's a tight deadline or it will be out of the statute of limitations," I replied as I tossed the file towards him for dramatic effect. I had no fucking clue whose file it was. For all I knew I could be claiming to represent a six-year-old who was suing her brother for ripping her Barbie's head off. I kept my poker face and watched to see what he would do.

He picked up the file and sat in the chair across from me. He leaned back and opened the file, reading the summary of the case. Damn it. My hands started sweating as I reached for my coffee. I was mid reach when he peered up and watched me, guilt forcing me to pull my hand back. It felt sac religious to drink coffee filled with booze while my uncle sat in front of me. Talk about a slap in the face to him after I had sworn to his face 2 years ago that I would stop drinking.

“So you can’t go because you’re working a case for a crooked cop that was caught red handed helping his wife embezzle from her place of business? An incident that happened 2 months ago. That they have on video,” he questioned as he stared at me over the top of the open file. “Seems to me that this is well within the statute of limitations, and quite frankly, an easy case to work given they have proof. Therefore, you’re going to the conference. We already paid your way. I just needed to know if Mia was coming so we could make her arrangements as well.”

“She won’t be attending,” I said curtly as I shifted in my seat and adjusted my tie. Suddenly it felt like the room was void of oxygen, the weight of his stare suffocated me.

“Why not?” He leaned forward and sat the file back where I had originally pulled it from.

“She’s been under the weather.” I lied.

“Well, surely she will be better by this weekend and can attend.” He pushed.

“I think she also had plans this weekend. Some gardening show in Boston that she wanted to go to with her friend, Jade.” The room grew hotter by the minute as I struggled to stay one step ahead of my uncle. He was purposely pushing for information about Mia and I was determined not to give more than I had to. How would I explain that my battered wife had vanished and that I was trying to find her so I could further silence her?

“What’s going on? You’re lying to me. What happened with Mia?” He raised his voice and leaned forward to invade more of my space.

"We're having marital problems. I wanted to try to go to counseling and spend next week with her, trying to reconnect. She blames the distance between us on my job and the late hours I've been working." I laid it on as thick as I could, knowing that my uncle would be relieved to hear that I was trying to make my marriage work after he watched my parent's marriage crumble as I was growing up.

He eyed me cautiously as he took in the information.

"Okay. Well, if that's the case." He stood up and pulled at his pant leg, forcing the material back down. He was a short, round man and suits didn't tend to agree with him. "Bring Mia by for lunch on Friday. After I talk with her, if your story pans out, then I'll let you off the hook for the conference. If she's not there for lunch on Friday then be prepared to pack your bags for D.C." He glanced down at my coffee mug and paused to look inside. He shook his head as he walked out of my office and closed the door behind him.

I let out a sigh and sunk back into my chair, relieved that he was gone. How the fuck was I supposed to bring Mia to lunch on Friday when I didn't even know where the fuck she was. I slammed my hand down on my desk in frustration, the pens in the pen holder rattled in response. It looked like I was taking an unwanted and incredibly inconvenient trip to D.C. next week.

Ten

Mia

The sun filtered in through the mini blinds as I rolled over and picked up my phone to check the time. 9:30. I couldn’t remember the last time I had slept this late but I was sure it had to have been when I used to live here. Back to old routines I thought as I sat up and stretched. My body was still sore from the other night, though I finally felt more rested. Thankfully sleep came easy to me last night, with Noah in the next room and no sign of Damian knowing where I was.

I stood under the hot water of the shower and allowed it to run over my body as I closed my eyes. For a moment I felt relaxed, and for once, at peace. I thought about my new life and tried hard to focus on making things the best I could this time around. If I stayed focused and cleared my mind, I could purposefully create the life that I wanted.

A shiver ran through me as I felt the water temperature change, a sign I had been in there long enough. I turned the handle to off and slid the glass shower door open to grab a towel. Now that I didn’t have the expectation of getting ready and looking a certain way for Damian, I was actually excited to get ready for my first day at my new job.

I decided to wear one of the new outfits I had picked up yesterday, hoping that a new outfit and new hair would continue to make me feel like a new woman. My jean shorts were a dark denim and fit loosely on my hips. I paired them with a white tank top that had a lace overlay on the front, hoping to keep it casual, while still dressing it up a bit. I didn't want to look like a slob or be unprofessional. Noah had mentioned a casual dress code but didn't elaborate any more than that.

My makeup was light, aside from the heaping amount of concealer used to hide the bruises. I tried to keep it from looking caked on and tried to highlight my eyes and lips to take the focus off of the purple bruise on my cheek. Maybe I would get lucky and Noah would have me working in the back where I wouldn't have to see or interact anyone. I'd hate to drive off business for him by scaring them with my beat-up face.

It was 10:30 and I had checked that there was a bus coming at 10:45 that would have me to The Vine by 11:00. I had given Noah the keys to the rental car yesterday before he left for his date. He had friends that were going up to Denver for the week and agreed to take the car back for me so I didn't have to figure out how to get it back. I shoved my phone in my front pocket and tossed the lipstick in my purse as I grabbed the spare key I had found next to the coffee pot this morning, as promised. I locked the door and made my way to the bus stop. It was a warm day, which made me want to sit outside and soak up the sun. Once I got to the bus stop, I closed my eyes and took a deep breath as I enjoyed the warm sun beating down on me while I waited for the bus.

My eyes opened and my head turned to the left as I heard the bus approaching. It screeched to a stop, the old thing grumbled in the process. If I had to bet, it was the same bus I used to ride as a teenager. I waited for the doors to open then boarded the bus as I paid my fare. There were a few seats open toward the back, so I made my way down the aisle and took a seat. I was surprised how many people were on the bus at 10:45 on a Monday morning so I turned to look out the window, avoiding eye contact and any opportunity to make small talk.

The bus inched down the road, stopping every few miles for passengers. There were two stops before the one I needed. I kept my eyes on the road, waiting for the stop before mine so I could stand and be ready to get off at the one I needed. As I stood, the elderly woman seated across the aisle from me looked up and fear flashed across her face. She subtly nodded toward a guy a few feet ahead of us who was standing against the pole with his back turned to his. He had a dark hoodie on with his head covered, which seemed odd given that it was already almost 80 degrees out.

She kept making eye contact with me as she tried to get me to acknowledge that I had seen the man she tried to warn me about. I felt scared as I watched the guy from behind. I had no idea who he was, but I prayed that it wasn't Damian. The bus slowed as it approached my stop and I clutched my purse tighter against my body as I held onto the bar above my head for balance. My body jerked forward from the impact of the stop and as I stepped forward, the man in the hoodie turned around and faced me.

I gasped as my hand went to my mouth, my eyes wide in shock.

"After you." He nodded with his head as his hands stayed in the pockets of his oversized hoodie. It made me wonder what he had in his pocket as I noticed the outline of something other than his hand. I stepped forward and got off the bus as I glanced over my shoulder to see where he had gone. Out of the corner of my eye I saw the dark figure run off into an alley and I let out the breath I had been holding. I was thankful that it wasn't Damian but he scared me nonetheless.

The guy appeared to be in his mid-twenties and had a deep scar across his right cheek. Underneath the hoodie I could make out a tattoo of a snake that wrapped its way around his neck. He had a black eye that was fading and a cut above his eyebrow. While I had been relieved that it wasn't Damian, I was still bothered by the guy and couldn't figure out why. My heartbeat continued to race as I looked for the building I needed.

I looked around at the businesses around me, some familiar from when I lived here, and some that were brand new. There was a vintage looking sign mounted on the outside of a newer looking building that was set back from the street. I squinted against the sun, my hand held up to block some of the glare and read: The Vine. I went in through the wrought iron gate and through a small courtyard that lead to the front entrance. Double doors greeted me as I pulled one open, surprised by how heavy it was. A bell chimed as I walked in and looked around the brewery. The atmosphere was warm and welcoming with a bar counter along the back wall offset by some high-top tables along the opposite wall. In the middle of the room there were long picnic tables with bench seats that filled the majority of the space, and double glass doors to the right that lead out to a beautiful, fully enclosed, outdoor patio. It felt calm and relaxing with cream colored paint on the walls and very strategically placed décor. I immediately knew that Noah’s mom was the person responsible for decorating and creating the ambiance, especially after seeing how decorated Noah’s guest room was.

A door off to the left of me opened and startled me as Noah walked out. I hadn’t paid attention to the door as it blended in with the wall, so it surprised me when he came out of it. There was nothing else on that wall, which made sense given that the room then opened up into the brewery. It was an L shaped room with bathrooms on the opposite wall, close to the entrance.

“Do you need a hand?” I asked as I saw Noah balance a crate with glasses on his hip as he made his way past the door.

“Nah, I’m good. Thanks though.” He sat the crate at the end of the bar as I made my way over.

“This place is beautiful, Noah.” I continued to look around as I admired the place I was going to be working at. When he first told me that it was a brewery, I had immediately pictured a dark, dingy bar environment.

“Thanks. It feels like home to me, I really enjoy spending my time here. Which is probably a good thing, given how much time I actually end up spending here.” He laughed and started unpacking the crate of glasses on the counter behind the bar.

“If you want to go ahead and put your stuff down in the break room, it’s the open area at the end of the hall. And there’s new hire paperwork that you’ll need to complete. Chase should be in his office, it’s the second door on the right.”

“Chase?” I struggled to pick up my jaw that I was sure had dropped to the floor.
“Yeah....”

I could tell that he knew that he was caught by the way he avoided looking at me and how his sentence dropped off. There it was. The other shoe finally fell. I was nervous and excited at the same time to see Chase, the combination of feelings made me a bit nauseous.

“Noah?” I arched an eyebrow at him as he tried to dodge my glance.

“Did I forget to mention that we are business partners? We bought this place together. Chase handles the operations, including new hire paperwork, and I handle the fun stuff.”

“Like flirting with drunk girls every Saturday night?”

“Sometimes they come in on Friday nights too.” He winked and my mood lightened some.

I shook my head at him as I pulled my purse over my shoulder and walked to the door that led to the back offices. I didn’t hear anything coming from the office as I made my way back to the break room. My plan was to sit my stuff down, get myself together, then go do my paperwork. I was so distracted that I didn’t hear someone coming out of the office. Immediately our bodies collided, and I was embraced by strong arms and a broad chest. I didn’t have to look up to know whose arms I had just landed in. I would have recognized the smell of his cologne and the feel of his embrace anywhere.

I pulled back and looked up into his dark brown eyes, feeling a flash back of my youth. For a moment it felt as if nothing had changed as he looked at me with concern, which was quickly replaced with a smile as he helped steady me.

“You always knew how to make an entrance,” he joked as he stepped back to allow me some space while maintaining a grip on my elbow so I didn’t fall. His smile stretched across his face and lit up the room.

“Well, you know me. Always the graceful one,” I joked back, making light of how clumsy I was. It was one of those traits that just never left, no matter how hard I tried.

“Welcome back, Mia. It’s nice to see you again.” He leaned back against the wall, his T-shirt pulled tight as his muscles flexed when he crossed his arms over his chest. His eyes were soft, genuine sincerity in his tone.

"Thanks."

"I have your paperwork ready to go over, whenever you're ready. You can put your stuff in any of the cabinets along the back wall, and feel free to put your lunch in the fridge." He pointed to the cabinets that lined the back wall as he walked into the open space with me. I had anticipated a regular break room with a table, fridge, and microwave but this was an actual kitchen with a full pantry, stove, microwave, fridge, and cabinets. There was a 6-foot table with 8 folding chairs scattered around it and off to the side was a single person restroom. Mounted to the wall across from the table was a decent size tv. To the left of the tv was a door that had a sign above it that said kitchen. I looked at it, confused, since we were technically already in a kitchen.

"We have a small food menu." He nodded toward the kitchen. "Pablo and Maria run the food side, and on occasion, their daughter Isabell fills in for them. They moved here a few years ago and ran a food truck that everyone loved. When we decided to open the brewery, we talked to them about going in together and they jumped on board right away."

"Wow, I had no idea. I thought it was just drinks." I shrugged, not having many details of what the job would actually entail until now.

"They handle all of the food stuff. You'll take the orders and put them into the system, then they'll prepare it and deliver to the tables. So you'll only have to worry about putting the order into the system and handling the drinks. It's pretty easy, I'm sure you'll get the hang of it right away."

"I'm going to head up front to talk to Noah about a few things, but it shouldn't take long. Go ahead and get yourself situated and I'll meet you in my office in a few." He paused to look back over his shoulder. "It's the one you tried to tackle me in front of a few minutes ago." He chuckled and walked down the hallway as I tried to blend in with the walls, hopeful that they would swallow me so he wouldn't see the blush that had turned my entire body a new shade of crimson.

Ten minutes had passed as I sat in Chase's office, admiring the rich colors he had chosen for his office furniture. A mahogany u-shaped desk took the main focus with a high back leather chair situated behind it. There were a few framed landscape photos hung on the wall behind him, enclosed in by floor to ceiling bookcases.

"Sorry, you know Noah, he likes to talk." Chase came around the desk and took his seat on the other side. I found myself fidgeting, nervous about his presence, and folded my hands in my lap.
Chase has always had this effect on me. Regardless of what we were doing or what had been said, I constantly felt so nervous and clumsy around him. It's like when you try to make the best impression you can but instead you make a total ass of yourself. That's me.

We finished the paperwork fairly quickly and Chase didn't ask any questions about the name I was using or the fact that I was using Noah's address, which meant that they had already talked. It made sense, it was business related and they both owned the business. I had no idea how many of the personal details they had discussed as friends. Chase wasn't asking any personal questions so I decided to just assume that he knew everything.

I spent the next few hours working with Noah, learning the computer system and how to enter the food items. The day seemed to go by in the blink of an eye and before I knew it, it was already almost seven. Noah was hustling behind the bar, trying to wait tables, and clean up behind the early dinner crowd that had come in. I jumped in where I could and took over waiting on the new tables as customers came in. Noah seemed pleased and we worked seamlessly until closing time at 9.

"That- was a freaking long day." He sighed as he locked the front double doors and turned the sign in the window to closed.

"Is it always this busy on Mondays?" I finished wiping down the last table and threw the washcloth over the side of the bin I had collected dirty dishes in.
"Yes and no. Right now we're busy with the start of summer break, all of the college kids are celebrating the semester being over before they head out of town for the summer. It'll die down in a few weeks then pick up again a month before the next semester starts. Some kids will stay here the entire summer, which means the weekends will stay busy."

"I'm sorry you ended up staying late, I had planned to get you out around 7," he said apologetically.

"I don't mind. It was nice to feel useful and help out." I pulled a hair tie out of my pocket and pulled my hair up into a ponytail to get it out of my face. "Besides, it looked like you needed the help."

I laughed as I recalled Noah trying to take an order while balancing a pile of plates in the other hand. Every attempt he made to jot down their order on his notepad, the plates would sway and threatened to fall. He had always been stubborn and reluctant to ask for help. Apparently, even with his own employees. I had seen the struggle and grabbed the plates from him on my way to clear another table.

"Well, thank you, I do appreciate the help." He smiled back at me as he worked on closing out the day in the computer system and emptied the cash drawer. I watched as he wrote a few things down on a slip of paper and tucked it in a bank deposit bag along with the cash that was bundled together with a rubber band.

"What else do we need to do?" I looked around, waiting for him to give me more duties.

"That's it, we're pretty much done. We'll grab our stuff from the back, then I'll take you with me to drop off the deposit." He zipped the bag shut as he made his way around the bar and we walked down the hall to the back offices. I grabbed my purse from the cabinet and met Noah in the hallway outside of his office.

We were at the front door and had already turned all of the inside lights off when Noah realized he forgot his cell phone on his desk and had to go back to his office to get it. He handed me the deposit and I heard him walk down the hallway as his steps faded. It was eerily dark outside, with very little light by the front door. I peered up and noticed that one of the lamps by the door had a broken light bulb, which explained the darkness. The other lamp was further away which shed some light, but still left the entrance to the door hidden in shadows.

Out of the corner of my eye I saw a quick movement in the shadows as my heart jumped into my throat. I looked over my shoulder for Noah when I heard a fist bang on the heavy glass of the door and found a man in a hoodie staring at me. His face was covered by the darkness which made it hard to see him.

"Open the door." He pulled his hand out of the pocket of his hoodie and pointed a gun at me.

"Now."

Terror flooded through me as I stared at the gun, unable to react to what had happened. My fingers trembled as they gripped the deposit bag tighter, his eyes watched my every movement. I waited for him to lift his head, even half an inch, so I could see if it was Damian. It had to be Damian, who else would be here, pointing a gun at me and demanding that I let them in? I knew he would find me.

My breaths came hurriedly as my ears echoed the sound of my racing heartbeat. His eyes flickered to look at something behind me, something that caught his attention. I was too afraid to move, paralyzed where I was. I waited for him to pull the trigger and for it to be over. I closed my eyes and waited. Any minute now and my life would be over. He would make sure of it.

I felt footsteps behind me and in a swift movement I was pushed out of the way and shoved behind a large plant in a ceramic pot by the doors.

"What the fuck are you doing here, Jimmy?" Noah continued to block me from seeing what was happening. Who was Jimmy? I slowly tilted my head to the side to try to see what was happening. Did Noah mistake Damian for someone else? I had to warn him, he had no idea what he was up against. I started to push forward when I felt Noah reach back and push me further back against the wall.

"Just give me the bag."

Bag? What bag? What was happening? I arched my back as I leaned back as far as I could and peeked through the plant leaves. They were big and thick, which provided good coverage to keep me hidden, but also made it hard for me to see anything.

"You know damn well that you're not getting the bag. You're not getting a damn thing other than a bullet in your ass if you ever come back here again." Noah reached behind him and I saw him pull a black handgun from the back of his jeans. He hid his hands down by his side as I watched him mess with the gun, all while keeping his eyes on the man. I glanced down at the bank deposit bag in my hand. I had completely forgotten about it until now.

"I ain't playin man. Just give me the fucking bag. You don't want that girl to get hurt- do you? Cause that's all on you man. You know ima take it from her the second her skinny ass steps out this door, yo." The guy started bouncing around and wiped at his nose with his free hand. The hoodie had shifted back off of his face and I gasped when I saw the scar on his cheek and the snake tattoo on his neck. It was the guy from the bus this morning.

"Look Jimmy, I'm getting real tired of your punk ass. I'm gonna give you 10 seconds to get your high as fuck loser ass off of my property." Noah turned to whisper to me while he kept Jimmy in his sight.

"Go call 911 and ask them to send Lieutenant Dickson. Let them know his kid is out and causing trouble here. Just tell them it's The Vine, they know where it's at." He nodded toward the office and I slowly crept along the side of the wall, staying out of sight, as I made my way to the phone.

I hated leaving Noah by himself with a crazy person who was high on drugs and had a gun. Noah seemed to know the guy and apparently kept a gun on himself, so I did as I was told. My heart was still racing as I sat in Noah's chair, unsure of what else to do. I couldn't go back up there and risk the guy seeing me and going crazy. That wouldn't be smart.

Ten minutes later I heard voices upfront and made my way up to the front.

"Sorry about the hassle, Noah. I wasn't told he had been released. He's predictable so my guess is that he wasn't out for long."

"No problem, Lieutenant. Just happy that no one got hurt."

I slowly walked up to where Noah was talking to a tall, muscular man, wearing sweats. My guess was that it was the Lieutenant. I felt his eyes take me in, unsure of who I was and why I was stalking around. He appeared to be in his fifties or sixties, though his physical appearance looked like that of a twenty-year-old.

“Hey.” Noah stepped to the side as I stood beside him. “Lieutenant Dickson, this is Amelia. Amelia, this is Lieutenant Dickson.”

I reached out and shook his hand as I offered Noah the deposit bag back. I felt uncomfortable holding onto it when I had just barely started that day, and it had already been the source of drama with the Lieutenant’s son.

“How about I give you two an escort over to the bank for the deposit?” He nodded at the bag as Noah took it.

“Nah, it’s okay. We will be fine taking it. I’m showing Mia the ropes tonight but she won’t be doing any of the night deposits. I’ll still be the only one who handles them.”

“It’s the least I can do for what happened.”
Noah smiled in acceptance as we followed the Lieutenant out and Noah locked the doors. The bank was literally across the parking lot so the escort consisted of him walking the short distance with us as he kept watch while Noah showed me how to slide the deposit bag into the night drop box on the outside of the bank. A loud thud echoed as we heard the bag land in the bottom of the box. I pulled the handle to open it one more time and looked inside, just to make sure it had really made it in. Noah chuckled as we walked back through the parking lot, said goodbye to the Lieutenant, and got into Noah’s 4Runner.

The first day had plenty of ups and downs and I felt exhausted. We stopped and grabbed dinner through a drive thru on our way home, both of us too tired to go sit down somewhere. Once we got home, I felt more relaxed as we ate our food and talked about old times growing up. He gave me the back story on Jimmy who had been in and out of the system since he was sixteen. Given that his dad was the Lieutenant, you would think that it would make Jimmy stop getting into trouble, but it seemed to only make it worse. Jimmy wasn’t afraid of the law, he was however afraid of his father. Noah continued to explain that Buck was also a body builder and had won numerous competitions, which explained his physique. Everyone in town knew Jimmy’s past and when they saw him pop up around town, they didn’t bother calling the police anymore. A call to Buck, and Jimmy was dealt with. Noah assured me that he would be locked up again, given that he was a felon in possession of a firearm. He wasn't the smartest and made no efforts to stay out of the system.

It felt normal getting back into the swing of small-town living where everyone ended up knowing your business, whether you wanted them to or not. While I desperately wanted to keep my business hidden, I didn't anticipate too many people would actually ask about it. There would be general questions about what life was like in Boston, and why I had decided to come back, other than that, no one would care about the other details. If I could lay low for a little while longer, that was all I would need to get my new life started on the right foot.

Eleven

Mia

I tilted my head back as Chase kissed his way down my neck, slowly moved over my shoulder, and down towards my breast. A shiver ran through me as I ran my hand through his hair and took in the scent of his aftershave. Our bodies were desperate to find each other, hands reaching for whatever they could find. I lifted my head and looked into his eyes, wishing he would fill the emptiness I've felt inside for so long now.

Our lips touched, a gentle kiss as he held his muscular body on top of mine. I watched as he slid his boxers off, his gaze steady on mine as he waited for a sign that I might change my mind. I smiled and licked my lips, confirming this was what I wanted. His smile spread across his face almost as quickly as he made his way back up on the bed and positioned himself next to me. This was it, this was the moment I had been fantasizing about since I was a teenager.

I jolted up in bed, a noise outside startled me awake. Noah's door opened and his footsteps faded quickly past my room as I heard him go to the front door. I got out of bed and opened my door, peeking into the hallway to try to hear what had happened. Noah came back down the hallway a few minutes later, his cell phone in one hand and his gun in the other. I would have thought that it would bother me with Noah always having his gun on him, but it actually made me feel safer.

"The neighbors next door are out of town and they forgot to put their trashcan in the garage before they left. Looks like it got knocked over. Probably a bear looking for food."

"Scared the hell out of me. I was sound asleep and that was a hostile awakening." I remembered the dream I was having about Chase and felt my cheeks flush. Noah quirked an eyebrow in response. He missed nothing.

"Good dreams?" The smirk on his face made me blush even more. It was impossible for him to know what they were about, and I hated that he could read me so well to know that I was embarrassed. His eyes quickly darted down to my chest and I looked down to find that in my time of need, my nipples had very pointedly betrayed me. I crossed my arms over my chest in an attempt to hide them. It wasn't cold so I couldn't blame it on that.

"Assuming that we are safe from hungry bears, I'm going back to bed." I tried to play it cool as I turned on my heel and walked toward the bed.

"Yeah, I'm sure you're eager to get back to that dream. Don't worry, I won't tell Chase that you were calling his name while you were sleeping. Wouldn't want his ego to get any bigger." He winked and tapped the wall a few times with his knuckles before walking to his room, closing his door behind him.

I walked over and closed my door, mortified that not only had I said Chase's name out loud while I was asleep, but Noah had heard it! The dream was random and I had no idea where it came from, but I definitely wasn't ready to analyze it with someone else knowing that it had happened. It made it even harder to forget now that Noah knew. I sat on the bed and brought my knees up to my chin as I hung my head in embarrassment.

The dream was good, I would admit that. It was damn good. A part of me wondered what it would really be like to be with Chase. Would he be as smooth as I had dreamt he was? Would he say the right things and do the things that would send me over the edge? For years I had wondered what it would be like to be with him, but then I met Damian and I put those thoughts out of my mind.

There was an unknown tension that I felt coursing through my body as I thought more about the dream. While part of it was physical from the dream being so arousing, there was a part of it that was mental and I couldn't figure out how I really felt about everything. I hadn't thought of another man since before I met Damian, and regardless of what he thought, I hadn't been flirting with anyone. I barely even noticed that they existed. While I didn't get much attention or affection from Damian, I also wasn't seeking it out.

It had been such a long time since I had a man show me any attention, I couldn't remember what it felt like. Maybe that was why the dream had made such an impression on me. A longing that I've had for years to be seen, and even more so, to be wanted. Something that no one had tried to fulfill. I felt guilty for wanting that from another man when I was a married woman. But on the flip side, I was married to a man who was trying to kill me, so I guess it wasn't the worst thing in the world to want to find someone who at least liked me.

Now that my mind had allowed these thoughts of Chase to enter it, I couldn't get rid of them. I wanted to see him. I wanted to flirt with him. A part of me wanted to be a free woman and not be tied to Damian anymore. A huge part of me wanted to explore what kind of woman I really was. I had been living a lie for so long, always focused on being who Damian wanted me to be, that I never allowed myself to discover who I really was.

I laid down and rolled onto my side, the clock on my cell phone showed it was 3 in the morning. My mind was overwhelmed with thoughts of Chase as I slowly drifted back to sleep.

****

It was after 8:00 Saturday night and it had started to pick up a little as the college crowd made their way in. There was a group of guys that had come in and took over 3 of the high-top tables in the back. They were laughing and joking, all putting on a show for the table of girls that were at one of the long tables across from them. Shortly after, four girls in short dresses and stilettos joined the guys and their attention was redirected as the other girls finished up and left. I vaguely remembered those days and part of me regretted that I settled down with Damian so quickly and never got to fully embrace that part of growing up.

I wiped down the bar for what felt like the millionth time. Not because it needed it but because I was constantly running out of things to do. Noah had taken the tables on the patio and I was given the tables inside, but so far there was only the one group and they already had their drinks so I was stuck killing time until more tables were occupied. As I worked my way from one end of the bar to the other, I looked up to see Chase walk in. He was off tonight so I wondered if he was here to talk to Noah, or if he ended up coming in to work. It was my first Saturday working and I hadn't figured the dynamics out in the time I had been there. I was just thankful that this Saturday was a lot better than last Saturday. It felt like more time had passed, things had happened so quickly. Part of me wondered where Damian was and if he was still looking for me. It felt unsettling that I hadn't heard anything from him and for a moment, I prayed that I had been better at hiding than I originally gave myself credit for.

One of the guys pulled out a barstool and slid it in Chase's direction. I watched as his eyes met mine as he pulled one leg up and over the stool in a fluid motion. The movement reminded me of the movements he had done in my dream and I felt my cheeks flushing again. I lowered my eyes and tried to escape the feel of his eyes on me. Noah came in from outside and made his way around the bar to work on closing out a tab. I smiled as he walked past me to the computer in the corner, his head quickly glancing in Chase's direction where my attention was still focused.

One of the girls at the table kept trying to get his attention and finally gave up when he refused to look her way when she called his name, over and over and over. Quite frankly, it annoyed me as well so I didn't blame him for ignoring her. I watched as she stood up, ran her hands down her leopard print dress that was painted to her body, and flung her red curly hair over her shoulder as she walked around the tables to where he was sitting. His eyes shifted to look my way before he looked at her. I knew Chase well enough to know the look on his face. But that also didn't make me any less jealous of this woman who was being so forward and aggressive with getting his attention.

Little miss provocative tramp, in her 5-inch heels, leaned in and whispered something in his ear. I watched as she brushed her lips against his ear and saw the way she pushed her breasts so they touched his arm. I rubbed the cleaning towel on the counter in circles as I worked to clean a water ring that had formed. It was far from dirty, but the ring had been driving me crazy.

Chase allowed her to continue whispering in his ear as his arm reached up and touched her elbow. She adjusted her body and angled it toward his, allowing him to lower his hand and grab her ass. I watched intently as I waited to see what Chase would do. What could she possibly be telling him that is taking so long?

Probably telling him all of the slutty things she wants to do for him. I rolled my eyes. I don't know if I was still annoyed with the other woman or annoyed with myself for how jealous I was acting. It wasn't like Chase had ever expressed any interest in me. If anything, I was mad because I felt he was cheating on me, when the only time we ever had a moment was in a freaking dream. I needed to stop watching and just focus my attention elsewhere but I found it impossible to stop watching.

I watched as the girl slid her hand up Chase's arm as he leaned in to talk to her. The way he's reacting to her made me wonder if they were an item or if they had ever dated. Chase seemed really comfortable with her now, a smile on his face with something she said. Why wouldn't he be dating someone? Chase was a sexy man, with a wonderful personality. I didn't have to stay in Haven Brook to know that all of the women were still lined up for their chance to be with him. I chewed on the inside of my lip as I continued to wipe the same spot on the counter as I watched him.

"You know, if that doesn't get that spot clean, let me know and I'll just get a new countertop." Noah shoulder bumped me as he nodded at where my hand was still rubbing the towel in circles. I watched as he walked past me to go say hi to the group at the table. Chase smiled when Noah approached and gently pushed the girl away from his ear. The look on her face confirmed she wasn't pleased about being interrupted. She looked Noah up and down and continued to glare at him as she made her way back to her chair at the other end of the table. She sat down and began talking to the other girls as Noah said something to Chase that made him look in my direction.

Embarrassed for getting caught and frustrated for being so easily attracted to Chase I decided to take a much-needed break and walked to the back. I needed to clear my head and get away from the thoughts of Chase from last night. It was just a dream, so why wouldn't it just go away already?

I decided to clean the bathrooms which meant that I needed to get the supplies from the top shelf in the break room. I pulled one of the chairs over and used it to help me reach everything except the glass cleaner that was sitting too far back and out of my reach.

“Need a hand?” Chase offered. I jumped at the sound of his voice, I hadn’t heard him come down the hall and didn’t know anyone else was in the room with me.

“Nope, I’ve got it.” Reluctant to accept any help, I reached as far forward as I could and grunted as I grabbed the bottle of glass cleaner. The amount of force it took to reach the glass cleaner was enough to rock the chair beneath me. My eyes went wide as I watched the chair wobble beneath me.

In an instant Chase was by my side as he grabbed the chair to hold it steady. He had one hand holding the chair down and his arm wrapped around my waist. I looked down at him, a gasp escaping my throat due to the sudden physical contact. Something changed inside of him as well as I felt his hand twitch and his eyes shift.

“Need help down?” he offered as he continued to wrap his arm around me.

“I think I’m good but thank you.” I attempted to turn around to step off of the chair, not much room to work with. His arm moved down slightly and was almost to where it was wrapped around my ass instead of my waist as he looked at me for me to change my mind and accept his help. I realized that if I continued to turn around and tried to get down, it would force his hand to be on my ass now instead of my waist. Apparently, Chase realized the same thing as he lowered his hand even further, watching for my reaction.

“You’re impossible.” I decided to avoid the opportunity for any kind of contact with Chase and swatted his hand away as I squatted and got off of the chair.

“And why is that?”

“Any opportunity for you to grab some ass. Trying to act like you’re being a good guy and do a nice thing but yet all you’re really thinking about is your ulterior motives.”

“Hey, I was just trying to help a friend so she didn’t fall on her ass.” He raised his hands up in self-defense.

“Please, I’ve known you long enough to know that look in your eye. Always the ladies’ man. I’m sure that girl up front is still waiting to jump your bones." I knew the second that I said it, I would regret it. Any jealousy or insecurities I had, I just laid them out in front of him. Put everything out there for him to start asking questions about why I would even care.

I turned around with the cleaning supplies in my hands to see Chase leaned back against the counter, arms folded across his chest, with one foot crossed over the other. Damn him for making everything look sexy.

"I really get to you, don't I?"

"What would make you say that?" I turned away from him, hoping that my face had returned to its pale color instead of the scarlet hue I was sure was still lingering around.

"In all of the years that I've known you, I've never known you to be so feisty with me. It's like you've got all of this extra tension built up and you're needing a release." He waited for me to look at him. I was going to kill Noah if he had told Chase about last night. It was embarrassing enough already, I didn't need Noah telling Chase about it. And Chase had to know, why else would he be acting this way with me right now? This wasn't like him.

"I could help with that you know?"

"I hate to break it to you, Sparky, but you couldn't be more wrong. And even if I was in need of a *release*, you're the last person I would be coming to." I tried to muster as much sarcasm as I could. It was hard to convince someone else when you know that you're lying. Even more so when you know that the other person knows that you're lying.

"You can call it what you want to Mia, but there's a chemistry between us. I feel it and I know that you feel it. Sooner or later you'll give in. And trust me, not only will you be coming to me for the release, you'll be coming for me."

"I can't believe Noah. When did he tell you about the dream?"

"What dream?" His interest piqued as he pushed off from the counter and walked toward me.

Shoot.

"It was nothing." I chewed my bottom lip as I forced myself to rearrange the supplies that I had been messing with on the table while trying to avoid looking at him.

"What dream?"

I blew out a long breath and looked up at him. He had a coy grin on his face as he waited for me to tell him about the dream. Over my dead body. There was no way that I was going to tell him that I had a sex dream about him. No thank you, I didn't need that kind of embarrassment, followed by immediate rejection.

"I'm waiting."

"I had a dream last night. And you were in it. End of story." I squared my shoulders as I said it, an attempt to make myself feel stronger towards him and not give in and tell him.

"What was I doing in the dream?"

"Will you just let it go? It was just a dream."

"Sounds like it was a good dream if it's got you this wound up."

"Are you doing that thing, where Noah tells you something- then you pretend that he didn't tell you so you can try to make me tell you myself?" I folded my arms over my chest, matching his stance.

He stayed silent as his eyes remained focused on me. He was purposely trying to make me squirm and to get information out of me. There was no way that Noah hadn't told him something about my feelings for him. Either as a teenager, or now. That had to be what this was about.

"Noah hasn't told me anything, Mia."

"Then why are you being so---- whatever this is?" I was reluctant to say flirty, what if I was reading too much into this? What if I was trying to force this to be something that I wanted, instead of something that it was?

"Interested? Flirting? Forward? Which word do you want me to use?"

"Whichever one is the truth." I licked my lips, a nervous habit I've had since I was a little girl.

"All of them are the truth. Noah didn't tell me anything. You did."

I thought back to when I might have accidentally said something to him that would elude to me being interested in him. Nothing came to mind. He wasn't at the house when Noah heard me through the wall.

Unless Noah told him, which he kept saying that he didn't, I didn't know how Chase knew.

"What are you talking about?"

"I have a gift, Mia. I always have. It's the natural ability to know when a woman is interested in me. And your body language has been doing a lot of talking." He stepped closer, the air around us changed.

"You watched me tonight when you thought I wasn't looking. You were engaged in what you saw, jealous of another woman who was talking to me. You didn't pull away when I touched you earlier. You blush constantly around me. And your nervous habits go into full force when I get close to you." He ran a finger over my lip as I chewed the bottom of it, freeing it.

"I know that you have barely been back almost a week and that you are going through something really difficult and traumatic. I'm not going to be a dick and try to make the moves on you until you're ready. I respect you, Mia, and I know that when you're ready- and you will be ready- we can try and see where things go. For now, I'm here for you as a friend, as family, as whatever you need me to be. But don't allow yourself to be embarrassed about what you're feeling. It's okay to allow yourself to be attracted to me. It's okay to want to explore how you feel about things. I know that you're still technically married, but you owe it to yourself to decide what you want and make that your priority moving forward."

The conversation took a completely different turn than what I could have ever imagined. Chase knew me better than anyone did when we were growing up. He always knew my nervous habits and knew when I was lying. I felt blindsided by hearing him admit that there could be something between us. How long had he been interested? Was he only interested because he thought I was? There were so many thoughts floating around in my head, I tried to make sense of them when I saw him grinning at me.

"You better get back up front or Noah is going to think we're back here having sex on his desk."

"Why would he think that?" I looked up at him with confusion. If they hadn't been talking about what Noah knew, then why would he say that?

"Because I threatened to fuck you on his desk after he sprung it on me that he had hired you." Chase walked past me and went back up front while I was left in the breakroom with his words floating around me.

Twelve

Chase

I sat at an empty table on the patio while Noah cleared the glasses from the tables that had just left. It was almost closing time and I wasn't ready to leave just yet. I spun the bottle cap from my beer on the table and watched it spin in circles as I glanced over my shoulder to check on Mia. She spent the rest of the night avoiding me as she took care of the tables inside. In an effort to escape Nadia, I came outside to hang out with Noah as he worked.

"Man, that girl really has a thing for you." Noah sat the last glass down in the bin and lifted it off of the table as he wiped it down.

"Who?"

"The red head that was all up on you when I walked in earlier."

"Nadia." I let out a sigh as I peeked around the wall and saw her still sitting at the table I left her at earlier. The majority of the group had left and she stayed behind with a few of the guys. Either she was trying to make me jealous of the other guys, or she was hanging around to see if I would take her home with me. I didn't care either way, my mind was still on Mia.

"Wow, how many girls were all up on you tonight?" Noah joked as he looked up at me with a knowing look on his face.

"None, just her." I dodged his stare.
"Oh, so that's why you had to ask which one?"

"And why did you disappear to the back after Mia went on her break?" I heard the judgmental tone in his voice, asking what he already knew.

I looked at him but stayed silent. He met my silence with his own as he gave me a judgmental look.

"Look, like I said before- just stay off of my desk." He shifted the bin as he added another dirty glass and looked at me. I tried to keep the smile off my face but it was relentless.

"So, Mia said you knew about the dream she had?" I figured now was as good of a time as any to probe and see what I could find out.

"Did she tell you about the dream?" He arched an eyebrow.

"She said that you would tell me."

"Oh really? I find that hard to believe."

"Why's that?" I leaned forward in my chair, hoping that he would give me some insight into what the dream was about. It was killing me to know that she had a dream about me and no one would tell me what it was about. And by the way she reacted to me knowing about it, I knew it had to be dirty.

"Because Mia nearly died of embarrassment when she found out that I knew what kind of dream it was. She didn't give me the details, and quite frankly, I didn't want to know." Noah rotated the bin to his other hip and walked toward the doors that led inside.

"I have plenty of sex to keep me entertained, I don't need to hear about either of your fantasies. If I were you, I wouldn't bug her about telling you about the dream."

"Why not?" I stood up to follow him inside.

"Because I would hate for her illusion of how great you were in her dream be tarnished by how cocky and egotistical you are in real life. She's not like the other girls that are always chasing you, you need to remember that." He opened the door and I followed him inside as I let that information sink in.

Noah was right, Mia was not like the other girls. She was in a class all on her own and that's what made her so alluring. I was tired of the girls that were always chasing after me. It might have been flattering when I was in high school but not anymore. Sure, I could have almost any girl, any time I wanted her, but that didn't mean anything to me.

I wanted someone who was a challenge for me. Someone who kept me on my toes. Someone who would make me work harder for things. Someone who would push me past my limits. Someone who would force me out of my comfort zone. Someone like Mia. Maybe it was the fact that I couldn't have her that made me want her, but deep down I felt like it was more than that. I had a crush on Mia as we were growing up, but that was adolescent teenage hormones mixed in with a hot teenage girl always around.

Noah locked the front doors while Mia was busy closing out the register and prepared the deposit for Monday. I watched as she worked, fascinated with everything she did. She kept her head down as she looked over the reports she had printed and pulled a pen from the messy bun she had put her hair into after the last customer left. A small strand of hair curled behind her ear as it laid on her neck.

She stood at the register, the report in one hand and the pen in the other. Frustration showed on her face as she absentmindedly tapped the pen on the counter. She shifted her weight and I took notice of how small but curvy her body was. Her jean shorts were loose to where they hung low on her hips but not too baggy where she looked sloppy. Just baggy enough that I could easily slide them off without any effort. She had a white tank top underneath a short-sleeved button-down plaid top that was left open. It was a sexy mix of country paired with city girl.

"Noah, I can't get the totals to match. Are all of the sales in the system?" she called out to Noah as he made his way over to the register.

He took the report from her and looked over the last few pages as she watched over his shoulder.

"Sorry, it looks like I forgot to close out the last tab. Let me do that real quick and then I'll reprint the report. We should be fine after that." He entered a few things in the computer as I watched Mia walk down the hall to grab the new report that he had printed.

"You know you don't have to stay, Chase," he called over his shoulder to me. I had sat at one of the high-top tables and purposely avoided leaving right away as I saw Nadia's car still in the parking lot.

"I'm killing some time."

"Is she still outside?"

"Who's outside?" Mia asked as she made her way back to the counter and handed Noah the report. She looked at me as she waited for an answer.

"Some girl he's trying to avoid. She doesn't want to take no for an answer." Noah emptied the cash drawer into the deposit bag and added the reports to the others Mia had originally printed.

"Oh, poor Chase, can't escape the women throwing themselves at him. It must be so hard having every woman wanting you." I was surprised to hear the cattiness in her voice but I liked that she was still jealous of Nadia.

"Not every woman." I looked up at her and met her eyes. She looked surprised and taken aback by my remark.

"Yeah, the elderly ones don't care too much for him." Noah tried to cut the tension as he walked past us and went to put the deposit in the safe.

Mia and I were alone for a few minutes and I desperately wanted to take advantage of the time I had with her. I got up from the table and walked towards her. Her eyes grew bigger as she watched me invade her personal space. I wanted to take things slow and not overwhelm her. I needed her to trust me, to know that I wasn't going after her because I was bored with my options. I wanted her to know that I was genuine and sincere.

"Mia, I'm sorry if I was too forward with you earlier. I never meant to make you uncomfortable." I stood in front of her and made sure she looked at me so she could see the truth in my eyes.

"Thank you." She shifted her weight as she folded her arms across her chest then immediately unfolded them. She was fidgeting and I found it interesting that she was so nervous around me. She could deny that she wasn't feeling anything for me but her body language told a completely different story.

"You guys ready to go?" Noah turned the lights above us off as he waited by the front door.

I walked behind Mia as we walked into the parking lot and saw Nadia's car waiting for me. I sighed as I ran a hand through my hair, I had no energy to deal with her tonight. I had purposely ignored her texts and calls while she was gone after she hung up on me last weekend. I wasn't one to play games, I didn't care how good the sex might be.

Noah and Mia looked at the car and then over at me. I rolled my shoulders a few times as I looked at the car. I felt Mia's hand take mine as she walked with me to my truck. I had no idea what she was doing but decided to just go with it.

"See you tomorrow, Noah." she called as he walked to his SUV, looking just as confused as I was. She walked to the passenger side of the truck, which faces Nadia's car, and leaned in close to me.

"Open the door and help me in. Be sure to run your hand over my ass as you help me in," she instructed as she waited for the door to open.

The truck was lifted so she needed help getting in either way, however I was more than pleased to follow her command as I helped her in and glided my hand over her ass. The feel of her skin felt hot against mine as I tried to etch this memory before it could fade.

Out of the corner of my eye I saw Nadia's car still parked and knew she was watching us. Her lights flipped on and cast a light around us. I looked back to Mia who was looking past me at Nadia. I was about to close her door when she turned her body toward me and grabbed my shirt to pull me closer to her.

She opened her legs to allow my body to be close to hers as she reached up and wrapped her arms around my neck. I held onto her thighs as I watched her eyes, trying to figure out what she was doing. Her hands gently pushed my head down as our lips met in a soft kiss. I felt her body tense the moment we made contact and tried to pull away. Her hold around my neck got tighter as she opened her mouth further.

I heard an engine start and knew that Nadia had left as she revved it as she passed us. If she was mad before, she was even more pissed now. I slowly moved my hands up Mia's thighs and let them gently wrap around her waist. I could feel her pulling away from the kiss as she released her hands from my neck.
I stepped back and allowed her some space as I looked at her to try to get a feel for how she was feeling. I had no idea what had just happened, but I wasn't about to complain. That kiss was completely unexpected and took me by surprise.

"You looked like you needed a little help getting rid of her." Her voice was quiet and shaky. I knew she was trying to process what had just happened.

"Thanks, I do appreciate the help." I had no idea what to say. I didn't want to be an ass and make it seem like I didn't welcome the kiss, but I also didn't want to take advantage of her and keep going if she wasn't interested.

I never really thought about what it would feel like to kiss Mia. I'm sure whatever I would have imagined it would have been like, would be a disappointment compared to what it was actually like. Her lips were soft and she tasted sweet.

"Um, so Noah just left and the buses don't run this late, do you mind giving me a ride home?" She looked up at me and I wished I could kiss her again. "I mean, you do kind of owe me." There was a teasing tone to her voice which made me relieved that she wasn't overthinking what had just happened.

"You saved me from having to deal with a crazy chick tonight, I owe you more than just a ride home." I waited for her to pull her legs in before I closed her door and made my way around to the driver's side. I smiled as I got in, my night just got a whole hell of a lot better.

Thirteen

Mia

I climbed the second flight of stairs and walked down the hallway until I found apartment 825. The apartment complex was larger than I had expected and was relatively new. I got lucky when an apartment opened at last minute and I was able to secure it with the money I had saved from my first paycheck. I was even luckier that it was fully furnished so I didn't have to worry about buying furniture.

I turned the key in the lock and opened the door to my new home. It was bright and airy inside with white walls and an open floor plan. As I stepped inside I found an island to my left with cabinets along the wall. There wasn't much in the kitchen and it was rather small, but I was thankful that it had a full-size fridge, stove, and dishwasher. I didn't need much counter or cabinet space. Off to my right was a linen closet. I opened it to look inside, feeling silly that I still checked behind closed doors.

The kitchen flowed into the living room which had a tv mounted to the wall directly across from the door. There was a plush couch and an armchair by the wooden coffee table that sat in the middle of the room. Just past the end of the couch was a sliding glass door that led out to a balcony. I could picture myself enjoying a few dinners sitting out on the balcony, watching the sunset.

I shifted the bags on my arms as I made my way down the hallway that led back to the master bedroom, guest bedroom, and bathrooms. It was a short hall with the master bedroom on the left, the guest bedroom on the right, and an extra bathroom at the end. I walked into the master bedroom and sat my bags down on the bed. There wasn't much in them, just the items that I had collected and brought with me from Noah's. He had offered to help me move and I laughed as I held up the bags that I had and assured him it was really just a one-person type of job.

I looked around, taking in the bedroom that I would be sleeping in. To the left was a king-sized bed with a cushioned headboard and a white down comforter that looked like it belonged in a plush hotel suite. There were two nightstands, one on each side of the bed, and a long dresser that stood against the wall across from the bed and was big enough to store all of my belongings.

I walked through the room and opened the closet that was partially hidden behind the bedroom door. It was a small walk-in closet but big enough to hold the clothes I had when I lived in Boston. I walked past the bed and made my way into the master bathroom. There was a shower tub combo in the corner, a toilet right next to it, and a vanity with a large mirror and sink that took up the majority of the space, but still gave me plenty of space for me to get ready in the morning.

It was still early in the day so I took a look around at what had been provided, and what I needed to get. I had the basic toiletries from living with Noah, but I wanted to get my own towels and sheets to make it feel more comfortable. By noon everything was unpacked and I had my list of things I needed to get. I grabbed my keys and tucked my cell phone in my pocket as I made my way down the stairs and into the parking lot.

Part of what attracted me to these apartments was that it was a new development so everything was modern and not likely to break. My apartment had a small washer and dryer added in the guest bathroom which meant I didn't have to constantly take my laundry anywhere, and it was walking distance to both The Vine and General Bob's.

The store was busier than I expected for a Saturday at noon. I made my way through the store, collecting the items on my list. I was almost giddy when I found an entire aisle of clearance home goods and grabbed some other items that I wanted. The towels that I picked were a charcoal color and on sale, the sheets were buy 1 get 1 half off. I had completely forgotten the bargain deals I used to love coming here for when I was growing up.

I added a small coffee maker, coffee, and some creamer, in addition to a handful of groceries to get me through the week. I had been tracking the cost of everything as I went, making sure I wasn't going over what I actually had to spend. I glanced down at the calculator on my phone and added on what I guessed would be the tax. I should still have $60 extra from what I budgeted, thanks to all of the clearance items. I was almost to the line to check out when I saw a display with different wines and decided to stop. I browsed each of the bottles, admiring the artwork on each one as I ran my hand over the label. I was about to put the bottle back when I heard a voice behind me.

"Didn't peg you for a merlot kind of girl. Figured you would prefer the sweeter wines."

I turned around to find Chase standing behind me, a handheld cart balanced across his forearm. His smile beamed across his face as he waited for my response.
"I was just admiring the artwork." I put the wine back on the shelf and turned back to my cart. I had been trying to avoid Chase for a full week after we kissed in the parking lot. Okay, so maybe WE didn't kiss. I kissed him. And told him to grab my ass. Now I was wishing I could just open the wine right there and stick a straw in it.

"It's a good wine. You would probably like the Moscato, it has a nice flavor and is pretty sweet."

"Okay, I didn't peg you for a sweet wine kind of guy." I rested my arms on the handle of the cart, unsure of what to do with myself. I hated that he made me so nervous. It was like going through puberty all over again.

"I drink it on occasion, depends on whose company I'm in." He smiled and I knew that he meant it depended on what girl he was with. As much as I didn't want to be, I was jealous again.

Not knowing what else to say I started pushing my cart around the display.

"Well, guess I'll see you around." I started walking past him when I heard his footsteps beside me.

"Noah said you got settled in your apartment today." He said it more as a statement than a question.

"Yeah, just getting the few things I need and I should be all set." I nodded toward the basket of my cart that was filled with more than what I actually needed.
"How about a housewarming dinner?" he offered as he kept pace with me as I made my way to the check out and got in line.

I didn't know what to say to his invite. I wanted to spend time with him but I didn't know if could trust myself not to make an ass out of myself again. There was this weird tension between us and I didn't think it would be a good idea for us to be alone together until it was gone. I was sure he was only interested because I had led him on last weekend. I sighed heavily as I remembered the details and the softness of his lips.

"Why don't you take some time to think about it and after you're all settled in, you can let me know when and we'll do dinner. I can even cook. Just let me know, no rush." I could see him backing off as he said it, a look of rejection on his face. I hated that I had caused that look.

"Okay, sounds good. Thanks." I smiled as I moved forward in the line and Chase walked off as he waved goodbye. Relief flooded me that I didn't have to worry about messing things up with him but I also felt disappointed that I didn't get to spend time with him. I paid for my stuff and made my way back to the apartment with bags lined up both arms. Note to self- only buy what you're able to easily carry back to your apartment. Times like this I missed having the rental car but was also relieved when Noah had one of his friends take it back to Denver to return it for me so I didn't have to keep paying for it.

It was almost one thirty and I had an hour before I had to leave for work. I threw in a quick load of laundry to wash the new linens and made myself lunch as I sat on the balcony and watched traffic go by. It was so peaceful and relaxing that I almost lost track of time. I glanced at my phone and checked the time. As I was getting up to take my plate inside I saw a text message pop up from Jade.

Jade: yoga?

I smiled at her text message and our new code word for Damian.

Mia: No yoga. You?

I waited as I watched the three dots bounce across the screen.

Jade: No yoga for me either. Talk later?

Mia: I get off at 10, talk then?

Jade: 10 it is.

I slid my phone in my pocket as I cleaned up my mess and went to work.

Fourteen

Damian

"It's been almost three weeks. THREE. FUCKING. WEEKS! Why haven't you found her yet?" I slammed my hands down on my desk as I stared at the pathetic client in front of me.

"Damian, I've told you that it's not that easy. For one- I'm not active on the force. Remember, that little thing about me being fired for embezzlement? That means no one wants to talk to or help a dirty cop. I have a few contacts that I can ask for help, but it's going to take time." Hank leaned back in his chair and stared at me. He was lucky that I agreed to take his case, not because I wanted to, but because I had stuck my foot in my mouth with Ronnie and said I was working on it.

Truth was the guy had no case. All I would be able to do for him was possibly pull some strings and get him a lesser sentence. I knew if I could get him and his wife to rat on the other manager that was also involved, I could get them a deal since it would take down the entire structure. But I wasn't going to tell him that until I got what I wanted.

Mia had been gone almost three weeks and it was infuriating me that I had no idea where she was. Hank confirmed her flight had gone to Denver, which was pretty useless information given that I knew that when I looked up her flight information at the airport. I needed him to find out more before people started asking about where Mia was. I had been able to keep Ronnie at bay while I was in D.C. last week but he had already started asking how Mia was feeling and I was running out of bullshit to tell him. I needed this to be over already.

"If you have connections then use them. Now isn't the time to play around with me, Hank. I'm not someone you want to mess with."

"Are you threatening *me*? You *really* want to threaten a cop?" He leaned forward in his chair, invading my space and trying to show force.

"*Former* cop. Remember your place." I shot him look that forced him back in his chair again.

"Find where she went. She's a dumb housewife, it shouldn't be this hard to find her, damnit!" I pushed the stack of papers next to his file off to the side in frustration.

"I'll keep trying but it's not like I have a ton of options. There are a lot of cities and towns around Denver- she could be in any one of them. She might not even be in Colorado anymore. Without more information, it's hard to know where she went. She's not using any of her credit cards, and nothing has popped up under Mia Stone."

"Look under Mia Johnson."

"Johnson?" Hank raised an eyebrow in question.

"Johnson is her maiden name. She might be using that instead."

I watched as Hank pulled out a pen and jotted the information down on a scrap piece of paper.

"I'll see what I can find and let you know." Hank stood up to leave and walked toward the door when I stopped him.

"You have a week. Find her within the next week or you and your wife lose any plea deal options."

"You're kidding me." The look on Hank's face said he knew that I wasn't.

"How am I supposed to find her in a week? I need more time than that."

"You've had a week to figure that out." I looked up at him as he lingered in my doorway. "Thought cops were supposed to be good at finding people?"

He glared at me as he opened the door and stormed out, slamming it behind him. I rubbed my temples as the headache I had been fighting the past few days started to build again. It was nine in the morning and I had a long day ahead of me so I needed something to get rid of it. I opened my bottom desk drawer and looked at the bottle of aspirin sitting next to the almost empty bottle of whiskey. I debated my options before reaching for the whiskey and added it to my coffee.

I stirred the whiskey in with a pen as my door opened and Claire walked in wearing a tight black skirt with a white button-down blouse that showcased her perfect tits. I looked her up and down as I took in the show she was putting on as she stalked toward me, one stiletto in front of the other.

"Mr. Stone, I have the Lewis file that you asked for." She laid it on my desk, reaching across me so her tits were in my face.

"What are you working on?" she purred in my ear as she leaned down and let her breath hover over my ear. I reached down and ran a hand up her bare leg, caressing my way up her thigh. I waited as she took a step to the side and allowed me to slide my hand up further.

She looked down at me, a smirk on her face. I scooted my chair back as she pulled away from my touch and hiked her skirt up, her bare pussy greeting me. She leaned forward and worked quickly on undoing my pants before she straddled me and slid my thick dick inside of her.

I watched as she let her head fall back as she bounced up and down, her tits almost popping out of her shirt. I reached forward and pulled her blouse open, unhooking the clasp on the front of her bra. Within seconds her tits were free and she watched as I leaned forward and pulled a nipple into my mouth. She rode me even harder as my teeth nipped at her other nipple, pushing both of us close to climax. I felt the buildup and knew I was close to coming.

Why the fuck hadn't I put on a condom before we started? I looked around frantically, knowing it was too late. She caught my eye and held my gaze as she drove herself down deeper on my dick, taking every inch of me inside of her. I tried to push her off as I was about to come but she grabbed onto my shoulders and held on even tighter as I came undone inside of her. She smiled a wicked smile as she watched, knowing that I came inside of her. Once I was done, she climbed off, fixed her clothes, and smiled as she walked out of my office, shutting the door behind her. It was the first time we had sex but something told me it wasn't going to be the last.

Fifteen

Mia

Saturday was so busy that Jade and I never got the chance to talk that night after I got home from work. I really wanted to talk to her and catch up but I was exhausted and she ended up with a last-minute date. We had tried to set aside time for a call on Tuesday but that fell through. So did Wednesday. It was Thursday morning and I sat on the couch, watching my cell phone as I waited for it to ring.

My phone vibrated in my hand as I saw Jade's name on the screen. Excitement filled me as I slid the button to answer the call.

"Hey, I'm glad we are finally able to sit and talk for a few." My tone was cheery until I saw the bruise on Jade's face and a mark on her throat. My stomach dropped. Her eyes were reluctant to meet mine and I started to panic that he was there with her. We hadn't text in advance so I had no way of knowing whether she was okay before I answered the call.

"Jade, did you go to yoga?" I asked as calmly as I could and angled myself to where the plain white wall was behind me. I didn't want anything to give away where I was or make it easier to find me. Although if he was there with her, I knew he would find a way to trace the phone number that she had called so it didn't really matter.

"No yoga. Not today." She met my eyes and there was sadness behind them.

I challenged her with my stare, still unsure of whether she was alone.

"I'm by myself," she assured me as she stood up and walked around her apartment like we usually do. "All clear."

"What happened?" Concern took over as I worried that Damian had done this to her. It was possible that it was also the guy she had gone out with Saturday night. Her eyes looked down at the floor, refusing to meet mine.

"Jade. Talk to me." I needed to know what had happened to her.

"Do you need me to show you yoga on my side?" Maybe she was concerned that he was there with me, though it seemed unlikely given how I was talking to her. I was desperate to do whatever it took to get her to talk to me.

"No, I know he's not there with you. I know because he just left my apartment." She looked up at me and I knew that he had done that to her.

"Oh my God, I'm so sorry." I fought back the tears that wanted to flow and forced myself to keep it together. "What happened? Tell me everything."

"He followed me home Saturday night from work. He had come into the bar while I was working and recognized me from lunch. He started getting angry and caused a scene so management kicked him out. By the time I left for the night, I didn't see him around so I went home. It was already late and I didn't want to panic you so I lied about having a date." She took a deep breath and I watched her bring her hand up to her neck.

"I wasn't expecting anyone this morning so when I heard someone knocking on the door, I just answered it. I didn't think anything about it. He pushed his way inside my apartment and pinned me to the wall by my throat. He kept demanding that I tell him where you are. I told him that I didn't know and that you hadn't contacted me so I didn't know where you went. He hit me a few times after he pinned me down and tried to strangle me, then he left. He said he'll be back soon to see if my story has changed."

I stayed staring at her for what felt like hours. My heart was broken knowing that I had put my only friend in danger. It was my fault that he had attacked her. It was my fault that he was coming back for her. I tried to think of what to do next when she started to speak again and interrupted my thoughts.

"Mia, I didn't tell him where you are. I didn't tell him anything, I swear. But he's looking for you. He knows that you went to Denver, he tracked your flight."

There was panic in her voice and I felt it in my blood. He would find a way to find me, no matter how hard I tried to hide.

"You have to leave Jade. Today. You have to go before he can come back for you. He won't leave you alone until he gets to me."

"Mia, I can't do that. I don't have anywhere to go. I don't have family. I don't have friends. Where am I supposed to go?"

"Come here." I blurted it out before I even thought about it. It was insane to ask her to come here and risk that Damian could follow her here. If he did that then I would have inadvertently lead him directly to me. But I didn't want Jade to have to be on her own. Honestly, I didn't want to be on my own either. They say there's safety in numbers so if I could get her here without Damian knowing, we could keep each other safe.

"Mia, that's crazy. You know there's a risk."

"I know. But it's the only thing we can do at this point. You're not safe there."

"How are we going to do this?" I could hear that she was reluctant to go through with this, I felt the same way. It was going to be tricky but we could do it.

"I'm going to work in thirty minutes, I'll call you at the cafe we used to hang out at when I first met you. Neither of the landlines will be on anyone's radar so we can avoid using cell phones. Can you be there in thirty minutes?" My voice was filled with hope and I prayed that we would be able to pull this off.

"Yeah, I can get there in thirty minutes."

"Take time to look around." I hinted so she would know to watch for him. "And take only what you need."

"I'll talk to you in thirty."

We hung up and adrenaline coursed through me as I got dressed and made my way to The Vine. It wasn't open for business yet but I knew that Chase would already be there. I walked as quickly as I could, making sure I got there a few minutes early. My mind was racing as I tried to think through the rest of the plans. I used my key to open the front door and immediately regretted that I didn't give Chase a heads up that I was coming in. I heard his footsteps coming down the hall as I locked the door behind me.

"Hey, everything alright?" He looked past me to make sure no one else was behind me.

"Yeah, can I use the phone?" My nerves were still on high alert which made me look twitchy and caused Chase to take notice.

"Of course. What's going on, Mia? Are you okay?" He led the way back to his office and stepped to the side with his hand extended so I could enter.

I made my way behind his desk and checked the clock. I still had five minutes before I was supposed to call. I rubbed my hands together, my body felt cold despite the summer heat.

"Mia- tell me what's going on. You're really freaking me out." Chase came around the back side of the desk and sat on the edge of it, facing me as I sat in his chair.

"I need to help my friend Jade. Damian attacked her this morning, trying to find information about where I went. She needs to leave but we couldn't talk about it on our cell phones in case he tries to trace the call."

"How would he trace the call?" Chase frowned as he tried to process what I had just told him.

"He's a lawyer and has connections. He had a tracking app installed on my phone so he's pretty good at navigating that kind of stuff. We don't want to risk him having a connection that can trace the call. It would lead him right to me." I glanced at the clock and waited. Three more minutes.

I unlocked my cell phone and opened Google. I had started to type the name of the cafe when Chase's hand reached out to stop me.

"Mia, there's an actual computer in front of you. Use that one." He nodded to his computer and I took the mouse to navigate to the page with their phone number.

I picked up the phone and called the phone number on the screen, praying that this would work. After the seventh ring I started to feel uneasy that my plan would backfire.

"Giovanni's Cafe," a woman huffed into the phone.

"Hi, I'm looking for a customer- her name is Jade. She's expecting the phone call."

"Ma'am this is a place of business, not a place for customers to receive personal phone calls."

I listened as she started to move the phone away and knew she was going to hang up.

"PLEASE! She's in trouble. Please don't hang up." I begged as loud as I could, praying she would hear me. There was a faint sigh on the other end and I knew she had heard me.

"Let me call out and see if she's here."

"No! Please don't do that. There's a chance that a man followed her there."

"Okay, what do you want me to do?"

"Um, can you tell me if there are any men there?"

"There's a handful."

"Any that are sitting by themselves or with a girl?"

"A few that are with a girl, none that are by themselves."

"Okay, do you see a woman with short black hair and a bruise on her cheek?"

"Let me take a look around. I'll be right back." I heard her sit the phone down and waited anxiously for her to come back.

"Nope. No women that match that description."

I let out a deep breath as I closed my eyes and pinched the bridge of my nose to keep from crying. I felt Chase's hand rub my back lightly.

"Hold on a minute." My head perked up as I waited for her to come back.

"You get the hell away from her. Right now!" She was screaming at someone and I could hear a man's voice faint in the distance. "You come one more step towards her and I'll whack you with this frying pan. Don't you mess with me, asshole."

There was commotion in the background and I struggled to hear what it was. I looked up at Chase who looked as confused as I was even though he couldn't hear what was happening on the other end. I looked around on his phone until I found the button for the speaker phone and pressed it. I put the phone on the receiver as we listened to the commotion that was still happening on the other line. I heard footsteps getting louder and waited.

"Alright, I found her. Here she is." The woman sat the phone down again and a few seconds later I heard someone pick it up.

"Yoga is cancelled today." Jade said with a sigh.

"Are you okay? What happened?"

"Some guy tried to steal this woman's purse as I was walking in and she went off on him. She's a feisty one." Jade laughed and I felt relieved to know that she wasn't the one who had been in trouble.

"Did you make it there okay? Any sign of him following you?"

"None that I saw. I took several side streets and checked behind me several times. I even cut in through a few stores and popped out the back exits. I think it's clear."

"Perfect. I'm glad to hear that." My breathing had started to return to normal as I knew she was okay.

"So what's our plan? I brought the things I needed and left the rest. If he goes by my apartment at any point, it will look like I still live there."

"That's good. I'm sorry, I know that it sucks to up and leave everything. I never wanted this to happen to you."

"It's okay, Mia. It's not your fault." She tried to reassure me but I knew 100% that it was my fault she had to uproot everything and start over.

"There's a couple ways to get here but I worry about you buying a plane or bus ticket, he might be able to track your purchases."

"I could rent a car and drive. It would take a while but I could do it."

"That might be the only way. But it would still be linked to your name." Frustration was building quickly as we tried to figure out a plan without much luck.

"I can try to get a different ID."

"There's no time for that and do you even know anyone who does that anymore?" I asked with uncertainty in my voice.

"No, but desperate times call for desperate measures."

"I can help, ladies." I heard Chase next to me and for a moment I had forgotten that he was sitting next to me, listening to the call.

“Who’s that?” Jade sounded alarmed and I immediately felt bad for not telling her that she was on speakerphone and he was in the room.

“Sorry, that’s Chase. I’m in his office.”

“Oh, that scared me.” I heard her let out a sigh.

“Let me make a phone call real quick and see what I can do.” He got up and walked into the hallway while Jade and I stayed on the phone.

There was a lot of background noise which made me relieved that she was surrounded by people while we talked. For the moment I didn’t have to worry about her. A few minutes later Chase came back into the office with his cell phone pressed to his ear.

“Perfect, thanks Marty, I owe you one.” He hung up the phone and put it back in his pocket.

“Jade, do you have a way to make it to the Budget rental car lot on Frost avenue?” He spoke loudly to make sure she could hear him.

“Yeah, it’s only a few blocks from here. I can walk.”

“Great. Head over there and ask for Marty. She has a car ready for you and it will be under Wendy Ryder.” He smiled as he said the name and I could tell he was proud of the name he had made up.

“How did you do that? Aren’t they going to need my ID?”

“It’s one of my mom’s close friends, she’s like family and she owed me a favor. Just check in with her when you get there and she’ll get you on your way. No paperwork or ID required.”

“That’s really nice of you Chase, thank you.” Jade sounded relieved which made me relieved.

“Oh and Jade?” He waited to make sure she hadn’t hung up.

“Yeah?”

"Everything is paid for already. I've taken care of the rental fees so you won't need to pay for that. Be sure to check the glove box when you get in, Marty said she will leave you a care package as well."

"That's amazing, thank you. I can't wait to meet you and personally thank you. Now I see why Mia loves you so much." I blushed at the words as Chase looked down at me and smiled. It was now apparent that I had been talking about him to Jade.

"Be careful, Jade. Make sure to always check your surroundings and please try to check in when you can from a pay phone. I'll see you as soon as you get here." I listened as she said goodbye, both of us knowing that we wouldn't hear much from each other until she got here. Sadness filled me as I worried about her making it out here safely. I still felt an enormous amount of guilt over her leaving.

I looked up at Chase as I slouched back in his chair. He never ceased to surprise me with how kind and generous he was.

"That was really nice, what you did for Jade. Thank you."

"I'm glad I could help." He smiled down at me as he sat on the edge of his desk.

"It was really nice of your mom's friend to do that for Jade. What's in the care package?" I asked curiously.

"I'm not sure to be honest. I gave her a quick summary of what was happening and she took care of the rest." He let out a breath before continuing. "She was a victim of abuse as well. Boston was where she went to escape and after her husband was locked up in prison, she vowed to always help others to pay it forward as a thank you to those who had helped her."

"Is she covering the cost of the rental car?"

"Nope, that I'm taking care of. I gave her my credit card information, she'll run everything on that. The only thing she will have to pay for is gas, but Marty said she was giving her the most efficient vehicle she had so it shouldn't be too much."

"Wow. This is just— it's all too much. Thank you for helping. I really appreciate it." I patted his thigh without thinking about it. I felt his hand reach down and grab hold of mine as he gently squeezed it.

My hand lingered on his thigh and as much as I knew I needed to move it, I couldn't find it in me to actually do it. My eyes reached his, a heaviness hung over them as he licked his lips. I swallowed hard as I continued to meet his gaze. My pulse quickened as I waited for him to make a move, too afraid to do it myself. His hand ran up my bare arm, sending goosebumps in its path. He kept his eyes locked on mine as I felt the heat from his touch spread within me.

He adjusted his position and stood in front of me, pulling me up to a standing position as well. We were face to face, close enough that our breath could be felt on the other's skin. His fingers found mine, a slow touch as he caressed my hands. He stepped closer, invading more of my space. My breaths became harder and came quicker as my body reacted to being in such close proximity with his. I felt him lean forward and closed my eyes as he came close enough to kiss me.

"Morning." Noah called as he walked down the hallway and stood outside of Chase's door.

Chase let out a frustrated sigh as I took a step back, embarrassed. He ran a hand over his face and looked back at Noah. The look on Noah's face was half surprised to find us there together and half amused that he had walked in on us.

"My bad." He chuckled as he walked past the office and went into his.

"I should get going." I said as I stepped to the side of him, grabbing my cell phone from his desk and sliding it in my pocket. He kept his head down as he nodded in response and stepped back so I could get past.

"Bye, Noah." I called as I made my way out of the building as quickly as possible and went back to my apartment.

Sixteen

Chase

Fridays were by far my favorite day of the week. It was the end of the work week, the start of the weekend, and today, I got to see Mia the majority of the day since she was working the day shift.

We didn't see each other much yesterday after Noah interrupted our almost kiss. By the time she came in for her shift, I was leaving for the day. While I wanted to stick around and try to get any time with her that I could, I decided it was best to leave and allow her some space.

Yesterday I felt the chemistry between us. I felt her body respond to my touch. The way she leaned in to meet me for a kiss. I could tell that she wanted it as much as I did. I was glad that she had let me be part of what she was going through with Jade, it felt like she trusted me. That was the most important thing for me, to make sure that she knew she could trust me and that she felt safe with me. We were making progress on both ends.

I sat in my office, trying to focus on the report I was supposed to be working on, distracted as I waited for her to come in. I knew that she was coming in at nine to work on projects before we opened at eleven. It was 8:50 and it felt like time was passing by slower than ever.

There was a noise up front as I heard the door open and close, followed by light footsteps approaching down the hallway. I looked up and smiled when I saw her walk by on her way to the break room. She looked sexy in a short denim skirt with a black lace tank top and sandals. Fridays were a good day for tips and she was wearing the perfect outfit to take home a full paycheck worth.

I stood up from my desk and smoothed down the blue polo I was wearing, more out of habit than actually needing to. She was turned away from me as she put her purse in the cabinet when I walked in. I leaned against the wall as I admired her from behind.

Her hair was pulled up into a high ponytail which left her neck and shoulders exposed. I longed to walk up behind her and kiss the bare skin. Her skirt sat low on her hips and covered her legs mid-thigh. The skirt was longer than what I saw most girls wear these days and I loved that it was still sexy without being slutty. It left plenty to the imagination.

I had been staring at her so intently that I hadn't paid attention to the fact that she didn't know I was in the room and accidentally startled her when she turned around.

"Oh my God!" Her hand flew to her chest as she braced herself against the counter.

"You scared the shit out of me. How long were you standing there?"

"Sorry, I didn't mean to scare you. Not long, I was just coming to see how you were doing today. Have you heard from Jade at all?" I stood up straight and shoved my hands in my jeans, hoping she would buy my bullshit about checking on her instead of the truth that I was checking her out.

"I haven't heard from her yet. I hope she's okay. It's just hard not knowing where she's at and what's going on. It sucks, it's all my fault that she's in this position." She walked to the table and held onto the back of a chair.

"I'm sure she'll be okay. She sounds like a really smart girl." I smiled genuinely to try to put her mind at ease.

There was a silence between us as we looked at each other. I knew she was thinking about what had almost happened yesterday, just like I was. I waited to see if she would bring it up as we continued our silent standoff.

"Well, I better get started on unpacking the new glasses before we open." She pushed away from the chair and walked to the boxes in the back of the room that held the new glasses I had ordered. Her back was turned to me so I took that as my sign to leave her alone.

"Sounds good, I'll be in my office if you need any help."

"Thanks," she said as she looked over her shoulder to smile as I walked back to my office.

I wanted to spend more time with her. Just being in close proximity to her made me feel excited. I hadn't felt this way about a girl- ever. It was new and exciting and I felt like a teenage boy learning about girls for the first time. It was embarrassing what she could do to me. She could ask for a unicorn riding an abominable snowman and I would figure out a way to get it for her.

Two hours had gone by and I still hadn't gotten any work done. I sighed in frustration as I leaned back in my chair and tossed my pen on the desk. I needed to clear my head and get work done but I couldn't focus for the life of me. I heard my phone vibrate on the desk and picked it up.

"Hey mom, what's up?" I hadn't called my mom in a week so I expected that she would be calling to check in on me.

"He's gone, Chase! I can't find him anywhere!" Panic filled her voice and I leaned forward in my chair as I pressed the phone closer to try to hear what she was saying.

"Who's gone? What's going on?"

"Liam. He got into a fight with Grant and I thought he was upstairs in his room. I called him down for lunch and he didn't come so I went to look for him and I can't find him. Chase, he's gone!"

"Okay, mom, try to calm down. I'm leaving now, I'll start looking for him. Have you told Grant?"

"No, I haven't told him yet. I didn't know if I should or not. What if he finds Liam and he runs again? The fight was pretty bad."

"What was the fight about?" I picked up my car keys and walked out of my office, poking my head into Noah's office. I covered the mouthpiece of the phone as Noah looked at me, knowing something was wrong by the look on my face.

"Liam took off, I need to go find him." I whispered to Noah. He nodded his head and waved me off as I walked out of the door and got in the truck.

"Liam was talking about Renee and felt like Grant wasn't listening to him, which he wasn't because he was still working from his phone. Liam accused him of forgetting about Renee and Grant lost his temper." My mom summarized their fight as quickly as she could and I knew right away where to go find Liam. I hung up with my mom as I drove towards the pond and parked my truck.

I jumped out and jogged over to the willow tree that Liam used to sit under with his mom. She used to bring him here for picnics when he was growing up and they would sit under the tree and watch the ducks swim in the pond. I saw him before he saw me so I slowed my pace as I quietly approached him. He looked up and saw me but made no effort to get up. His face was red and splotchy, dried tears on his cheeks.

I sent a quick text to my mom to let her know that I found him as I walked over and sat down in the grass next to him. I looked out at the pond and waited for him to talk first.

"How did you know I was here?" He sniffled and wiped his face with his T-shirt.

"I know how important this place is to you. It's where you go when you want to be close to your mom." I kept my eyes ahead of me as we talked and picked at the cool grass under my legs.

"Why doesn't my dad miss her?" He looked up at me with tears in his eyes. I wrapped him in my arms as he sobbed into my shoulder. I held him as tight as I could, wishing I could take this pain away. I waited for him to calm down so I knew I had his full attention before speaking.

"Liam, your dad misses your mom more than any of us could ever know. He would have done anything in the world to make her better if he could. Hell, any of us would have. He fought so hard for her, to try to save her, and now, he fights so hard for you. To keep you happy. To keep you safe. To keep you from knowing how much he misses her." I watched as he looked up at me, listening to the words I spoke.

"Why doesn't he want me to know that he misses her?" Innocent eyes looked up at me and my heart felt like it might crumble.

"Because his heart is broken, champ. When your mom died, a part of your dad went with her. I think he's still trying to figure out just how big that part was." I let out a jagged breath as I fought back my own feelings. Liam stayed silent and looked back toward the pond as I continued to talk.

"Your daddy may not talk about her much, but it's not because he doesn't want to. It's because it makes him sad that she's not here. And he doesn't want you to see that he's sad. He wants to be strong for you, and to him, that means that he has to be brave."

"Brave for what?"

"Brave for you. So that you know how to be strong as well." I looked at the pond and tried to think of the right things to say to make him really understand.

"Your daddy loved your mom more than anything, then they had you, and they found that they could love someone even more. You became their entire world. So believe me when I say that your dad loved your mom, and he struggles with how much he misses her every single day. He sees her when he looks at you. We all do. And we're so blessed because in a way, we still get to have a piece of her here with us because we have you." I smiled and watched him smile back at me.

"Your dad is a wonderful man, Liam, and he will go to his grave constantly trying to prove to you how much he loves you. He works hard to try to provide the very best he can, to give you the life him and your mom always dreamed of giving you. Try to be patient with him, he's still trying to figure out how to do this on his own." I hugged him again and hated that this even had to be a conversation. Liam deserved to have his mom as much as my brother deserved to have his wife. It was a real shitty hand that they were dealt.

"Thanks, Uncle Chase. You always make me feel better." He reached up and wrapped his arms around me to hug me.

"Anytime champ, anytime." Moments like this warmed my heart as we stayed sitting next to each other and watching the ducks. We took turns sharing a memory of Renee as we laughed and cried, then laughed some more.

An hour later I saw Grant's car pull up. Liam hung his head as his dad approached and I shot my brother a look that told him to go easy on the kid. His eyes were red and I could tell that he had been upset as well. He smiled softly at me as he approached, taking Liam in to get a feel for his mood.

"Can I join you guys?" he asked casually as Liam avoided looking at him. I nodded subtly and Grant sat on the other side of Liam. I debated whether to get up and give them some privacy but when I started to move my brother shook his head no.

"Liam, I would like to say I'm sorry for what happened earlier. I never should have yelled at you, and I'm sorry that I wasn't giving you my full attention." Grant held his posture stiff and continued. "I promise that it won't happen again."

Liam looked over at his dad and rested his head on his knee as he pulled his legs in and cuddled them.

"How can you promise that? You're always too busy with your job." Liam hid his face in between his knees.

"Not anymore." He paused as he waited for Liam to respond.

"You know why?" Grant leaned forward to try to make eye contact with Liam.

"Why?"

"Because I quit my job." Grant smiled a huge smile as Liam's head popped up.

"Really?!" Liam was excited as he looked back and forth between me and his dad.

"Really. I decided that I didn't need to keep working crazy hours and I didn't want to miss out on the things that were happening in your life. I want to be there for every moment, I don't want to miss anything." Liam reached over and hugged Grant so hard he almost knocked him over as Grant laughed.

"That's the best news ever dad. But what are you going to do for a job?"

"Well, it turns out that your school had a position open for a P.E. coach so I took it. I'll start when school goes back in the fall. Until then, I'm going to be the assistant coach for your little league team. Which means we'll get to spend a lot of time together!"

"Wow! That's great! Did you hear that Uncle Chase?" He beamed up at me with pure happiness in his eyes.

"I sure did. I told you, didn't I?" I smiled at him as I winked, knowing that Grant would wonder what we had talked about.

"Yeah, he figured it out." Liam laughed as his dad grabbed him and tickled him.

I said my goodbyes as I made my way to the truck and went back to work. Grant and Liam were skimming stones across the pond when I left and I was relieved to see their relationship getting stronger. I was proud of my brother for quitting a job that he loved in order to be the dad that his son needed. He was a great dad, he just needed to prove it to himself.

Seventeen

Mia

It was after two when I saw Chase come in and make his way to his office. Noah went back to talk with him but I had no idea what was going on. Chase had seemed upset when I saw him leave earlier but I didn't dare ask Noah about it. I was trying to lay low and let things settle between us before Noah started to think something really was going on with Chase and I.

The last few hours of my shift went by quickly as we got busy during happy hour. The tips were good and I was thankful that I would have some extra cash if needed. While I knew I would have steady paychecks, I felt uneasy about Damian going after Jade to try to find me so I didn't want to get too comfortable and not have a way to run if needed.

I wrapped up the last few tables I had been waiting on and closed their tabs as I waited for them to leave so I could clear their table. Noah had started taking over the new tables, the system we had created worked flawlessly. It was thirty minutes before my shift ended when I saw Chase come up front and sit at the end of the bar. I was about to walk over to wait on him when I saw Noah grab a glass and fill it before sliding it to Chase. I couldn't hear what they were talking about over the noise of the room, but it looked like an intense conversation as

Chase spoke to Noah. Before I could look away I felt Chase's gaze land on me and felt trapped in it.

There was something different in the way he looked at me. It wasn't anger, maybe more frustration? My body tingled as I held his gaze for another second before breaking it and looking away. I made my way under the bar top to avoid having to walk over to where they were talking and went to clean the tables that had just left. I was cleaning the last table when I saw Chase head back to his office. I loaded the few glasses into the bin and walked over to the bar and sat it on the back counter. There were only a few glasses in it so Noah told me to leave it there and he would take it back later when it was full. I double checked to make sure all of my tables were closed out and cleaned before I walked back to the break room to grab my purse.

As I walked through the door, I saw Chase walking down the hallway toward his office from the break room. There was still that look in his eye and something told me that something inside of him had changed. Maybe it was whatever he had left to deal with earlier? I couldn't imagine it was the one beer he had and hadn't even finished. He smiled when he saw me, a devilish look on his face. I tried to quicken my pace to get past him when he reached his arm out to the side, blocking my path.

"Where you going so quickly?" His voice was low and sexy.

"I'm done for the day. Just grabbing my stuff so I can get out of here." I took a step back as he took a step forward, his arm still extended to block me. I felt butterflies in my stomach as my body reacted to the physical contact with him as his arm was still touching me.

"Why? Do you have something more pressing to do?" He kept his voice low, drawing me in with each word.

Interesting choice of words as I thought about all of the things I would like him to press into me right now. I felt my face turn red at the thought and knew that he noticed.

"Do I make you nervous?" His finger reached up and gently caressed my jawline as I looked up and found him watching me.

"Nervous? No. Excited is more like it." The words were out of my mouth before I realized what I said. His eyes watched as the blush crept down my neck, my eyes focused on anything other than his face.

“Excited? Well, that’s an interesting choice of words.” His arm slid down the wall some to where his hand was low enough to reach mine. I watched nervously, waiting to see what he was going to do next.

“Excited....” he tried the word out on his tongue as he licked his lips. The movement caught my eye and I felt his gaze upon me as I stared at his mouth. I felt my lips involuntarily part as I wished he would lean in and kiss me.

“I’m pretty sure there’s a better word for what you’re feeling right now. Guessing by your body language, I would say that excited is an understatement.”

There was something arousing about how he was talking to me and how he was taking control of the situation. It was different than how Damian controlled me. It was sexy. I felt wanted. I felt desired. I wanted him to keep going even though he made me so nervous. It was excitement mixed with anxiety mixed with arousal all in one.

“Okay, maybe more than excited.” My voice was shaky and far from sexy, unlike his. He kept this smooth, sexy vibe and I was jealous that I could barely get words out right.

“I want to hear you say it. Tell me Mia, what are you feeling?” He smirked as he said it. His eyes met mine and held them in place as I read the challenge on his face. He was purposely pushing me and I could tell that it was exciting him as much as it was me.

“Aroused.” I whispered as I looked down towards the floor. I could feel my cheeks heating as the words flowed freely from my mouth. My body tingled in response.

With the tip of his finger he gently raised my head and forced me to make eye contact with him again.

“Aroused.” He bit his lip after saying it. “And how does that make you feel?” His eyes turned dark and I could see the desire in them.

“Wet.”

I watched as he swallowed hard, caught off guard by my response. He slightly shifted his weight but kept the same position, blocking my path. He kept his eyes on me but remained silent which made my anxiety build. Had I said too much? Was he put off by how candid I was? All of a sudden it felt like our flirty game had ended.

"Like I said, I need to go." I pushed against his arm but the damn muscular thing didn't budge.

"So you're aroused and wet." He leaned in close and whispered in my ear, "What does it feel like?"

"You know what it feels like." I snapped, immediately frustrated with myself for allowing him this control. I thought I wanted it but now I was worried that it was only going to lead to my own embarrassment.

"I want to hear you say it," he pushed.

"I don't have time for this." I pushed harder against him, trying to move his arm so I could get by him. In a quick movement he turned me around so my back was up against the wall. He leaned in, resting his chest against mine, and pinned me against the wall with his forearms flat against the wall. "Say it."

My breathing quickened and a flush of heat took over my body as I responded to his touch. I tried to focus on anything other than the throbbing sensation that had started to build up.

"It feels like you could stick a finger inside me right now and find out just how wet I am." I whispered as I closed my eyes and tried to regulate my breathing. If that was what he wanted, fine, I would give it to him.

"What if I wanted to stick my tongue inside and taste it instead?" He whispered in my ear.

My eyes shot open finding him studying my face. I didn't know what to say, no one had ever talked to me this way before. And I found that I really liked it. Just as I tried to regain my composure, I felt his lips on my throat, slowly making their way to my collar bone. A moan escaped my throat as my hands made their way into his hair and I tilted my head to allow him better access.

"Do you want to feel my tongue inside of you?" He whispered as he pressed his body against mine. His hand slid down the wall and gently caressed over my breast while his legs spread my legs to hold me in place. In an instant I could feel just how ready he was for me. I moaned in response and heard a low growl in this throat.

"Say it out loud, do you want to feel my tongue inside of you, sucking and licking up all of the wetness?" He nipped my ear as he said it. The dirty words rolled around in my head while my body responded to them.

"Say the words Mia."

"Yes..." I felt like I was practically panting, I could come undone at any moment. The way he touched me mixed with the things he said to me were like a toxic combination and I wanted another hit.

"Yes what, Mia? I want to hear word for word what you want me to do to you." His lips continued kissing their way down my shoulders and hovered at the top of bra, teasing me as he pulled the fabric away from my skin with his teeth and ran his tongue over my nipple.

"I want to feel your tongue inside me. I want to ride your hard dick until you come inside of me. I want all of it." My breathing got heavy and faster as I grabbed his shoulders and arched my back, allowing him access to grab my ass. I felt his hands move over the fabric of my denim skirt, pulling it up in the process.

"Chase…." I whimpered as I allowed myself to give in to what was happening. Everything felt so good, I didn't want it to stop.

"Fuck, Mia." He groaned as he pushed his erection against my thigh.

The door opened as Noah walked in, stopping in his tracks as he saw us up against the wall. I immediately pushed Chase off of me and pulled down my shirt as I looked away from Noah.

"I thought you left?" Noah asked as he carried a crate of glasses to the back shelf. "Looks like I walked in on an interesting discussion." A smug smile sat on his face as he stared at Chase. Chase lowered his head and shoved his hands in his pockets.

"You walked in on nothing," I assured him as I made my way to the break room and grabbed my purse and keys. I was thankful they had both made it back up front as I made my way down the hallway and out the double doors. What had I just done?

Eighteen

Chase

"Want to explain what that was all about?" Noah asked as he sat the crate of clean glasses down behind the bar and wiped his hands on the front of his jeans.

"It was nothing." I looked past him to avoid making eye contact.

"Oh really? So, Mia is usually that flushed and flustered when you guys aren't doing anything, just talking? And, I'm assuming the bulge in your pants is because you're happy to see the new sampling glasses that just came in?" Noah raised an eyebrow in question. "Or maybe you're just happy to see me?"

I rolled my eyes and tried to hide the laugh that threatened to make its way out.

"You can play dumb and you can avoid talking to me about it right now, but we both know that you're going to give me the details of what just happened."

"And why would I do that?" I asked as I tilted my head to the side. I was dying to know the answer to this one.

"Because you tell me everything. Because you have a tendency of fucking things up with women and I always have to come to your rescue later. And honestly, it's easier if I can just fix shit before you get the chance to mess it up. Maybe I should just go finish whatever you "didn't start" with Mia. Save us all some time, have a little fun?" He wiggled his eyebrows suggestively and it took everything I had not to throw something at him.

Being best friends since we were six years old meant that he knew all of my buttons and exactly how to push them. I focused my attention on the tv across the bar to avoid giving Noah the response he was waiting for. He knew that I've had a crush on Mia since we were kids and now that she was back, he never missed an opportunity to take a jab at me about the only girl I wasn't able to get.

"Wow, I would have expected you to make some joke about kicking my ass by now." Noah commented, interrupting my thoughts. "She must really have a hold on your balls."

"First of all, no one has a hold on my balls. Second, me kicking your ass is never a joke- unless you want to hear the punch line." I smirked so he got the point.

Noah chuckled as he walked by and patted my shoulder.

"Tonight's going to be a slow night, why don't you take off and see what kind of trouble you find for me to bail you out of later?" Noah offered with a smirk.

"Sounds like a great idea to me, leaving your crazy ass to run this place. Call me in the morning after you've let it burn to the ground so I can call the insurance company and get started on the claim." I grabbed my cell phone from the counter and made my way out of the door as a group of college girls came in. I glanced behind me to see Noah's head perk up at the sight. He was absolutely hopeless.

I didn't have plans, which was odd for a Friday night. I could go to the gym and burn off some frustration or I could go home and obsess about what happened with Mia in the hallway. No matter how hard I tried, I couldn't shake the image of her letting me touch her. The way she responded to me was such a turn on. I didn't know how she would react, but she definitely surprised me. If I thought I had it bad for her before, it just got about ten times worse. I drove the short distance toward my house when a thought suddenly hit me and I made a U-turn. My plan was either going to work in my favor or bite me in the ass.

Growing up we all used to go to Paul's Pizza on the weekend and it soon became Mia's favorite. She was never big on going to parties and loved the nights when we would pick up a pizza and stay up late watching movies.

It was 6:15 and she had already been gone 45 minutes so it was a risky move, but one that I was willing to try if it meant that I could spend some time with her. I made my way to General Bob's and grabbed a bottle of the wine she was looking at the other day while I called in a to go order at Paul's. I wasn't sure what Mia had and didn't have at her apartment so I grabbed the basics- paper plates, napkins, and a corkscrew for the wine.

I was antsy while I waited inside Paul's for my order to be ready, counting down the minutes until I could try to see Mia. I didn't know if she was home, though I couldn't imagine where she would go. She wasn't very social since she had been back, especially since she was trying to keep a low profile. A young girl with freckles called my name as she smiled and handed me the box.

The drive to Mia's apartment was quick which I was thankful for. The traffic was never bad here but Friday and Saturday nights tended to be heavier with people getting out of the house and looking for something to do. I parked my truck and grabbed the box of pizza and the bag from General Bob's as I made my way to her apartment. I was as anxious as a teenage boy about to have his first kiss as I stood outside her door, trying to keep my hands from sweating as I knocked on her door and held my breath as I waited for her to answer.

Nineteen

Mia

It was 7:00 on a Friday night and I was wearing yoga pants and drinking wine out of a coffee mug. Had my life become pathetic or had I reached a new level of adulting? I wandered into the kitchen to look for suitable options for dinner. As I opened the fridge, I had hoped to find some sort of actual food, but instead I was greeted by milk, coffee creamer, and a half empty bottle of wine. I let out a sigh as I leaned against the open refrigerator door and debated whether to walk to the store to grab something to make for dinner, or to order takeout. I glanced down at my comfy clothes and decided takeout was the winner.

I closed the fridge and opened the drawer in the island that stored the takeout menus and began sorting through them when the doorbell rang. I stood still for a moment, waiting to hear a voice or for a sign that it might be someone at the wrong apartment. A few seconds later came another ring. I walked over to the door, determined to tell the person that I wasn't interested in whatever they were trying to sell, only when I opened the door I found that I was in fact, very interested.

Standing in front of me was Chase holding a pizza box and a bag from General Bob's. I looked at him with confusion, unsure of why he was there. He had offered to have a housewarming dinner but I had never accepted and we definitely hadn't made any plans.

"Can I come in?" He asked, interrupting my thoughts.

"Sorry, I should have called first, but I was worried you would say no and we really need to talk." He smiled and I knew I wasn't going to be able to say no.

"And what exactly do we need to talk about?" I asked with a sigh as I leaned against the open door. I was happy to see him but I didn't want him to know that, especially not after what had happened earlier. This was a slippery slope and I needed to try to stay on my feet as long as I could.

I saw him look down as he took in the outfit I was wearing and immediately wished I was wearing anything other than yoga pants and a tank top. Perhaps if I had been expecting company, I would have even put a bra on. I felt vulnerable with him checking me out but I squared my shoulders and tried to play the part of uninterested and unaffected. I continued to lean against the door, blocking his entrance as he looked past me to the wine glass on the counter next to the take-out menus.

"It appears I have a solution to your problem." He nodded towards the counter as he held onto the pizza box which I imagined was starting to get uncomfortable holding. It was big and bulky and he was still holding the bag in his other hand. He adjusted the angle at which he was holding the box and I saw the Paul's Pizza logo on the top of the box. I tried to hide a smile as I remembered our nights growing up, spending the weekends eating pizza and watching movies. It was sweet that he had remembered how much I loved Paul's Pizza.

"And what's that?" I asked with a sigh as I tried to feign interest. He handed me the pizza box and when I reached out to take it, he did some sly maneuver that turned me around so we were both inside the apartment.

"I played it safe and got a plain pepperoni pizza. I remembered that was your favorite growing up, so I hoped that hadn't changed. I mean, if you don't like pepperoni then this has to end now." He raised his eyebrows as he waited for my response.

"What has to end now?" I was confused. He was being sexy and charming and it made me feel drunk around him. Maybe it was the aftereffects from earlier still playing with my head.

"This flirty banter we started earlier. The start to our rocky but incredible relationship. The one with the mind-blowing sex," he said with a huge grin as he rocked back on his heels.

"There's no relationsh-," I started to protest but my words were cut off by his fingers over my mouth.

"Shhh, you're just hangry. Let's talk about it over pizza. Then we can move on to more important topics, like finishing our conversation from earlier." He was really in the zone tonight and I started to worry that I would end up giving in to his charm.

"You're so impossible." I mumbled as I closed the door behind him.

"That pizza better be worth all this." I walked past him and sunk down on the couch, curling my legs underneath me. I already knew that it would be, but still, I had to play the part. I couldn't lay all my cards out on the table this early on.

I watched as he maneuvered around the kitchen, unpacking the items he brought. Paper plates, napkins, wine, a corkscrew. He was prepared, I had to give him that. I waited on the couch as he brought two plates over with slices of pizza on them and sat them down on the table. He smiled as he went back to the kitchen and opened the bottle of wine. His brow furrowed as he looked around for wine glasses then turned back to me.

"There aren't any. I've been using a coffee mug." I nodded toward the one I left on the island. He smiled and grabbed another mug from the shelf above the sink and rinsed the one I was using. A few minutes later he sat the mugs of wine on the coffee table as he sat in the armchair across from me.

"You haven't answered me." I covered my mouth as I spoke in between bites of pizza. "What do we need to talk about?"

I reached for the mug to wash down the pizza when I was startled by how full the cup was. The wine was filled to the top, almost overflowing. I looked at him as he smiled again and nodded for me to have some wine while he chewed his bite.

"Thirsty?" I asked, looking for an explanation as to why the glass was so full.
"Liquid courage."

"Why do you need liquid courage?"

"It's for you, not me," he replied in between bites. "We're going to finish our conversation from earlier and I'm guessing you may need some liquid courage in order to do so."

"First of all, there is nothing to finish discussing. Second, I don't need liquid courage to talk about anything." I was lying and I knew that he knew it just as much as I did.

He stayed silent as he leaned back in the chair and wiped his mouth with a napkin as he finished his slice. There was a smirk on his face and it was driving me crazy.

"What?" I asked with more annoyance than I had intended to.

He continued to stay silent as he watched me. I felt like I was put on display and it made me feel anxious. I watched as his eyes roamed over my body and I wondered what he was thinking. He shifted in his seat and adjusted his jeans which drew my eyes to body. He was completely relaxed yet his muscular body looked rigid and solid. I remembered the feel of it on top of mine earlier in the hallway. The way his arms braced me against the wall, strong, yet gentle. It was a turn on to watch him take control of the situation and push me to tell him what I wanted. No one had done that before and I was still aroused by it. If I could rewind time I would go back to that moment in the hallway and play it on repeat, but in slow motion.

I licked my lips as I remembered the feeling of his lips on mine. How soft and gentle they were as they waited for my permission. My breathing changed as I relived the moments in my head, forgetting that he was sitting right in front of me while I continued on with my daydream.

A few minutes later my thoughts were interrupted by the sound of him clearing his throat. Startled, I looked up and made eye contact with him, knowing I had a frozen deer in the headlights look on my face. There was no way to hide what I had been thinking about as I felt the blush creep up my skin.

"Wanna share what you're thinking? Or should I guess based on how long you've been staring at my body and the flush in your cheeks?" His grin spread across his face as I forced myself to look away. I took a few big sips of wine, emptying my mug.

"May I?" he asked as he held up the bottle of wine, ready to refill my glass.

"Yes, please." I smiled a nervous smile.

"So the liquid courage is helping already." He chuckled.

"What makes you think that?"

"You're not being as feisty or looking at me like you want to rip my head off."

"Well you are pretty frustrating most of the time. Perhaps your personality flaw is leading to a drinking problem on my end. I maintain my innocence in this situation."

I watched as he got up and took the empty plates to the trash after I declined his offer for more pizza. Between the two slices I had and the wine, I was getting full, fast. I watched as he came back and sat at the other end of the couch instead of sitting in the armchair. My body instantly reacted to his presence and silently I wished that he would sit closer.

"I would venture to say that innocence would be far-fetched at this point, but I'm happy to play along," he joked. "However, the fact that you find me frustrating leads me to believe that I am in fact *frustrating* you."

"Here we go again." I sighed, taking a long sip of wine.

"Why can't you just admit that you're attracted to me?" He turned his body as he leaned toward me. "Given that you're not wearing a bra, and it's 80 some degrees out, I can tell for a fact that you're aroused at this very moment. Just like you were aroused earlier when we were in the hallway."

Embarrassed, I quickly grabbed one of the throw pillows and pulled it up to my chest.

"Attraction, my friend, is overrated." I took another sip and finished the wine left in my glass. "You can be attracted to lots of people but not want to do anything about it."

"So what is it about me that makes you not want to do anything about it?"

"I'm not really into one-night stands and I know what kind of guy you are. You like the challenge but once you get what you're after, you're done. You show up unannounced on a Friday night, I can only assume what you're really after." He sat in silence as he waited for me to continue.

"I haven't been with a lot of guys, Chase. And the last one I was with is trying to find me so he can kill me. I can't afford to let my guard down and let you in, only for you to run off after you get what you wanted. That's not fair to me." Apparently liquid courage was what I needed so I could tell him how I really felt.

I was scared to trust anyone again. And even though I had feelings for Chase and I was attracted to him, I didn't want to be another notch on his belt. I wanted it to be something more but I wasn't sure that I was even in a place to try to make it something more. No matter which way we played it, I was bound to be the one to get hurt in the end.

"You really think you know me that well?" He slid over closer to me on the couch. "I showed up here unannounced because I couldn't get you out of my head from what happened earlier. Trust me when I say that I had plenty of offers for tonight and I can have any of them with a quick reply to their text."

"That's not the point." Feeling frustrated I got up and took my mug to the kitchen sink. This was getting too complicated, too fast. I heard his footsteps behind me as I kept my back turned to him.

"What is the point?" He came up behind me and placed his hands on each side of my hands on the sink. I could feel the heat from his body behind me. All it would take was one small step backwards and I would be in his arms, leaning against his chest where it felt safe. I tried to focus on keeping my body rigid so I didn't give in to what my body really wanted.

Gently he moved my hair to the side and slowly kissed the back of my neck. I closed my eyes and soaked up the feeling while it lasted.

"What's the point, Mia?" he murmured as he ran kisses along my neck and onto my shoulders.

"That it's complicated. That it's wrong. That I'll be the one who gets screwed in the end."

"Baby if you want me to screw you, I have no objections to that request. I'll gladly screw you any way you'd like and as many times as you'd like. I'm just waiting for the green light." I could hear the flirtiness in his voice and knew that he was teasing me. He pulled away from me as he turned me around to look at him.

"I know that it feels complicated, Mia. I don't want you to think that I'm discrediting how you feel. But I have no intention of hurting you. I don't want to see anyone other than you. You're not a piece of ass that I'm after. This is more than that for me." His eyes searched mine, pleading for me to hear his words. "I know that you're technically still married and that it's scary to want to be with someone else, I get it. I really do. But I feel the way your body responds to me, Mia. And I know you feel it too."

"It's getting late. Thank you for the pizza and wine, I think it's time for you to go." I looked down to avoid having to see the hurt look on his face. I watched as he stepped back and ran his fingers through his hair in frustration.

"Okay, Mia. If that's what you really want, then I'll go. I promised that I would never try to push you or make you feel uncomfortable, and I meant it. But promise me that you'll take the time to think about yourself and what you really want. You deserve better than what you're allowing yourself to have, Mia. And at the end of the day, it's not me, that's okay. I'm still going to push for you to have the best, to have what you deserve."

He let out a deep breath as he walked past me, our hands grazed each other, and the door closed behind him.

I locked the door behind him and tried to get myself together. I was disappointed in myself for pushing him away when really I wanted nothing more than to spend time with him and let myself have all of the things he wanted to give me. I leaned my back against the door as I slid down it and sat on the floor thinking about what had just happened.

Twenty

Chase

Well, tonight definitely didn't turn out how I had hoped it would, though it's not like I was expecting for her to take down all of the walls she's built up and suddenly declare her undying love for me.

Frustration had started to build even more as every approach I made with Mia seemed to turn into a dead end. I tried to take things slow with her and be the best friend that I've always been, someone that she could lean on and trust. Then Noah reminded me that she would never see me as anything other than a brother.

So then I tried subtle flirting with her but that seemed to confuse her even more. For whatever reason, she refused to believe that I could be interested in her or that I would be flirting with her. Finally, I decided to lay it on even thicker to make sure she got the point, which she did, even if she didn't want to admit it. I saw the way her body reacted to my touch and to the things that I said to her. And for a fraction of a second, she responded to me and told me what she wanted. It was raw and dirty and such a turn on. I wanted nothing more than to give her everything she could ever ask for. I would go to my grave fulfilling every single one of her sexual desires if she would let me, there was no doubt about that.

But it was more than that. I wanted more from Mia. I wanted the girl that I grew up with and fell in love with. The girl who liked to cuddle on the couch while eating pizza and watching movies. The girl who would get the giggles and laugh so hard that she would snort. I wanted to protect her from anything that could ever hurt her and make her feel safe again. In the end, it didn't matter what I wanted if she didn't want those things in return. My mind was too busy to go home and obsess over what had happened so I made my way to The Vine.

It was fairly busy for a Friday night and Noah was behind the bar flirting with a blonde who appeared to be overly drunk and barely legal.

"Head outside. There's a taxi waiting for you." I nodded toward the door and watched her pouty face as she grabbed her purse and stumbled toward the front doors, nearly falling on her way out.

"Gee thanks." Noah muttered as he picked up a bar towel and wiped off the countertop after she left.

"Sure thing."

"I was being sarcastic."

"And I was keeping you from going to jail for over-serving Malibu Barbie and having to explain that you thought it was still consensual sex, even if she is passed out."

Noah grinned ear to ear, knowing that I was right.

"So, what brings you in on a Friday night, in such a delightful mood, I might add?" Noah questioned with one eyebrow raised.

"Don't want to talk about it. How bout you stop playing shrink and offer me a drink?"

Noah picked up a glass and worked the towel through it as he dried it before walking to the tap and filled the glass. He slid it across the bar as I reached out and grabbed it.

"I take it things didn't go well with Mia tonight?" He leaned back against the counter behind him and crossed one leg over the other.

"What makes you think I went to go see Mia?"

"Because you're in a shitty mood and you're only ever in this shitty of a mood when you don't get your way. What happened?"

I took a deep breath and let it out as I took a drink. The cold beer felt good going down.

"She has this guard up and I get it. I really do. But she's known me since the 3rd grade, you would think she would know what kind of person I am. I hate that I'm making this effort and she doesn't believe me. She's so determined that I'm just after sex and that she's the only one that will get hurt in this. I've tried telling her how I really feel but she doesn't hear me." I avoided looking at Noah as he watched me, listening to what I said as I regretted saying it out loud. I wasn't one who liked to tell others about my problems, but with Noah, it was different.

"She's been through a lot. I'm not going to tell you what she's told me because it's not my place to tell you but trust me when I say that you can't imagine what she's been through. Right now she needs a friend, Chase. I know that you are in love with her, but she isn't ready for that right now. I don't know that she even knows what love is. He broke her in more ways than one. She's going to need time to heal. And WHEN she gets into another relationship, she's going to need someone who understands and respects what she went through and who is willing to take things at the pace that she wants to go." He leaned forward and I could feel his eyes on me. I looked up at him as he continued.

"She doesn't know what any guy wants from her at this point. To think that you'd be any different is hilarious. You may walk on water with other women, but as far as Mia is concerned, she wouldn't care if you drowned. Right now she's focused on protecting herself and you need to respect that."

Noah was right. It wasn't anything that I hadn't already told myself but hearing it from him made me put it into a different perspective. If I really wanted Mia then I had no choice than to back off and hope that when she was ready, she would come find me. I didn't want to keep pushing her and risk pushing her away completely.

"Sometimes I hate talking to you about stuff." I glanced up at him, looking smug as he looked down on me.

"I know, but you know that I always give you the best advice." He winked and I almost snorted as I laughed.

"Oh really? Is that why just the other day you told me that I had to stop acting like her friend and start flirting with her if I wanted her to notice me? And now look where we are!" I pointed at him as I laughed and he held his hands up in defense.

"Hey, what can I say? I was going off of her having a sex dream about you, I thought it might help if you flirted with her."

"Maybe you should have told me about the dream before I unloaded my charm on her." I teased, hoping he would finally tell me about the dream.

"She never told me anything about it. I only know she had a dream about you because she was flustered about it and I had heard her calling out your name in her sleep."

"That's good to know." I felt satisfied to know that at least the dream version of me was having better luck with her.

"I wouldn't get too excited there champ, only her subconscious seems interested at this point and it only lasted all of two minutes. I'd hate for you to have to try to last long in real life." He ducked as I picked up the towel and whipped it at him.

I could hear him laughing from under the bar as he slid his way down and out into the open, escaping any additional attacks I might launch on him. I pulled some cash out of my wallet and slid it under my empty glass as I made my way toward the doors, nodding as Noah waved from one of the tables as I left.

Twenty One

Damian

I sat in my office and tapped my fingers impatiently while I waited for Hank to come in. This was not how I wanted to spend my Saturday night, but shit needed to get done. I looked down at my phone to check the time, again, when I noticed a new text message from Claire. My finger slid over the button to open the message when a picture of Claire's naked tits popped up on the screen. That was a nice surprise, to say the least, though it didn't calm my temper with Hank being late.

It was almost 6:30 and my blood pressure was rising as I counted the minutes that he was late. I reached into the bottom drawer and pulled out the new bottle of whiskey I had brought with me. I was just about to unscrew the top when I heard the front door open. I grumbled under my breath as I put it back in the drawer. There was a light knock on the door followed by Hank's big ass head peaking in.

"We said 5. It's 6:30." I glared at him as he made his way in and sat down across from me.

"I know, I'm sorry. My contact I've been working with was able to get some more information for me, that's why I was late." He crossed his leg over his knee and leaned back in the worn-out leather chair.

"It better be worth it," I warned as I waited for him to get on with it already. He was lucky I had given him a week to get the information before I threatened to pound his head into the concrete outside.

"We ran Mia Johnson through the system but kept hitting dead ends. As you know, she isn't using any of her credit cards and has been off the radar." *No fucking shit, Sherlock.* How the fuck did this guy ever make it through the academy? Did they not have standards anymore?

"Then we ran her social security number and found that she legally changed her name eleven years ago from Amelia Johnson to Mia Johnson." He smiled as he waited for my reaction. *Keep waiting, kid, keep waiting.*

"And why exactly do I care about that?"

"Because Mia Johnson isn't showing up anywhere, however Amelia Johnson is currently employed and renting an apartment in Haven Brook, Colorado." He smirked as if he just proved the earth was round. My hand twitched as it fought the urge to reach across the desk and smack it off of his face.

"Where is Haven Brook?" I asked as I thought back to whether she had ever mentioned her hometown while we were dating. It didn't ring a bell, so I assumed she hadn't told me where she was from. Just like how she apparently never bothered to tell me her real name either.

"It's a few hours from Denver. Small town but growing in size, especially over the recent years. They recently added some new apartments and some condos are going up later this year by the golf course they are adding as well."

I rolled my eyes as Hank spoke. Who the fuck cared about any of that? I asked him to find my wife, not plan my next vacation. I couldn't wait to be done with this asshole.

"I didn't ask for a fucking tour guide to tell me about the town, dumb ass." I sighed heavily as I rubbed my temple from the headache he was inducing. "Who's your contact?"

"I have a cousin who works in law enforcement in Eastern Point, it's another small town near Haven Brook. I decided to have him search Colorado since that's where her flight landed."

"How far is that from where she's at?" I looked down at my phone as another text message popped up from Claire. While I appreciated the dirty texts she would send me, she was starting to get too clingy. I slid my phone to the side of my desk and waited for Hank's response.

"It's about an hour away."

"Good. Tell him to drive out there and find her. He's not to approach her or have any contact with her. I want to know where she's at, what she's doing, and what her routine looks like."

I wanted to pack up right then and there and get on a plane to Colorado so I could end this bullshit right now but I couldn't do that. I had a charity dinner to attend tomorrow night that the firm was hosting and I was damned if I was going to try to explain to Ronnie why I wasn't going. He was already watching me like a hawk and stopped by the house unexpectedly to talk to Mia. It was getting harder and harder to come up with lies and I needed to be able to sneak out of town without anyone noticing I was gone. My plan would never work otherwise.

"I can't ask him to go down there, he has a wife and kids!" Hank threw his hands in the air.

I felt the vein in my temple throb as I glared at him. *Did he seriously just say no to me? Did he forget who the fuck he was dealing with?*

"He doesn't have an option. Either he gets down there and watches her for a few days and reports back to me, or I bring him on charges of obstruction."

"Obstruction? How so?!" Hank's voice rose along with my temper. I slammed my fist down on the desk, causing Hank to jump in response. I watched the look on his face change as I turned toward him.

"You don't think that I can link him to the missing money? Who knows, he might have even tried to bribe me to try to get you a lesser sentence." I raised an eyebrow as I challenged him. I didn't even know about his cousin until 5 minutes ago, it's not like I had any time to dig up any dirt on the douche bag.

"You dirty son of a bitch!" Hank lunged forward in his chair, knocking the pen holder over in the process. I watched as it spilled across my desk, regret on Hank's face as he watched it happen.

I didn't get the feeling that in general, Hank was intimidated by me. He was a cop and surely had dealt with far worse than the likes of me. However, Hank was intimidated by me because I was the ONLY lawyer who was willing to take his case when all others had declined, knowing they would never win. I planned to hang that over his head as long as I needed. He didn't need to know that I had been stuck with his case. He held out hope that I had taken it because I thought I could help him, and that was all that I needed to keep him hooked.

"You have no proof, and you know it!" His face was red with anger which amused me.

"Who do you think people are going to believe, Hank? A crooked cop who was caught on video stealing cash from his wife's work, or an upstanding lawyer who has a clean track record?" I raised my eyebrow even further to challenge him to correct me. I watched as he worked his jaw back and forth in frustration.

He leaned back in his chair as he shook his head at me, disgust on his face. I could care less. All I cared about was finding Mia and tracking her movements. I needed someone to watch her until I could get there myself and take care of things from there.

"So what's it going to be Hank? Are you going to call him and get me in contact with him, or do I need to start working on paperwork?"

He shook his head as he lifted out of his seat and pulled out his cell phone. I watched as he pressed a few buttons and put it on speakerphone as we waited for the guy to answer. After five rings I assumed it would go to voicemail when I heard a male voice answer.

"Hey Lenny, it's me." Hank let out a deep breath as he glared at me over the phone.

"What's up?"

"I need another favor. I have you on speakerphone. I'm at my lawyer's office, he's the one that we're trying to find the information on the girl for."

"Okay...." There was hesitation on the other line.

"His name is Damian and he's gonna tell you what he needs. You guys will be in contact from here on." Hank reached over and handed me the phone. There was silence from Lenny as he waited for me to talk.

"Lenny, I need you to drive down to Haven Brook and follow Mia for a few days until I can make it down there."

"And why exactly would I do that?" His attitude instantly pissed me off. Now was the time to play my hand and see what would happen.

"Because I know you took money from Hank, from what was embezzled. He's on the hook for a Class B felony, I wouldn't want to be linked to any part of that if I were you." There was an edge to my tone.

"Son of a bitch." He sighed heavily. "I didn't want to take the money. My wife is sick and the medical bills are piling up, we didn't want to lose the house."

Bingo. I had both of them where I wanted them. I had no idea that Hank had given him money. Bluffing paid off. I heard Lenny fall silent on the other end as he waited for me to play my hand.

"Then I guess if you don't want to do jail time, you better do as I'm fucking asking you." My tone was harsh and void of any empathy. I had my own problems, I didn't care about him or his wife.

"Fine. What do you want?"

"Drive there tonight. Watch her but don't approach her or let her know that you're there. I want to know where she lives, where she works, what she drives- I want to know everything. Who she talks to. Where she goes." I let out a deep breath frustrated that I had to give this incompetent moron step by step instructions instead of doing it myself.

"And find her phone number, I know she has a new one. I want an update from you as soon as you find her and we’ll take it from there with step by step directions.”

Silence lingered on the other end of the line and for a moment I wondered if he hung up on me. I prayed for his sake that he didn’t. That would’ve been a fucking stupid move to make on his end.

“Got it?” My voice was deep and controlled as my knuckles turned white from how hard I gripped the phone.

“Yeah, I got it. Text me your info and I’ll send you an update as soon as I find her.”

There was an edginess to his voice as I heard the line disconnect before I had a chance to say anything further. He had no idea who he was dealing with. I tossed the phone back to Hank and nodded my head toward the door for him to leave.

A few minutes later I heard the front door open and close and knew I was finally alone in the office. I reached down and pulled out the bottle of whiskey. I waited for the familiar burn as it passed down my throat and watched the phone as I called Claire. The phone rang twice before she purred hello as she answered. I rolled my eyes as I stuffed the bottle back into the bottom drawer and closed it. I needed a release and with her I didn’t have to work for it, which made it somewhat worth it to deal with her pathetic little show.

“Be naked with your ass up on the bed when I get there in 10 minutes.” I hung up the phone as I left the office, the tension from the day soon to be relieved.

Twenty Two

Mia

It was slow for a Saturday night, even with the few tables that had made their way in for dinner. I dropped off a couple of beers at a table and scanned the room as I made my way back up behind the bar and looked for any sign of Jade. I hadn't heard the door chime that someone had come in, but I was so anxious to see her that I found myself obsessing over when she would get there. The last update I had received from her was a quick text message last night: yoga tomorrow at 6:30.

I had my back turned as I entered the order into the system and waited for the receipt to print. Out of the corner of my eye I noticed someone approach the bar and sit down, my body already on full alert. I didn't have to look behind me to know who was there. He had this natural ability to draw me to him without trying. A small smile formed on my lips as I tore the receipt off and slid it onto the mini clipboard and turned around to face him.

"Hey." His tone was happy though I could hear a level of uncertainty in it. We hadn't talked since I asked him to leave my apartment last night, and I had avoided him the majority of the day today when he showed up unexpectedly to work. I smiled and waited for him to smile back, unsure of what to do. There was an awkwardness between us and I hated it.

"Do you want something to drink?" I asked as I glanced behind me at the beers on tap, unsure of what he was in the mood for.

"Just water, please." I was surprised that he didn't want a beer but thought better than to ask him about it. I needed to figure out what the lines and boundaries were going to be between us and that meant that right now I needed to stay his friend and keep my distance. But how do you act like a caring friend while wanting to be more than friends, without acknowledging that you want to be more than friends? The door chimed behind me and I was thankful for a distraction from my thoughts. I leaned to the side to get a look at the door as I placed the glass of water in front of Chase, my eyes still focused on the door.

"How's it going today? You seem a little distracted."

I looked over to find him watching me with curiosity on his face. He has always had a way of reading me without me having to say much so it was no surprise that he would notice the change in me today.

"Jade is supposed to be here today. She text that she thought she would be here around 6:30 and she's supposed to meet me here. Every time I hear the door, I get excited that it might be her." I sighed as I watched another young couple walk in and make their way out to the patio area. "It feels almost surreal that she's going to be here soon. That I'll get to see her again and that she made it safely." I let out a sigh and slid my finger over my phone to check for any messages or calls from Jade. Nothing. I looked down at the time. 6:45. I felt my face drop as my anxiety started to rise. What if something had happened to her and she wasn't going to make it after all?

"I'm sure she'll be here soon. You know traffic sometimes gets jammed up on the way in, maybe she got stuck in it?" His voice was gentle which for a moment made me feel better.

"Maybe." I turned my head away to look out at the patio. Noah's head tilted back as he laughed at something one of the girls said as she ran her fingers up his arm. For a moment I was jealous that I would never have that kind of a life. My life would always be clouded by fear that Damian would find me. It had been three weeks since I had left but only a few days since he had gone after Jade looking for me which left me with little hope that he would give up on finding me.

The front door chimed again and I looked over to see Jade walk in, her eyes scanned the room as she looked for me. Once her eyes landed on mine, we both smiled and I let out the breath I had been holding. I quickly made it around the bar as she came running over and pulled me into a hug. For a moment nothing else mattered and no one else was in the room, just her and I. Happiness filled my heart as I held her, knowing that she was okay. My body trembled as the emotions continued to flow through me.

“Jade! I’m so happy to see you! You’re really here!” I shrieked with excitement as she smiled back at me.

“I’m so happy to see you too, I’ve been worried sick about you since you left.” She ran her hand up and cupped my cheek as she wiped away a tear that had made its way down my face. “This place is ADORABLE, Mia. I love it here!”

“You’ve only been here a few minutes, how can you love it already?” I laughed as I let go of her and walked the short distance to where Chase was sitting, watching us.

“Jade, this is Chase. Chase, this is Jade.” I introduced them as Jade sat on the barstool next to Chase and they shook hands. I heard the door to the patio open and watched as Noah made his way up to the bar, unaware of Jade sitting next to Chase. He came around the corner and went to say something to Chase when I saw his eyes light up at the sight of Jade. I laughed as I watched him try to put together what was happening.

“Hi, I’m Noah.” He smiled as he extended his hand out to Jade, completely oblivious to the fact that Chase and I were there as well.

“This is Jade,” I offered as he turned to look at me, surprised that I was standing there.

“Ah, the best friend from Boston. Nice to meet you.” He smiled the smile that usually melted girls’ panties and I waited for Jade’s reaction.

“Nice to meet you too.” She pulled her hand back, completely unphased by the interaction. Usually women were smiling back at him and batting their eyes, but not Jade. I wasn’t sure if she even knew he was still there. I let out a chuckle at the same time as Chase. Our eyes met and instantly we both burst into laughter, knowing that we were both thinking the same thing.

“What’s so funny?” Noah looked between both of us, waiting for the punchline to our joke.

"Nothing." I smirked as I tried to avoid his look, afraid that I would laugh even harder if I made eye contact with him. In all of the years that I've known Noah, I have never seen him meet a woman who wasn't instantly into him. This was refreshing to say the least.

"Did you have any trouble getting down here?" Chase asked as he turned on the barstool toward Jade and shifted the focus from Noah's subtle rejection. Noah let out a soft sigh as he raked a hand through his hair and went to enter his sales into the system.

"Everything seemed to go fine. I didn't notice anyone following me and I ditched my cell phone in Boston before I got into the rental car." Jade reached over and squeezed Chase's hand for a second as she took a deep breath. "Thank you again for what you did for me with the rental car. I can't imagine how I would have been able to leave so easily if it hadn't been for your help."

"Of course, it was no big deal. Did you get the care package in the glove box?"

Jade let out a laugh as she nodded yes. "Yes, thank you."

"So, what was in it?" I probed, relieved that she was finally here. I watched her as she talked and tried not to focus on the fading bruises that were left on her body because of me.

"There were the essentials that came in very handy- cash, a few gift cards for gas, some snacks, and a few CDs." She tried to hide a giggle as we all waited for her to keep going. "The CDs were nothing but songs about hating men. I think my favorites were a toss-up between Miranda Lambert's Kerosene and Mama's Broken Heart." Laughter erupted as I tried to picture Jade driving by herself along the open highway, belting out country songs. As long as I had known her, she was always a rock kind of girl so I couldn't see her jamming out to country.

"Sounds like Marty." Chase smiled warmly.

"Well, you must be tired after driving for a few days. Do you want to go get settled in at my place? I should be home in a few hours but you can make yourself at home until I get there."

"That sounds great, thank you." She smiled as I pulled my keys out of my pocket and handed them to her. It felt really good to have her back in my life and to know that she was safe. I gave her directions to my apartment, followed by Noah's offer to personally escort her there, if needed, and watched as she walked out and headed for my apartment. My heart felt full that my best friend was back in my life and that she was safe.

The night continued by at a fast pace as Chase stayed working on something in his office and Noah stayed on the patio with the bachelorette party. The bachelorette party was heading out around 8:30 which left the place practically empty. Noah left with the girls and asked that I close by 9 and be out by 9:30. I practically squealed with excitement to get to leave early and go hang out with Jade. There was so much that I wanted to catch her up on with Chase and everything that had happened since we last talked. It felt like it had been such a long time since we were able to really talk to each other and I missed that connection we had.

At 9:00 on the spot, I went up front and locked the front doors, relieved to be done. As I made my way back toward the bar, I felt a vibration in my pocket and pulled my cell phone out to find a text message from Chase. For a moment, I had forgotten he was still back there and I hadn't told him that we were closing early tonight.

Chase: When Noah takes a break let me know.

Mia: He left 30 minutes ago to go with the girls from the bachelorette party. I just closed the front and plan to be out of here in 30 minutes. Might want to call him on his cell.

I sat my phone on the counter and grabbed the towel and cleaning supplies to clean the last few tables that had left. I quickly worked the towel across the last table, lifting the sugar packets to clean underneath them. As I moved them back across the table my arm bumped the bottle of cleaner, causing it to roll across the floor. It rolled quickly under another table, finally stopping further back than I could reach. I sighed as I pulled my skirt down a little then got down on my hands and knees to crawl under the table to get it.

"Fuck, Mia." I peered over my shoulder to see Chase standing behind me, arms crossed over his chest in frustration.

"Sorry, I didn't hear you come in."

"Do you have any fucking idea what you're doing?" He ran a hand down the scruff on his face as he let out a low muffled growl.

"Picking up the bottle of cleaner?" I offered my cheesiest smile as I stood up and sat the cleaner on the table between us.

"You can't wear a short skirt like that then be running around here on your hands and knees with your ass in the air Mia."

"Why not?" I chewed my bottom lip as I looked up at him, his eyes hooded. My stomach clenched and I reminded myself that I was venturing into more than friends territory the more I flirted with him. Even if it was subconscious.

"Because you make it really hard for me to not pull you over here and fuck some sense into you. Damn it, Mia," he growled.

"I didn't know anyone else was in here, I'll try to be more careful with cleaning up next time." I had hoped to lighten the mood but given that he didn't seem to be budging on his side, I picked up the cleaning supplies and carried them back down the hallway to put them away. I could feel his footsteps in line behind me.

"Look Mia, about last night-"

I held up my hand to cut him off. I had beat myself up about it all night last night and didn't want to get into it with him tonight. I just wanted to give it some time and hope that my attraction to him would subside. He deserved better than a woman who was hiding from her husband and may have to up and leave at any given moment.

"No Chase, we're not talking about last night."

"And why the hell not?" I could hear the frustration in his voice as I felt his glare on me.

"Because now isn't the time to try to discuss it. Things are complicated and I don't imagine they are going to get any easier." I sighed as I looked up at him. I needed to walk away and clear my head. To stop letting him look at me the way he was. The way that made me want to let down the wall I had been working so hard to build.

"Things are only hard if we make them hard. I like you. You like me. I find you attractive. You think I'm pretty hot as well. What is so hard about that?" He stepped to the side as I made my way down the hallway, expecting him to reach out to stop me. Surprisingly, he didn't. My stomach dropped a little bit and I scolded myself for wanting the physical contact from him.

"It's just hard, okay? I need to go finish closing." I walked past him and let the door close behind me as my heart ached for shutting him out. I fought so hard all of my life to find someone who would love me and now that I had someone who wanted to, I wasn't able to let them in.

I was finishing with closing up front when I felt my phone vibrate in my pocket. I stuffed the report into the deposit bag and zipped it closed as I pulled out my phone and looked at the screen. I had thought that it might be Chase, disappointment hitting me when the screen said Unknown instead. I debated on whether to answer the call since I didn't know who it was, then remembered that Jade's phone shows up as Unknown in my phone. I smiled as I slid the button to answer the call.

"Hey!" My voice was more cheerful than usual, the smile still prominent on my face.

"Hello, Mia." My blood ran cold as I stilled, Damian's voice paralyzing me. I must have heard wrong. There was no way that he would be calling me. How did he get my number? I stayed silent for what felt like hours when I was interrupted by the sound of his voice.

"Cat got your tongue?"

"How did you get this number?" I whispered, unsure of what else to say. Cautiously I looked around as I turned my back against the counter. My eyes continued to scan the room as I waited for him to talk.

"You know what's funny- when you get stuck defending a crooked cop and suddenly they have access to a lot of things. Like birth names and social security numbers that show where you're currently renting a new apartment," he taunted. "You know what's not funny? When your wife leaves you and you have to spend three weeks trying to chase her down."

I heard the tone in his voice as I remembered the fights we had right before I left. My skin felt cold as goosebumps ran up along my arms. Suddenly the warm evening night had an icy chill to it.

"That makes me fucking angry. And you *know* that I don't like getting angry, Mia."

"What do you want Damian?" I used the tone that I knew would work with him. The one that was direct and to the point, without sounding like I was actually standing up to him. It was what helped me to dodge fights that could have been a lot worse than they were. I needed to know where he was as much as I needed the air which suddenly felt too thick to breath.

"You know what I want. I want what is mine." He paused for a minute as silence filled the empty space. "I thought I had made myself very clear, there is no *you* without *me*."

His words were heavy and I could hear the weight of the whiskey on every breath. He would drink so much that it became harder and harder for him to speak as his words got jumbled and the alcohol numbed his body.

"Damian, just let me go. Please. You don't want or need me. You're happier without me." I pleaded as I slowly walked the short distance along the bar until I reached the window. I pulled my body back as I tried to stay hidden in the shadows while I looked around outside for any sign of him.

"You think you know what the fuck makes me happy?! You haven't made me happy in years," he scoffed. "This isn't about what makes me happy, Mia. This is about taking what is fucking mine and dealing with your behavior. I've warned you…." His voice trailed off as I continued to search the darkness.

"It would seem that you've forgotten your place, dear *wife*," He spit out the word wife as if it disgusted him. "You come back home, dress like a slut in your little denim skirt, and think that I won't find you? You're even stupider that I thought."

His words send a chill down my spine. I clutched a hand to my heart as I gripped the phone tighter, desperate to find him. If he knew what I was wearing, that meant he could see me. Even if I couldn't see him. My body trembled as the fear coursed through me, shredding every ounce of hope I had built up the last three weeks of surviving him.

A movement outside caught my eye and I leaned forward slowly, no longer worried about keeping myself hidden since he obviously knew where I was. Across the street sat a man on the bench at the bus stop with a cell phone in his hand. My heart raced as I stared at the figure partially hidden in the shadows of the night sky. I continued to watch in horror as he lifted his hand and waved at me. It was a slow, creepy wave. The kind of thing that haunted you in horror movies, only this was real life. I brought my hand to my mouth as I fought the urge to let out a scream.

The line was quiet as I waited for Damian to talk. Anxiety built as I watched him sit in the darkness, stalking me. My breathing became shallow as I strained to listen for any sign of movement on the other line, desperate for him to say something. He continued to sit at the bus stop, no effort to come over to where I was. The longer he stayed silent and didn't move, made me even more uncomfortable. He was being unpredictable and it was eating at me.

"Don't you know it's rude not to wave back?" His voice broke my concentration as it brought me back to the phone call.

The door to the back offices opened and I realized that I had completely forgotten that Chase was still there. I turned to look at him, thankful that I wasn't by myself. My eyes were wide as I kept my phone pressed against my ear and let out a shaky breath as I turned my attention to back to the window. All of a sudden the bus stop was empty. I leaned forward as I pressed the phone harder to my ear and searched the area, not seeing any sign of him. My heartbeat quickened as I tried to find him, unsure of where he had gone. Knowing that he was here and that he knew where I was, but that I had no idea where he was, made my stomach churn.

"Remember, you can run, but you can't hide." The line disconnected and I stared at it, bewildered. Then I realized that this was all a game for him. He could have come for me long ago and already ended this. He wasn't the kind of man who waited for the right time, he was reckless and careless when he didn't like something. But he had warned me the night that I left that this was a game for him; *how about a game of hide and seek? You TRY to hide, and I'll let you wait in fear before I come to find you.*

I knew that he liked the idea of torturing me, it gave him a sense of control and made him felt powerful. The physical attacks had gotten worse, but I started to fight back and he didn't like that. What I hadn't expected was that he would move on to playing mind games.

I felt Chase walk up beside me, concern on his face as he tried to assess the situation. I stayed staring out the window as I held my cell phone close to my chest.

"Mia, what's going on?" His voice was low as he looked out the window with me.

"He found me." I turned around and looked up at Chase, desperate to feel safe but not sure that I ever would as long as Damian was after me.

“Is he here?” Chases eyes went wide as he stepped past me and looked out the glass doors that led to the patio. Fear paralyzed me as I watched Chase go back and forth between the windows and doors, looking for a sign of Damian.

“Mia, is he here? What did he say?” There was an urgency in his voice and I struggled to try to focus on what he was asking, my mind still reeling from his words.

“He’s here. He found me. He knows what I’m wearing. He’s watching me.” My words stumbled out of my mouth as I tried to get everything relevant out at once.

“Where is he, Mia? Did you see him?” Chase stood directly in front of me and placed his hands on my shoulders as he pulled my gaze into his. His eyes searched mine as if they would hold the answers that my mouth couldn’t get out.

“There was a man sitting across the street at the bus stop. I couldn’t see him very well. But he waved. This really slow, creepy wave.” I tried to imitate it the best I could. “Then he told me it was rude not to wave back. I couldn’t see the guy, Chase, but it had to be him, right?”

“Mia, get your things, we’re leaving.” His hand touched my lower back as he guided me. He stayed by my side as we put the deposit in the safe and grabbed my things before making our way to the front door. I felt relieved that I had him there with me so I didn’t have to face Damian alone, but I was also terrified of what Damian might do to him. Guilt weighed heavily as I thought about how selfish I was being by allowing him to help me.

“I can’t go home.” I whispered as we walked to the front door. “He’s coming for me. He’ll kill me this time.”

I looked down at the floor, sadness and despair taking hold of me. Just hours ago I had been so happy and excited, now I was back to where I had been three weeks ago. Jade! I had completely forgotten that Jade was at my apartment. The apartment that Damian said he knew about. What if he was there right now? Panic rose as I worried about Jade and how I would get to her before Damian could.

"You're not going home," Chase leaned forward to look outside before opening the door. He was on high alert, just like I was. "You're coming home with me so I can keep an eye on you and protect you."

"He knows where I live, Chase." My eyes looked past him into the darkness outside, wondering if he was out there waiting for me. "Jade is at my apartment." I swallowed hard as I lifted my head to look at him.

"We'll take care of it, Mia. Don't worry, you guys are safe here." He leaned forward and kissed my forehead, taking away some of the worry and stress that was suffocating me.

I took a deep breath as he opened the door and we walked the short distance to his truck as I looked around, waiting for Damian to come out of the shadows. I got in his truck and waited for Chase to close the door behind me while I checked my cell phone for any missed calls or texts from Jade. So far nothing. Chase opened the driver's side door and climbed in, locking the doors before starting the truck. I watched as he pulled out his cell phone and called Noah, allowing the call to go through the truck's blue tooth so he could drive.

The truck pulled forward and I nervously looked around, wondering which vehicle Damian might be in. Would he simply follow us and continue to stalk me? Would he ram the vehicle and push us off the side of the road like I've seen in movies? My mind was running wild while I listened to the phone ringing throughout the cab.

"You have the WORST timing. Someone better be dead." Noah muttered into the phone.

"Well, Damian's in town and found Mia. So how's that for bad timing?"

"What the fuck? What happened? Is she okay?" Noah's tone had immediately changed and I listened as it went from noisy to quite as he left wherever he was when he first took the call.

"She's fine, she's with me. I'm taking her to my place but we need to check on Jade. She's at Mia's apartment. He knows where she lives."

"I'm on it. Let me know when you guys get home."

"Will do. Get me an update on Jade ASAP."

"You got it."

The call disconnected as I sent up silent prayers that Jade would be okay. Guilt overwhelmed me as I thought about how hard she fought to make it out here, only to have Damian show up at the same time. Maybe she would have been better off staying in Boston, instead of uprooting her life to come to Haven Brook. It seemed anyone I cared about became an instant target for Damian and that thought killed me as I looked over at the man next to me.

Twenty Three

Chase

There was a brisk chill in the air that made me feel even more alert as I drove toward my house. I had no idea what Damian looked like, and frankly, I was kicking myself for not looking him up sooner. But having lived in Haven Brook all my life, I knew pretty much everyone who lived here, including the new families that had moved in over the past few years. It was rare that a single person moved into town, and when they did, the town talked about it. I had a feeling that I would immediately know Damian the moment I saw him, for that exact reason. He would stick out like a sore thumb.

The drive from The Vine to my house was short and usually only took me about ten minutes, but I decided to take the long way to make sure no one was following us. As I pulled onto the one lane highway that leads out of town, I felt Mia's eyes on me

"Where are you going?" she asked confused.

"I'm taking the back-way home to make sure we aren't being followed." I glanced in my mirrors repeatedly as I took the exit onto the dirt path that would eventually lead back to my house. The road was barely a road, more of a beaten path that some of the locals took when they wanted to go off roading. There were no streetlights and the closest house was miles away and not visible through the thick forest of trees. I knew these roads better than most who lived here and knew that the likelihood of encountering another car would be slim, unless we were being followed. I was more likely to encounter wildlife, which was another item added to my list of things to watch for.

The road was dark and quiet as we made our way along, the sound of dirt and gravel crunching under the tires filling the cab. I wanted to talk to Mia about what had happened but I didn’t want to push her until she was ready to talk about it. Noah knew what had happened and why she left but he’s never said anything to me about it, other than to allow Mia to tell me herself. And now, I needed to know what happened. In order to protect her, I needed to know what this guy was capable of.

“Growing up with Noah, I had to know all of the back streets and places to hide when he’d get into trouble,” I tried to break the silence by offering an explanation of why I took this road. “Which you know with Noah meant we were traveling these roads every weekend. This road will actually take us to my house and I’ll be able to see if anyone has been following us before we get there.” I watched her shoulders rise and fall as she listened, knowing that her mind was still somewhere else.

The road wound around a few bends before it finally came to an end. I slowed as I approached the fork in the road and followed it to the right. The ten miles of dirt road had been clear of any other drivers and I hadn’t seen any headlights in the area which meant we hadn’t been followed. A few miles down the road and I turned left onto the road that wound up the side of the mountain, leading to my house. I loved that my house was secluded from the others with at least an acre between each house and the mountain as my backyard. It gave me the country feel that I wanted while being ten minutes away from the modern conveniences that I enjoyed.

I pulled into the paved driveway and looked around as I scanned the area before I pressed the button to open the garage. Once I made sure everything was clear I pulled in and waited for the garage door to close behind us before getting out and helping Mia out of the truck. I could feel the heat from Mia’s body behind me as I entered the six-digit alarm code and waited for the beep to confirm it was turned off. She fidgeted with the hem of her shirt, a giveaway that she was nervous. While I was relieved to have her there with me so I could protect her, I felt bad that we hadn’t had a chance to talk about what had happened last night. I had been trying to talk about it but she shot me down every chance she could. The alarm beeped, indicating that it had been turned off.

"Nice place," Mia commented as she stepped into the open space as we walked inside. She stepped to the side, out of the way, unsure of where to go.

"Thank you." I smiled as I set the alarm behind me. I wanted to make sure she felt safe with me, even if I never set the alarm except for when I left. "Let me show you around since you'll be here with me for a few days."

She smiled as she waited for my lead. It felt weird having Mia in my house, especially knowing that she would be living with me for at least a few days. I felt nervous like a teenage boy who was hoping to go to first base for the first time but not having any clue what to do. I ran my palms down the front of my jeans as I took a few steps into the open space that served as the living room and kitchen, looking around to see where to begin.

"So this is the living room," I pointed toward the couch and love seat that surrounded a distressed wood coffee table. The TV hung mounted on the wall above the fireplace which was next to the door that led to the garage. "and this is the kitchen. Obviously." I felt so awkward as if she couldn't tell that it was a kitchen. I wanted to smack my forehead for sounding like such an idiot. I watched as she walked by the island that separated the kitchen from the living room and ran her fingers along the smooth granite top. She leaned to the side to glance out the sliding glass door that led to the wrap around porch and I saw a shimmer of disappointment cross her face when she realized it was too dark to see anything.

"There's a full wrap around porch. This end has a hot tub and the grill, the front has a swing and a few rocking chairs that my grandpa and I used to sit in when I was a little boy," I explained as I turned on the porch lights for her to see outside. A soft smile formed when I mentioned my grandpa and memories of us hanging out with him when we were growing up crossed my mind.

"You've done a lot with this place. I barely remembered where it was when we were driving here, but now that I'm inside, it feels like we're ten years old again."

"My grandpa always wanted to fix it up and make it more modern before he died but he never got the chance. I started working on some of the renovations, like the porch and the fireplace, before he passed. He helped when he could, otherwise he would sit and tell me stories while I worked.” Talking about my grandpa had never been easy for me since he passed but talking about him with Mia felt comfortable and easy.

“He would have loved all of this. You did a really good job.” She squeezed my forearm gently as she walked away from the sliding glass door and waited for me to continue with showing her the rest of the house.

“Thanks, I really appreciate it. I figured the least I could do was finish the dreams he had for the place after he left it to me.” I laughed a nervous laugh and waited for her response. Everyone had made me feel like I was some entitled prick that took his grandpa’s house and destroyed it after he passed. Little did anyone know that my grandpa had left me the house, completely paid off, along with a hefty savings account to finish the projects that we had hoped to work on together. I worked hard at The Vine to earn my keep, even if I didn’t have a mortgage to pay. It was a constant struggle to feel like I had to justify myself to others and prove that I worked just as hard as anyone else.

“I’m sure he was relieved to know that you would take care of it and continue to work on the things he didn’t get a chance to do with you. There’s nothing wrong with that, Chase.” She paused to look up at me as I walked closer to her. “Anyone who really knows you, knows that you busted your ass to help your grandpa with this house, while also helping your mom take care of your brothers after your dad passed, AND while trying to start your own life. Anyone who tells you any different is an idiot and you shouldn’t be surrounding yourself with people like that.”

In just a few minutes she took the years of guilt and worry that I had been harboring and destroyed them with her words. No one has ever made me feel like I was a good person for taking over my grandfather’s house and continuing his projects. This was one of the reasons why I loved her. She was always real and honest with me, and she had a way of making me feel good about myself when others tried to knock me down.

I smiled down at her and for a moment I felt that connection between us again. The one that no matter how hard I tried to avoid it, forced me to want to pull her into my arms and kiss her. Her face was filled with mixed emotions as I watched her smile then look away, unsure of where she should look.

"So this hallway leads to the bathroom and bedrooms." I nodded toward the hallway as we started to walk in that direction, hoping to get past the awkward tension that had filled the room.

"The guest bedroom is here on the right, the bathroom is across the hall on the left, and at the end of the hall on the right is the master bedroom and bathroom." I stepped to the side to let her look into the guest bedroom. Confusion crossed her face as she leaned in further and pulled back out, her eyebrows pulled in.

"The room is empty."

"Yeah, I don't have many guests."

"Oh. Well, no problem, I can sleep on the couch." She licked her lips as she tugged at the bottom of her shirt again.

"You're not sleeping on the couch." I turned her to face the master bedroom and gently placed my hand on her lower back to guide her in.

"Then where am I supposed to sleep?" She looked up at me inquisitively.

"In the bed." I shoved my hands in my pockets as I leaned against the door frame and nodded toward the bed.

"Chase, I am not sleeping in your bed."

"Why not?"

"Because I don't want to put you out and make you sleep on the couch."

"I won't be sleeping on the couch."

"Then where are you going to sleep?"

"In the bed."

"In the bed?"

"Yup."

"I'm not sleeping in your bed with you." She walked across the room and turned to look at me with her arms crossed over her chest.

“Why not?”

“Because that would be….. weird. Awkward. Hard….”

“How so?” I was really enjoying watching her squirm. It was cute. If she really didn’t want to share the bed with me, that was fine, I would sleep on the couch. But I was having fun with the back and forth and watching her reaction to it.

“Because- it’s just- it’s hard.”

“Most women find that to be a good thing.” I raised my eyebrows suggestively. “Just saying.”

I watched as her face turned a slight shade of pink as the blush made its way down her neck.

“You’re impossible.” The smile she tried to keep off of her face gently pulled up at the corners of her mouth before she looked away.

“What, are you afraid that you won’t be able to keep your hands off me if we share a bed? Mia, I’m a man, not a piece of meat…”

I waited for a sarcastic answer to come out of her mouth but instead I saw a look of guilt on her face before she quickly looked away. While I hadn’t expected that to be an actual reason for her to not want to share the bed with me, I was quite flattered to know that she felt that way.

“I’m kidding, Mia. Not to worry, we don’t have to share the bed. However, you will be sleeping in it either way. I won’t budge on that.” I smiled as I pushed off from the wall and joined her in the middle of the room.

The bathroom was immediately off to the left as soon as you entered the bedroom and was a pretty decent size for how old the house was. I had remodeled the bathroom after my grandpa had passed away and gutted the entire bathroom. The old, outdated tub was replaced with a walk-in shower and the hard wood floors were replaced with gray rustic looking wood planks. Across from the shower was a full wall mirror that sat above a double sink with a few drawers beneath the counter. The counter ran along the length of the wall which created a four-foot space by the bathroom door that was open. Aside from a small wastebasket, there was nothing else in this space which made the bathroom feel more open. The remodel took longer than I had expected due to some water damage that I didn't know about, but it was one of my favorite projects that I had completed so far.

I watched as Mia took in the master bedroom and looked around. It wasn't a big room but was big enough to fit a king-sized bed that was centered along the wall with the bathroom and had a nightstand on each side. There was a huge bay window that took up the outside wall with three panes that curved outward with a plush bench seat and throw pillows beneath it. Growing up I would often find my grandma sitting on the bench seat crocheting or reading a book. Someday I pictured my future wife doing the same.

Across from the bed was a TV mounted to the wall above a chest of drawers. All of the furniture in the room was a dark oak color with light brown paint on the walls. The master closet was more space than I would ever need and was tucked away next to the dresser. Most women would probably complain about how small it was but I loved that I didn't have a ton of room to store unnecessary crap.

"Well, that's everything," I said as I watched her walk around the room and peek inside the bathroom. "Feel free to make yourself at home."

"Thanks, Chase, I really do appreciate it."

"Of course." I smiled warmly at her as the reminder loomed in the air about why she was there to begin with. It wasn't because she had finally given in and decided to be with me. It was because her husband had tracked her down and wanted to kill her, which instantly killed any thoughts I had about having Mia to myself in my house.

"I'm gonna go check in with Noah, I'll let you get settled in if you want." I didn't know how to make things any less awkward and hoped this would be a good chance to get away before it got worse. I knew she didn't have anything with her other than her purse but still, I wanted to give her some space to try to feel as comfortable as possible at my place.

"Thanks." She smiled nervously as she chewed her bottom lip, looking at the chair sitting next to the dresser by the window.

"Alright, I'll be in the living room if you need me." I tapped my knuckles on the doorway a few times as I made my way down the hall, leaving her to have the space she needed. Having her in my house might be even harder than I thought.

Twenty Four

Mia

The night flew by in a blur and my head was spinning as I sat on the edge of Chase's bed and tried to sort through what had actually happened. My worst fear, the one that I always knew deep down, in the back of mind, that it would come true, had happened. Damian found me. I shouldn't be surprised, though I had hoped that he would be too drunk to actually be successful. But then again, once Damian had his mind set on something, no amount of alcohol could stop him.

I sighed as I pulled my cell phone out of the front pocket of my denim skirt and checked the battery which was almost dead thanks to the constant missed calls from what I assumed was Damian. It was hard that Damian and Jade both showed up as unknown in my phone so I didn't know who it was that had called. Finally, Noah and Chase decided that it would be best if Jade called Chase if she needed anything since Damian didn't have his number. I sat my phone on the nightstand, next to my purse when I suddenly realized that I didn't have anything with me other than the clothes on my back and whatever might be in my purse. Anxiety started to loom over me as I thought about how crazy and foolish it was of me to come back to Chase's house. The idea of having someone else around made me feel safer, though the idea of sleeping in his bed made me feel nervous.

He had joked about me not being able to keep my hands off of him, and while he was joking, the blush on my face had given me away. I wanted to kick myself for the reaction he was able to draw out of me so easily. If I could just NOT be attracted to him, things would be so much easier. But as I was quickly learning, nothing in my life was easy right now.

I walked down the hallway and found him sitting on the couch with his cell phone in his hand. He looked serious and I wasn’t sure if I should interrupt as I tried to sneak past him to the other couch.

“Hey.” He smiled up at me as he slid his phone onto the coffee table and watched me sit down across from him.

“Hi.” I pulled my legs up under me while trying to be as ladylike as possible in my skirt. “Have you heard anything from Noah on Jade?”

“I just got off the phone with him a few minutes ago. He checked out the apartment and everything looked fine. He offered to stay with Jade, she said no. He offered her to go stay at his place, she said no. He offered to buy her a pizza, and as you can guess, she said no.” He laughed as he glanced down at his cell phone, a text message notification lit up the screen.

I pulled my eyes away. I didn’t want to be nosy, even though curiosity was getting the better of me and I really wanted to know who the text message was from. It was a Saturday night and he was a single guy, I should have assumed that he might have a date. Instantly I felt bad for being there and for possibly ruining plans that he might have had to cancel.

“I’m sorry, I feel bad if you had to cancel plans tonight because of me.” I nodded toward the cell phone on the coffee table.

“I didn’t have any plans.”

“Okay.” I didn’t know what else to say and the awkward tension from earlier surrounded us again.

“It’s an alert that the pizza I ordered is out for delivery. I thought you might be hungry, and figured pizza might be a safe bet.” He stood as the doorbell rang and I watched as he went to the door and peeked through the peephole before opening it.

A tall, lanky teenage boy with red curly hair tucked under a baseball hat that was too big for his head stood on the other side with a pizza in one hand and a small bag in the other. Chase smiled as he handed him the cash and told him to keep the change. He closed the door and carried the box and bag over to the island, tilting his head as he nodded for me to join him.

I got up and made my way to the island as Chase grabbed paper plates out of the cabinet and sat them in front of us. I waited as he opened the box, extending it toward me to take a slice. The kind gesture of him ordering food for us without asking made my heart full. He was always going above and beyond to take care of everyone else, it made me feel sad that he didn't have anyone to take care of him. I pulled the slice onto my plate and grabbed a napkin from the pile that was in the bag with the packets of red peppers and parmesan cheese.

Chase smiled as he carried his plate over to the coffee table and sat it down. I started to follow, feeling uneasy to just make myself at home, when I felt him watching me.

"You can go ahead and make yourself comfy on the couch. I'll bring us some water, unless you want something else. Beer? Wine? Tea? Whiskey?"

"Water is fine, thank you." I sat on the couch and pulled my legs up under me as I waited for Chase to come sit down before I started to eat. The couch was soft and worn in which made me want to curl up in it and go to sleep. Everything about Chase's house made it feel warm and homey. I felt like I could feel really comfortable there if I could ever get past my attraction to Chase. Everything I touched reminded me that he had touched it too and that thought played at the corners of my mind, entertaining ideas that I had been trying really hard not to have.

"Thank you for the pizza, this is delicious." I took another bite and allowed the fragrant aroma to fill my mouth and satisfy my taste buds. In all the years that I had been gone I was convinced that nothing would ever bring me back to Haven Brook, except maybe pizza from Paul's Pizza. I might even sell my soul for a slice.

"You're welcome."

We sat in silence while we ate and for once, it wasn't an awkward silence. I was relieved for that. I sat my empty plate on the coffee table and leaned back against the couch as I curled up into a soft throw pillow. Between my overly full stomach and the mental exhaustion from the day, I was ready to crash out right then and there. My eyes felt heavy as I laid my head back and closed them.

"Do you want to go get ready for bed?" Chase interrupted my thoughts as I fought the urge to give in and go to sleep. I knew he didn't want me to sleep on the couch but right now, I couldn't imagine that anything would be as soft or as comfortable as this.

"I don't think you can pry me from this couch. It's officially accepted me as its own." My eyes were still closed though I could sense that Chase was close from the light scent of his cologne. It was always light and subtle but my body reacted to it as soon as it smelled it, a smell that had been etched into my memory long ago.

"I don't think it would be hard for anything to accept you." His voice was soft and sincere, a gentleness that I didn't always see from him.

Reluctantly I pushed the pillow to the side and stood up, my body protesting as I moved away from the warmth and comfort of the couch. I smoothed down my skirt as I stood and remembered that I still didn't have anything with me other than what I was wearing. I frowned at the thought of sleeping in my skirt and tank top but it was better than stripping down to my bra and panties in front of Chase.

"What's the matter?" he asked, mimicking the frown I had been making.

"I was just thinking about how I don't have anything to sleep in that would really be appropriate." My voice trailed off as I ran my hands down the front of my skirt and tucked my chin.

"You can borrow something of mine. I have t-shirts and sweats you can wear, though they might be a little too big."

"Thank you. I'm sorry for being such a pain."

"Mia, you're far from a pain. I have several shirts and sweats, I think I can spare some for you to wear tonight. Don't worry about it." He smiled as we walked to the bedroom. I sat on the bed while he pulled a few things out of the closet, holding them up in the air then shaking his head and putting them back in the closet. A few minutes later he came out with a few shirts and a pair of sweatpants folded over his arm and handed them to me.

"Sorry, I tried to find the smallest shirts I could find. I'm hoping that you won't drown in these." He shrugged as he held them out to me. I tried not to laugh as I took them and made my way into the bathroom, closing the door behind me. It was cute that he was so worried about having clothes that would fit me when I was more worried about having clothes that would be too provocative.

I stripped off my tank top and skirt and folded them neatly before setting them in a pile under the counter. The shirt was a little baggy but it fit, and more importantly, it smelled like Chase. I pulled the drawstring on the sweats as tight as it would go and was pleased that they sat low on my hips without falling off. For a moment I felt comfortable and relaxed.

As I opened the bathroom door I found Chase by the closet, shirtless as he bent over to pick up his boots he had kicked off. He was wearing nothing but jeans and socks and I had an unobstructed view of his perfectly ripped body. I imagined he spent a lot of time working outside without a shirt as he had a sun kissed glow. I couldn't imagine how he stayed so lean and fit, with literally zero body fat, when all I've ever seen him eat is pizza. He must spend a lot of time at the gym or maybe he only eats bad when I was around.

He cleared his throat as he pulled up his sweatpants which sat low on his hips and showed off his taut muscles on either side of his abdomen. I had been so consumed with my thoughts that I hadn't paid attention to the fact that I had subconsciously watched him undress, or that he had caught me. I felt his eyes on mine as I tried to pull away.

"Ready for bed?" He came toward the bed and sat his watch on the nightstand next to his phone. It was awkward because I didn't know if he was really planning to sleep in the same bed as me and I didn't want to have expectations either way. Part of me hoped that he would so that I would feel safer, but part of me hoped that he didn't so I didn't feel any temptation to cuddle up against him in my sleep. I didn't want to have to make the decision or to ask him to sleep somewhere else, especially since this is his house and I was an unexpected guest.

"Yeah, are you?" I asked as I looked up at him as if he was going to make the decision on where to sleep.

"Sure am." He walked over toward my side of the bed as I climbed in and pulled the covers up over me. I watched as he bent down and fumbled around beneath the bed. I had no idea what he was doing but his head was next to mine as he smiled and continued to fumble around.

“Liam always ends up losing this.” He reached further and finally grabbed whatever he was trying to reach. A beat-up baseball bat appeared next to him as he stood up and positioned it next to the nightstand. “Use this if anything spooks you or if you need it. I’ll be on the couch so just yell and I’ll be right here.”

“Chase, you don’t have to sleep on the couch.” All of a sudden it felt like I knew what I wanted before I could stop my mouth from saying it.

“It’s okay, I don’t mind. I want you to be comfortable and to get some rest.”

“I think I would actually feel safer with you in here, with me.” There was a new level of nervousness in my voice and I couldn’t tell if he picked up on it or not.

“Whatever you want, Mia. I don’t mind sleeping next to you if that’s what you want.” His eyes were soft as he waited for my response.

“That’s what I want.” I reached over and pulled the covers back on his side of the bed as I watched him turn off the light switch by the door and climb into bed. The bed shifted as he climbed in and I realized that I had been wrong earlier. The couch wasn’t the most comfortable thing in the house. This bed was. My body relaxed into the softness of the bed and I wondered how many women were responsible for wearing down the mattress to make it this soft. Having Chase next to me made me feel safe and allowed me to rest for a little bit without having to worry about Damian. It was reassuring that if he did find me at Chase’s house, at least I had someone else here with me so I didn’t have to face him alone. That thought had been floating around in my mind from the moment I got into Chase’s truck and had kept me calm throughout the evening. I was thankful for a friend who took me in, no questions asked, and created a safe place for me.

Twenty Five

Chase

The soft snore of Mia sleeping made me feel at peace that she was getting the rest that I hoped she would get. I couldn't imagine what she was feeling after everything that had happened but I could see that she was struggling with how to process all of it. Throughout the night I watched as she checked her phone, silencing it as it rang. I didn't have to ask to know that it was Damian calling her repeatedly.

She seemed distracted and while I still wanted to talk to her and make sure she was really okay, I knew it wasn't the right time to do so. She needed to work through whatever she was trying to work through, and I sensed that part of it was her trying to figure out her feelings toward me and being alone with me in my house.

I had caught her watching me undress and part of me wanted to act on the look in her eye and satisfy every single desire she had. But now wasn't the time or place for that and I needed to remember that she needed me to be her friend, not her distraction. I had seen this plenty of times with other girls. They would be upset about something that had happened, didn't want to deal with it, and ended up in my bed. It's easy to trick yourself into thinking that you want something when you're so desperate to try to get away from something else.

Mia was still living in fear of Damian, even if she was comfortable at my house with me. I noticed how she flinched when the doorbell rang when the pizza was delivered. How she startled when she hadn't heard me walking toward her until I was already right beside her. She was afraid and she had every right to be. I just hated that there wasn't much that I could do to alleviate that fear for her. Until things were resolved with Damian, she wouldn't have any escape from that fear.

It was close to midnight and I still hadn't been able to fall asleep. It wasn't that I couldn't sleep having a woman lying in bed next to me, it was that I couldn't fall asleep knowing that *Mia* was lying in bed next to me. I had dreamt of this day for years, though never due to these circumstances. My body was tired and my eyes were heavy but my mind wouldn't shut down for me to go to sleep. I was never one to be scared of anyone or anything but tonight I found myself overly alert to every little noise. It was unlikely that Damian would be able to find her unless he tracked her cell phone, which was a possibility. I wasn't about to take any chances and assume that random noises couldn't be him.

"No…. please… stop… you're hurting me… please…. stop…I can't breathe…." I rolled over to look at Mia as she continued to mumble in her sleep. I gently tried to shake her to wake her up but her body felt limp and she didn't respond.

"Not my stomach. You're going to kill the baby. Damian, please stop. The baby."

My heart lurched forward in my chest as my mind tried to process the words she just said in her sleep. I desperately shook her, trying to wake her from the nightmare she was having, praying that it was only a dream.

"Mia, wake up." I shook a little harder and rubbed my hand up and down her arm. "Mia, you need to wake up. You're having a bad dream." My heart felt like it was going to beat out of my chest as I continued to try to free her from the dream.

She gasped and jolted forward on the bed, her hand clutching her stomach as her eyes scanned the room. I quickly reached over and turned on the light on my nightstand as I saw her turn toward me. Tears were rolling down her face as she searched mine.

"You're okay, Mia. It was a bad dream. He's not here." I reassured her as I scooted closer to her and wrapped an arm around her. "You're safe, he's not here."

I could feel her body tremble against mine as she cried, my heart continued to break for her.

"Shhhh…." I whispered in her ear as I held her as close as I could. I rocked her gently back and forth as I tried to comfort her.

"It's okay, Mia. I've got you. It's okay."

"Shhhh…." I wanted to comfort her as much as I could but I had no idea what to say to make her feel better so I continued to hold her and hoped that she would feel my love through my touch. I could feel her breathing slow down some as she took a jagged breath as she leaned away from me.

"I'm sorry. I had a bad dream." She wiped her tears away with the back of her hand.

"It's nothing to be sorry about. Are you okay?"

"Yeah. Sometimes he haunts me in my dreams." She let out a shaky breath.

"I can see that. Do you want to talk about it?" I tried to be as gentle as possible. I didn't want to push her, especially with how upset she was.

"What did I say in my dream?" She worked her lower lip back and forth through her teeth as she waited for my response. I didn't want to remind her what it was about if I didn't have to, why make her relive it while she was awake? But part of me felt like maybe she really needed to know so she could try to work through it.

"You sounded like you were fighting Damian." I sighed. "You told him to stop, that you couldn't breathe. Then you mentioned that he would kill the baby." I looked up at her, hoping that she would assure me that it was only a dream. A nightmare that lived in her subconscious and wasn't a part of her reality.

Her eyes filled with a sadness I had never seen in my life, not even when my dad died, or when my grandpa died. A sadness of someone who lost more than their share from someone who purposely wanted to hurt them. I wanted to reach out and hold her. Take her in my arms and never let her go.

"Mia…." My eyes pleaded for an answer.

"I wasn't trying to get pregnant. I mean, we weren't trying. I didn't mean to get pregnant. I was surprised that I could get pregnant." She folded her hands in her lap as she looked down to tell me what had happened. “I was 8 weeks along when I found out. We had just started to have problems, it wasn’t anything like what it was when I left. I was hopeful that having a baby would fix things between us, make him love me again.” A tear rolled down her cheek as her eyes continued to look down at the bed.

“He wasn’t happy about the baby. He accused me of getting pregnant by another man, insisted that I had an affair. I couldn’t believe it. This was a few days after he had hit me for the first time.” She looked up and met my eyes for a quick second before she looked away again. It killed me that she allowed herself to feel so much shame for this.

“We got into a fight that night and of course, he had been drinking. He had pinned me to the wall and had his hands wrapped around my throat to where I couldn’t breathe. I didn’t think about it, I just brought my knee up and caught him in the groin. He let me go and I fell. I was worried about the baby as I tried to crawl away from him while catching my breath. He was pissed that I had kneed him and he caught me in the hallway and kicked me a few times in the stomach. I knew then that the baby was gone.”

I felt my jaw clenched as she told the story, my knuckles white from gripping the sheets in anger. How could a man ever hurt a woman like that? Before I had hoped to find Damian so I could stop him from hurting Mia. Now I was obsessed with finding this prick so I could make him pay for what he did to Mia.

“Mia, I am so sorry.” I didn’t know what else to say. There were no words that could ease her pain of what she physically went through at the hands of her ex.

“Thank you.” She took a deep breath and looked up at me. “I know it sounds horrible, but in a way, I’m thankful that I lost the baby. It just means that he can’t hurt it.”

I nodded and pulled her in for a hug as she started to cry against my chest. I wrapped my arms around her as tight as I could without hurting her and allowed her to let herself fall apart. My heart was broken for her.

“Mia, it doesn’t sound horrible. It sounds like a good mother who wants to protect her baby from harm. It wasn’t your choice what happened to you or to the baby. He’s a terrible man and one day he will pay for what he's done. Trust me."

I could feel her body relax into mine and after a few minutes her breathing evened out. Gently I rubbed her back in circles, the way my mom used to do when I would have a bad dream when I was little. Fifteen minutes later I heard the soft sound of snoring and knew that she had fallen asleep in my arms. Part of me didn't want to let go of her, but I knew that she would sleep better laying down than to stay curled up in my arms all night. Gently I rolled her to her side and pulled the covers up over her. She looked small and frail as she laid in my bed, swallowed up by clothes that were too big for her. I reached down and placed a gentle kiss on her cheek as I rolled over and laid down next to her. I was exhausted but after hearing what had happened with Damian, I wasn't about to go to sleep and leave her vulnerable. Reaching over, I grabbed my cell phone from the nightstand and googled Damian Stone. I had a few hours to kill which meant I had time to learn everything I could about the little douche bag.

Twenty Six

Mia

I opened my eyes and tried to adjust to the darkness of the room, trying to figure out where I was. Disoriented, I looked around and saw Chase asleep next to me with his arm sprawled out across my abdomen. I remembered crying and having him comfort me, but I didn’t remember falling asleep. Then it occurred to me that I must have fallen asleep on him and he rolled me over so he could get some sleep.

I slowly slid his arm off of me and laid it down by his side as I quietly got out of bed and went to the bathroom. All of the water that I drank during dinner had finally worked its way through me as I fumbled with finding the light switch. I crossed my legs as tight as I could while my hand made its way across the wall, relieved when I found the switch and turned the light on. The bathroom tile was cold on my feet as I sat on the toilet, trying to be as quiet as possible to not wake up Chase. I flushed the toilet and prayed that I wouldn’t wake him up as I quickly washed my hands and took a glance in the mirror. My hair was a mess and my blue eyes were red and puffy from crying. Not the best look by any means.

I tiptoed back to bed and slowly got in. The bed shifted with my weight and I held my breath as I slid under the covers, trying to keep my movements small so I didn’t wake him. After ten Mississippi’s I took a deep breath and rolled onto my side to check my phone. The clock reads that it’s 4:00 in the morning and I wondered how long I had been asleep. I had lost track of time earlier and didn’t know how long I was up with Chase after my nightmare.

My stomach churned as I thought back to that night and the fight that cost my unborn child its life. I hadn’t told anyone that I was pregnant, except for Damian. Chase was the first person I had ever talked about that night with. It was one of the hardest things I had gone through with Damian because I couldn’t get past the guilt of costing someone else their life. An innocent baby died because of me. I couldn’t get past the sadness of not being able to protect my own child against their parent, something that I vowed to do after the childhood I had. A heavy disappointment had hung over me and I had forced myself to make peace with it because there was no other choice. I would never wish for a child to die, especially the way I lost mine, but a small voice in my head told me that my child was better where they were, in a place where no one could ever hurt them again. I rolled onto my back as I let out a sigh and felt the bed shift as Chase changed positions. From the corner of my eye it looked like he was still asleep.

“You ok?” he asked groggily with his eyes closed.

“Yeah, sorry, I was hoping not to wake you. I needed the restroom.”

“You can wake me any time. But I wasn’t actually sleeping so you didn’t technically wake me.”

“Why weren’t you sleeping?” Concern filled me as I worried that his inability to sleep was due to me being there.

“I wanted to make sure that you were safe.” There was a tenderness to his voice that pulled at my heart.

“I’m sorry. I feel bad that you’re not getting sleep because of me. I’ll be fine, you should get some sleep.”

“Trust me, I’m fine without sleep. I would rather that you get sleep.”

“You sure you’re ok?” He pressed.

“Yeah, I don’t usually sleep well lately so I tend to be up throughout the night.” I explained with a shrug even though it was too dark for him to see it.

“You slept pretty good while you were laying with me, wanna try that again?" There was a hint of flirtiness to his voice that I had missed. I playfully swatted at his arm, embarrassed that I had fallen asleep on him earlier.

"Seriously though Mia, it's ok to let yourself be vulnerable with me. I would never hurt you. I'll go to my grave trying to prove that to you."

"I know, Chase. I appreciate how much you care for me."

"Then why do you fight me so hard on wanting to be with you? I can prove to you however you want or need me to that it's not just about sex with you Mia." He gently rubbed his hand over my arm. "I mean, I definitely want to have sex with you, don't get me wrong." He laughed. "But I want more from this, not just sex."

"Why do you want me?" The words were out of my mouth before I could think about it or stop them.

"Why wouldn't I want you?"

"I'm not the sexy, flirty girls that you go out with. I'm not some successful businesswoman. There's nothing about me that stands out or makes me different."

"Mia, you are everything that I could ever want in a woman. You're gorgeous. You're sweet. You're caring. You're giving. You're rowdy as hell when you want to be. You keep me on my toes. And you're the definition of sexy. You don't need the slutty clothes or the over the top hair and makeup to make you sexy. You're sexy wearing my t-shirt and sweats, Mia. If you need proof of that, I'm happy to show you." He reached down and adjusted his sweats as he raised an eyebrow. "Trust me, it's not easy having you in my arms and not being able to actually touch you."

I giggled as I cupped my hands over my mouth and looked down at the bed where the covers were hiding him. Slowly he lifted the covers and I saw the outline of a bulge in his sweatpants. My eyes went wide as I looked up at him. He subtly licked his lips as he dropped the covers over himself again and rolled onto his side to look at me.

"If time is what you need, Mia, then time is what I will give you. But please don't walk away from this because you have some absurd idea in your head that you're not good enough for me."

"I tried to be sexy once with Damian." I don't know why I felt like telling him this but for whatever reason I felt like I wanted to open up to him and finally let someone in. "I had cooked dinner and when he came home, I greeted him wearing nothing but an apron and high heels. He took one look at me and told me that I looked ridiculous and to go put some clothes on as he took his dinner to his study and closed the door. I was so nervous before he got there, it was the wildest thing I had ever done. After that I was so embarrassed that I never wanted to do anything like that again. It's hard to feel like you're sexy when someone is always telling you that you aren't, you know what I mean?"

"He's an idiot. But then again, we already knew that." He smiled and chuckled. "Do you know what I would do if I came home and found you wearing nothing but an apron and high heels?"

"What?"

"I would pick you up and carry you into this bedroom, laying you down on this bed so I could look at how sexy you look while I take off my clothes. Then I would slowly go down on you and show you that you taste better than anything you could make in the kitchen. I would fuck you with your apron on until you couldn't take anymore Mia. And then we would go eat the delicious meal you made, get some energy back, then I would spend the rest of the night making love to you."

"You make it sound so easy." I tried to slow my breathing as I clenched my thighs together, turned on by the erotic picture he just painted for me.

"Mia, it is easy," he said gently. "He's taken plenty from you already, don't allow him to rob you of your self-confidence. There's an incredibly sexy woman in you and I'm dying for her to come out and see what she wants."

I thought about what he said and how his perception of the world is so different than anything I've been used to for the past few years. I yawned as I felt the tiredness start to take over again. Before I could think about what was happening, I felt Chase grab me and pull me into him, my back perfectly nuzzled against his chest.

"What are you doing?" I asked over my shoulder as I made no effort to move.

"Making sure you get some rest. Now go to sleep."

A smiled formed on my face as I allowed myself to relax against him, our breathing synchronized. Soon after I felt the change in his body as he drifted off to sleep, a soft snore filled the air above my head. I wished I could turn around and watch him as he slept, knowing that he would look as peaceful and beautiful as he did when he was awake. My eyes grew heavy as my body gave in and I fell asleep cuddled up against his warm body.

Twenty Seven

Mia

Sunday and Monday went by relatively quick while I spent time at Chase's house even though I was still anxious about where Damian was hiding. I would get a few calls from unknown numbers but didn't bother to answer them. If they were Damian, which I figured they were, he didn't bother to leave a message, which was fine by me. Sunday morning we stopped by my apartment to check on Jade and I grabbed a few things that I needed. Everything looked fine and Jade assured us that she wasn't afraid to stay there by herself. We made sure she had Chase's number programmed into her phone if needed before we left and ran to the store for some groceries for the next few days. I had no idea how long I was going to be staying with Chase but neither of us seemed to want to rush my departure.

By Tuesday morning we were both feeling antsy being cooped up in the house for a few days so Chase suggested a drive over to Lakeside. While we could have been productive and gone into work, we decided to spend a few days away from the office and clear our heads while enjoying some fresh air. Noah assured us that he had it handled and they had a temp who came in to help when needed who had been looking for some work which gave us a good excuse to take a few days off.

Lakeside was smaller than Haven Brook and I don't think it had grown any since the day I was born. It was a cute small town with a beautiful lake that we used to fish for trout in growing up. The drive out to Lakeside was relaxing as I rolled my window down and hung my hand out of the window, allowing the warm breeze to dance over my body. I closed my eyes as I leaned my head back against the seat and felt the warm sun on my skin. For a moment I left all of my worries behind me as I got lost in the peaceful silence as Chase drove.

An old George Straight song played softly on the radio as the sound was muffled by the sound of tires crunching over gravel. I opened my eyes and smiled when I saw the lake in front of us. It was even more beautiful than I had remembered with green grass leading to the bank and tall trees casting the perfect amount of shade by the water's edge.

I waited for Chase to turn off the truck before I swung my door open and hopped out. It was so quiet and peaceful, not a single other person there except for us. I looked over at Chase as he smiled at me and walked with me to the shady spot in the grass that we used to hang out at when we would come here.

"This feels like I'm back in high school." I plopped down on the grass and stretched my legs out in front of me as Chase sat down next to me.

"Yeah, it really does." He plucked a few pieces of grass and ran his finger up and down the blade as he looked out at the water.

"Thanks for bringing me out here today."

"Of course. It's nice to get away from it all sometimes."

Silence filled the space between us as we looked out at the calmness of the water. I would come here a lot growing up when I wanted to get away from my mother. She would always pretend to freak out, claim that I had ran away, just so she could get attention. Chase and Noah would always end up making their way out here and would claim they came to go fishing and didn't know I was here. They've always looked out for me, as long as I've known them.

"Sometimes I wish I could just live at the lake." I sighed as I took in a deep breath of fresh air. "Never have to worry about anything again."

"I don't know about that." He looked at me out of the corner of his eye and I could see the start of a smirk.

"What's that supposed to mean?"

"Well I'm sure after a few days even the fish would smell better than you. And then no one would want to come here because some smelly girl ruined the atmosphere for everyone else." His grin spread across his face as he turned toward me.

"I would not smell!" I playfully reached across and swatted his chest as his hand caught my arm. An electricity zinged between us and I considered pulling my arm away as he gently pulled me forward. We were close enough that I could smell the cleanliness of the soap from his morning shower. I took a deep breath trying to inhale as much of him as I could as he tilted his head and brought his face closer to mine. Slowly I lifted my head and turned into him, planting a soft kiss on his lips.

The kiss was tender and left me wanting more as I felt him slowly pull away from me and move his arm away from mine. I instantly missed the physical contact and wondered what had made him pull away. Secretly I wondered if I actually did smell worse than the fish even though I had a nice long shower that morning.

"I'm sorry, Mia." He looked at me as he spoke softly.

"For what?" I leaned back on my arms and tried to distract my body from the longing it felt to reach over and touch him again.

"For kissing you."

"Is it because I smell worse than the fish?" I tried to lighten the mood as he laid down next to me and rested his head in his hands.

"Do you think you smell worse than the fish?" He arched one eyebrow as he looked up at me, a smile making its way back into his gorgeous face.

"Not particularly. But you're the one who pulled away, so who knows?"

"You don't smell worse than the fish," he chuckled. "I was just trying to be respectful and not step over the line."

One thing that I really admired about Chase was that he was a real gentleman and I always knew that I could trust what he said. But part of me wanted to see what it felt like to just give in and stop being afraid. To have one reckless moment and live life without worrying about the repercussions.

"I appreciate that, thank you." I leaned forward and pulled my legs in toward me as I played with the grass nervously. "But I didn't mind it." I bit my lip as I avoided looking at him. It was the first time I was genuinely admitting that I was interested in him and part of me worried that I would still be rejected.

"Oh yeah?"

"Yeah." Another deep breath. "I don't want to constantly live my life in fear, Chase. I just want to live in the moment for once. To act on impulse. To feel like I'm actually living. To kiss you and feel you against me." My voice trailed off as I tried not to get too far ahead of myself.

"It's okay to want those things, Mia. You deserve to have a life that isn't lived in fear." He sat up and scooted closer to where I was sitting. I could feel the fabric of his jeans against my bare leg, sending shivers through my body.

"Tell me what you want, Mia." His voice was soft and low as he reached over and gently used his finger to turn my head toward him.

"I want you." My eyes searched his as they looked for him to assure me that he wanted the same. There was a darkness that shadowed his as I watched him lean into me and close his eyes as he pulled me in for a kiss.

My lips parted as they accepted his tongue, eager to explore my mouth as one hand made its way into my hair while the other slid down my back and pulled me down onto the grass. I wrapped my arms around his neck as I pulled him closer to me as his muscular body hovered over mine. My senses were overwhelmed with my body wanting more of him.

I started pulling at the hem of his shirt to pull it over his head as I heard him chuckle as he rolled off of me and took his T-shirt off. His perfectly toned body was within my reach and my fingers ached to touch him.

"Aren't you a little minx?" he teased with a wink as he tossed his shirt to the side.

"I've waited a long time for this."

"Same here." He leaned down and kissed me again as he wrapped his arms around my waist and rolled me on top of him. I shifted my position and was pleasantly surprised when I felt the bulge beneath me through his jeans. My eyes went wide as he smiled and licked his lips.

"Your turn." He nodded and waited, though I had no clue what he was waiting for.

"My turn? For what?"

"You wanted my shirt off, now I want yours off." There was something so incredibly sexy about the way that he said it. Maybe I was just high on endorphins, everything he said sounded sexy.

I watched as he watched me reach down and lift my tank top over my head and toss it to the side as I stayed straddling him wearing a black lacy bra and denim shorts.

"Very nice. I like it." He reached up and ran a finger along the lace trim on top of the cup that barely covered my breast.

"But I think I would like it even more if you took it off."

"I thought this was supposed to be fair- you remove a piece of clothing, I remove the same piece?" I joked as I tried to build up the confidence to do it.

"Well, we can play it that way. But you do have more clothes on than I do, which means I'll be naked before you. And I'm already bare chested, you're not."

"Fine." I sighed as I tossed my hair over my shoulder and leaned my head back as I reached behind my back and unclasped my bra. I slowly pulled each bra strap down my shoulders as I held the cups in place with one hand, watching his reaction as I teased him. His eyes were fixated on my every move and I found myself getting more turned on by it. His hands slowly made their way up my hips and along my stomach as I let go of the bra and allowed his hands to cup my breasts.

I could hear him moan as he gently rubbed each one as I tilted my head back and leaned against his legs that were propped up. His fingers rolled each nipple as he leaned forward and sat up, taking his time licking my neck down to each breast and pulling a hard nipple in.

My body felt on fire with every touch, I wanted more. I looked at him as I parted my lips and leaned forward for a kiss. Taking control, I gently forced him back on the ground as I worked his belt buckle free underneath me. I slowly kissed his jawline down his neck as his hands continued to work their magic on my breasts and my hands worked to unbutton his jeans. I could feel his erection bulging through the thick fabric and I yearned to have him inside of me.

One swift movement and he had rolled me over and laid me on my back once again while I watched him jump up and unzip his pants. He watched me as he kicked his boots off and slid his jeans down, stripping him of everything but his boxers. My legs slightly spread as I watched him come toward me, a hunger in his eyes.

His lips softly kissed my stomach as he slid my shorts down, pulling my panties along with them. I laid completely naked in front of him as he slowly looked me up and down before meeting my eyes.

"You're so damn beautiful." He whispered as he reached down and pulled off his boxers, his thickness taking up the majority of his hand. Slowly he laid down beside me and gently kissed me as he pulled me closer to him.

"How do you want it?" he murmured between kisses.

"I don't care as long as it's inside of me." I moaned as I heard a low growl from his throat. I felt his arms pull me onto him as he laid on his back and braced me with his legs. I watched him as I slowly lifted myself as I reached down and guided him inside of me. A hiss escaped his lips as he shut his eyes and his hands gripped my hips tighter. I stilled for a moment while I allowed my body to adjust to his size before I started to rock back and forth, creating a perfect friction.

We watched each other as I rode him through to my release which was the most intense orgasm I had ever had. I studied his face as he closed his eyes and he chewed his lip as he got closer. His fingers dug into my hips as I continued to push down on him and followed the changes in his body as he tried to hold off as long as he could before letting go and climaxing. His body shook beneath me and a smile crossed my face, satisfaction that I was able to take him over the edge. Exhausted I collapsed onto his chest as he kissed my forehead and rubbed my back. We didn't say anything. We just allowed ourselves to get completely lost in the moment as we stayed entangled in each other.

The drive back to Chase's house was quiet as we held hands the entire way back, both too tired to talk about much after spending the day soaking up the sun and making love. The sun was beginning to set as my stomach rumbled, a gentle reminder that we still needed to eat dinner. As we pulled into the garage I noticed a strange look on Chase's face as he looked around before putting the truck in park.

"What's wrong?" I asked as I looked around, unsure of what was bothering him.

"It's probably nothing, but the alarm should have beeped twice when we pulled in, and I only heard it beep once."

"What does that mean?"

"It means that the alarm was turned off. A single beep indicates that a door is opened, or in this case, the garage door was opened." He looked around while the garage door stayed open and the truck was still running. It felt like he was ready for a quick getaway if we needed one and that made me feel uneasy as I wondered if Damian had figured out where I was after all.

"Is it possible you missed the first beep because the windows were rolled up when we pulled in?" I asked with hope in my voice.

"It's a possibility. But I have the alarm system linked to my blue tooth, so I hear the beeps in the truck as well."

My eyes darted around the garage as I looked for any signs that someone had been in the house. I had only been staying there for a few days so it wasn't likely that I would be able to tell if anyone had been there but I continued to look anyways.

"Look, we don't need to panic yet. I'll call the alarm company and confirm if the alarm was set before we left. That will put us at ease once we know for sure." He pulled out his phone and held it to his ear as he waited for them to answer.

I stared out the window as I chewed my fingernail, anxious for Chase to get confirmation of whether the alarm had been set. His home had felt so safe to me from the moment I walked in the door and now I felt like that could easily be stripped away from me. It had only been a few days since Damian had called and even if he hadn't followed us the first time we came to Chase's house, it didn't mean that he hadn't followed us at some point since then.

"Okay, thank you. I appreciate your help." Chase let out a big sigh as he pressed the button to end the call and turned in his seat to look at me.

"They confirmed that the alarm was turned off when we left earlier and hasn't been set since then. I must have turned it off earlier when we left, thinking that I had set it."

It made sense but it still made me feel uneasy. I tried to remember whether I had seen him set it before we left. Did I hear it beep? Did I see him set it? I couldn't remember.

"You ready to go inside?" he asked as he turned the truck off and took the keys out of the ignition. I nodded as I got out and followed him inside as I looked behind me one last time.

Dinner was quick and easy which was nice given that we were both still tired from the day. Around ten we decided to call it a day and went to bed. Within minutes of my head hitting the pillow I was out and floating around happily in a blissful dream.

The clock on the nightstand showed 3:00 am as I was startled awake. I sat up and tiredly rubbed my eyes before looking around. The tv was still on with an infomercial about vitamins playing. Everything looked fine but I still had an overwhelming uneasy feeling. Slowly I scanned the room again when a dark shadow in the corner caught my eye.

My heart started to race as I peered into the darkness and found the outline of a person sitting in the chair by the window. I held my breath as I waited for them to move. It was too dark to see much other than a shape but it looked large enough to be a man. Large enough to be Damian. I felt my body stiffen as I waited for him to make his way over to the bed and attack me, but he just stayed sitting there. Every second felt like it was moving in slow motion as I continued to wait.

A shadow moved along the wall and I squinted to try to see what it was. Was it his hand? Was it a gun? My breathing quickened as I felt the adrenaline rush through me as I gripped the blankets around me. What was I supposed to do? Should I wake Chase and risk Damian hurting him? Should I take off and run out of the room so Damian would follow me and leave Chase alone? My mind tried to go through the options as quickly as possible when I felt Chase move on the bed next to me. I looked down as he looked up at me with a smile on his face. Once he noticed the look on mine his mind registered something was wrong as his eyes darted to where I was looking. I nodded toward the chair as I pulled the sheet up to my chest and pushed myself further back against the headboard as if the feel of the soft material would comfort me. Chase quickly rolled over and pulled the gun out of his nightstand, pointing it at the chair as he flicked on the light.

My eyes immediately focused on the chair and my heart dropped when I saw that there was nothing there other than a few throw pillows, and some laundry that was piled up on top of the pillows. My hand clutched my chest as I looked over and over, unable to process how it could have looked like a man when it was really just a pile of laundry on top of pillows. I let out a long sigh as I leaned back against the headboard and listened as Chase made his way through the rest of the house, checking to make sure everything was okay.

"Sorry, I think my mind was trying to play tricks on me tonight." I offered as an explanation as he put the gun away and climbed back in bed.

“Not a problem at all, I’m glad we were able to check things out to make sure they were okay.” He leaned over and gently kissed my cheek.

“I never knew laundry could be so terrifying.”

I heard him chuckle as he adjusted his pillow and laid next to me, propped up on his elbow.

“Not to worry, we can work on it in the morning. I’m sure you’re wanting some clean clothes to wear since you’ve run out of what we brought from your apartment.”

“Yeah, that would be nice. Sorry for leaving them under the bathroom sink. I was trying to be as out of the way as possible.”

“What are you talking about?”

“My dirty clothes. I’ve been leaving them in a small pile under the counter in the bathroom, so they are out of the way.”

“Mia, there are no clothes under the sink. The clothes you’ve been wearing are the clothes that are piled up on the chair. The clothes that startled you.”

What was he talking about? I hadn’t put any clothes on the chair. Everything had been folded and piled neatly under the bathroom counter, out of the way. I looked over at the chair and tried to figure out what exactly was on it but it was hard because everything looked like it was balled up in a messy pile. I looked over at Chase as I expected him to tell me it was some weird joke he had played on me but he kept looking at me as if I was the one who was losing it. Maybe I was?

“Why did you put my clothes on the chair like that?” There was so much confusion, none of this made any sense. Maybe he didn’t want my clothes piled on the floor so he moved them? But why didn’t he just tell me and I could have put them somewhere else? And why was he acting like I was the one who put them there?

“I didn’t touch your clothes, Mia. They were like that when we got home earlier. I thought maybe you put them there because you were getting ready to do laundry.”

"I didn't move my clothes. And I wouldn't have put them on the chair like that." I pointed toward the chair as I chewed my lower lip, unsure of what was happening.

"Are you sure?" His tone was calm as he reached over and held my hand. The look on his face made me feel like he thought I was crazy.

"Of course I'm sure." My tone came out more defensively than I had imagined but none of it made any sense to me.

"Okay, I'm sorry. I wasn't trying to accuse you of anything, Mia."
"I'm sure because that right there," I nodded toward the chair, "is something that he would have beat me for if he saw it. Damian didn't allow anything to be untidy, dirty laundry included."

I looked up at Chase as he gently squeezed my hand.

"He knows I'm here."

Twenty Eight

Damian

It had been nice to hear Mia's voice the other night when I called. Not because I missed her but because I enjoyed hearing the fear in her voice as she pathetically begged me to leave her alone. Wah wah wah. Cry me a fucking river. It was after seven on Wednesday night and I was irritated as fuck as I waited for Lenny to send me the last bit of information that I needed so I could get on the road and get to Haven Brook. This had gone on long enough and I was ready to put an end to it.

I had already printed the information that I needed on where Mia's apartment was and Lenny was supposed to be getting me the additional information that I asked for on Chase, the stupid prick who was trying to sabotage my plan. Leave it to Mia to go running to someone for help and making this even harder. Why couldn't she get it through her head that I wasn't going to stop until I had what was mine? Had I not made it clear?

This morning I had called into the office and convinced Doris I was too sick to come in to work. I faked a cough as many times as I could and pretended to be drowsy when she asked if I wanted to speak to Ronnie to let him know. There was a mandatory meeting that afternoon that I would miss but I didn't give a flying fuck. I needed people to think I was out sick so no one would notice if I was out a few more days as I left town.

The sooner I got to Haven Brook, the sooner this could all be over and I could be done with Lenny and Hank. As smart as Lenny should have been, he was still fucking up little things when he could. Part of me knew that it was simply to spite me. Like letting Mia see him at the bus stop when I told him to make sure she didn't see him. Lucky for him I was quick on my feet and played it off as if it was me, waving at her, which added an additional level of fear that I was disappointed that I hadn't thought of sooner. I didn't bother to worry too much about Lenny- I just needed him to finish the things I had asked of him, then he would get what was coming to him.

I glanced over at the printer as it finished printing the items I had sent over when I heard the doorbell ring. Who the fuck was there? I sure as hell hadn't been expecting anyone. I tried to ignore it as I heard it ring again. And again. And again. My temper rose as I pushed back my chair and stormed out of my office and flung the front door open.

"You don't look sick to me." Ronnie stepped inside and tucked his hands into pockets as he looked around.

"Yeah, well, I am." I leaned into the open doorway, leaving a path for him to go back the way he came. "What do you want?"

"I came to check on you. Doris said that you called in but she didn't give me much information, so I figured I would come see how you were doing since you missed a mandatory meeting this afternoon. Figured you ought to be on your death bed and I should come say my goodbyes." His eyes narrowed in on mine and I could tell he wasn't planning on leaving until he got whatever it was he was after. Apparently stubbornness ran through our veins.

"I haven't felt well all day. Fever. Cough. Stomach cramps. Throwing up. You know, the typical flu stuff that knocks you down for a few days."

"Interesting.... I don't usually wear jeans, button down shirts, or steel toed boots when I have the flu. Most people tend to live in sweats when they are that sick." He shrugged and looked into the kitchen.

"Where's Mia?"

My eyes darted up to his as I tried to come up with an excuse of where she was. I could lie and say that she was already in bed but I doubted that he would believe she went to bed this early. I could say that she was sick too but he would want to check on her. I could say that she was out of town but I couldn't remember if I had used that excuse with him recently or not. I felt him staring at me as he tried to read me, something he had done since I was a boy and had started getting into trouble at an early age.

"She's out."

"Out where?"

"With her friend. I don't know where they went."

"You don't know where your wife went?" His eyes narrowed as his brow furrowed. "The one that basically has to check in with you every time she goes to the bathroom. And you don't know where she is?"

I felt my blood pressure rise as quickly as my anger. I wasn't prepared to have to talk about Mia tonight nor I had I expected my nosey ass uncle to drop in and ask about my estranged wife. Fuck!

"I didn't feel good enough to care. Now can you just leave so I can rest?" I ran my hand through my hair as I sat on the arm of the couch and nodded toward the door.

"Damian, something is going on and I want to see Mia." He sat on the couch and planted his feet in front of him as he waited for my answer. "Now." His tone was stern and it pissed me off. Where the fuck did he get off coming over here uninvited and demanding to see my wife?

"She's not here so that's not really a possibility. Why don't you go and I'll leave a message for her to call you when she gets back?" There was an edginess to my tone and I knew he would pick up on it. It wasn't the first time I had ever challenged him and it wouldn't be the last time.

He stood up and sighed as he looked me square in the eye.

"Did she finally get tired of dealing with your drunk ass and decided to leave you? Is that what happened?"

My nostrils flared as my jaw clenched, anger coursed through me as I stared at him. How dare he fucking ask me that. He stared back at me, a challenge in his eyes as he waited for me to say what we both already knew. Problem was that he didn't need to know what had happened or that she had left me. And now that he knew, that was another problem that I needed to solve. I took a deep breath and tried to unclench my first that was balled up at my side.

"I knew it wouldn't be long before she came to her senses and left you. It was only a matter of time." He shook his head and as he turned to face me my fist made contact with his temple and knocked him to the ground. Everything played out before me in slow motion as his head whipped back and he fell backwards, his head hitting the edge of the coffee table on his way down.

There was a pool of blood that had formed around his head while his body laid lifeless on the hardwood floor. I watched as I waited for him to move, ready to deliver another blow if that was what it would take to keep him down. My breathing was heavy as the adrenaline rushed through me, giving me the high that I had learned to love so much. There was something about being in control that just really got to me. I could feel it in my blood and it felt almost as good as the few times I had partied too hard in law school and fueled myself with cocaine to make it through.

After a few minutes of Ronnie staying sprawled out on the floor I decided to move on with my night and started throwing the things I needed into the car. I debated what to do with Ronnie as I couldn't just leave him there in case he eventually came to and decided to go run his mouth to someone about what had happened. That wouldn't be good. There weren't any other options as I drug his limp body through the garage and loaded it into the trunk. It would add on a little extra time to find a place to dump him but at least it would get one thing marked off the list.

I grabbed my cell phone off of my desk and grabbed the file with the printed information that I needed. A quick pat of my pocket confirmed that I had my care package to keep me awake for the drive out there.

There wasn't time to bother with eating or sleeping until all of this was done and over, and the sooner, the better.

I climbed in the car and waited for the garage door to open before backing out. The night sky was already dark, much to my relief. If I could get a head start while it was still dark then I had a better chance of no one knowing that I had left. I didn't need anyone else putting their nose in my fucking business.

The two-lane highway was nearly deserted this time of night, especially since we lived in the suburbs and there wasn't much traffic out here to begin with. I leaned back against the leather seat as the line of trees whipped past me so fast they were nothing but a blur. I needed to dump Ronnie's body further out so if it washed up somewhere it would be harder for them to find if he was reported as a missing person.

I was twenty minutes away from the next town and considered whether to dump Ronnie's body or wait for another town. If I dumped him now then it was still close enough that they might find and identify him easily. If I waited then I ran the risk that he might come to, if he wasn't already dead. I didn't care enough to check before I stuffed his fat body into the trunk.

The exit was quickly approaching as I saw the sign for it on the right. As I debated whether to take the exit something darted out onto the road in front of me, forcing me to jerk the steering wheel hard to the right to avoid hitting it. I knew better than to over correct but there was nothing that I could do about it as I felt my body jerk to the side as the car spiraled down the steep side of the hill and plunged headfirst into a tree. The airbags deployed immediately upon contact and my head was whipped back and forth from the impact. There was a loud ringing in my head as I reached up and tried to push the airbag out of my face before it suffocated me. The car was stuck with the hood wrapped around the tree and the back end up in the air which forced me further into the airbag. I reached over and fumbled with the armrest until I got it open and pulled out a ball point pen, praying it would work. I quickly stabbed at the airbag, deflating it as I gasped for air.

I had to get out as I looked around for the best way to do so. The car was totaled which made the doors hard to open since the frame had been crushed in. I fumbled with my seatbelt as I slowly got it undone and tried to steady myself from falling forward. There was a heat under my feet as I struggled with the door handle, unable to push it open. Panic started to flood me as I saw flames under the hood of the car. My hands worked at the door handle again but the lock was jammed. I desperately searched around for something to break the window with as I watched the flames get higher as they moved in closer. I was running out of time, only seconds before the car would be completely engulfed in flames. I let out a deep breath as the heat spread over me and darkness took over.

Twenty Nine

Chase

The door slammed shut as Mia walked out my front door and didn't bother looking back. This wasn't the way that I had wanted to start the morning I thought as I rubbed a hand down the scruff of my jaw. I was exhausted with the past few days wearing on me.

Mia hadn't been the same since Tuesday night with the whole laundry fiasco which lead to some tension between us all day Wednesday when I didn't freak out about it the same way she did. There was no sign that anyone had been in the house so it made it hard for me to believe that Damian would find where I lived, break into my house without my knowing, move Mia's clothes around, then sit and wait for her to freak out about it. From what Mia had told me about the guy I didn't imagine he was going to just sit on the sideline and play games with her. None of it made any sense to me. If he was there, why hadn't he physically come for her?

By Wednesday evening she was still obsessed over Damian being at the house and kept insisting that he must have been there while we were at the lake. I assured her that I had already checked in with the security company and no one had been in or out of the house the entire time we were gone. I could tell that she still felt uneasy about it but there wasn't anything else I could do to try to prove it to her.

I hated to see her so afraid. It broke my heart. I wanted to offer her the peace and comfort she had a few days before she ever got the call from Damian but there was nothing that I could do now. I knew that she was just as exhausted as I was. Hell, probably more, from not sleeping at night. She was in this state of defense, constantly waiting for something to happen.

This morning was no different other than she seemed to reach a new level of irritability with me and decided to go back to her apartment so she could have some space and clear her head. I hated the idea of her being alone, even if Jade was still staying there with her. It made me feel better having her near me so I could protect her if needed.

I leaned back against the couch as I felt my cell phone vibrate in my pocket as I fumbled around and pulled it out. A new text message from Mia came through.

Mia: I made it to my apartment.

I was happy to hear that she had made it home safely, especially since she had refused my offer to drive her. I had never met anyone as stubborn as Mia, especially when she was mad. My fingers moved quickly as I sent a response thanking her for letting me know. I kept it short and simple which felt like what she wanted right now.

The house felt different without Mia there which made me miss her. There was no way that I could just sit around all day in a quiet house and think about her so I grabbed my keys and headed into work. I needed something to keep myself busy and help pass the time.

Noah was in a good mood when I got there which was a pleasant surprise given the attitude I had been getting from Mia the past few days. I stayed in my office the majority of the morning, catching up on things from the few days I had been out. Thursday's were always slow which was a nice break while I got caught up. By 2:00 my head was killing me from the lack of sleep and excess caffeine I had downed at my desk. I still didn't feel like going home but needed a break from work stuff so I took the time to mess around on the internet.

There wasn't anything in specific that I was looking for but somehow I ended up logging into my home security account online and pulled up the entry log for Tuesday. I stared at it for a few minutes as I looked at the general log which showed when the alarm was turned on and off over a 24-hour window. It felt like I was missing something but I just couldn't put my finger on it.

Just as I thought I was onto something I heard Noah open the door that led back to the offices and call for me. I let out a deep breath as I got up to see what Noah wanted, leaving the screen open on my computer.

Hours later I finally made it back to my office after helping Noah with the evening rush after Stacy, our temp, had gone home sick at last minute. While I loved to stay in my office and work the numbers, sometimes I really loved being up front and interacting with people. There were quite a few groups of college kids that came in tonight, laughing and hanging out, that reminded me of hanging out with Noah and Mia. We got into a lot of trouble but we sure had fun doing it.

I could hear Noah putting the deposit in the safe as he finished closing everything up front. It felt late even though it was barely 9:00, but I was ready to go home. I went to turn my computer off when I moved the mouse and the screen to the security system page popped up. I had been so busy up front that I had forgotten that I was looking for something.

Part of me wanted to say forget it and go home, knowing there wasn't anything I would find out of the norm anyways. A bigger part of me told me that I needed to look into it more. I sighed as I sat down at my computer and clicked the tab for a detailed report for Monday and Tuesday since we had been home all day yesterday. A 4-page report popped up as I moved my mouse over the print icon and selected it. I didn't have the energy to look at it now but wanted to have the physical copy in case insomnia kept me up again tonight and I needed something to read. A few seconds later the printer spit out the pages as I grabbed them on my way out of the office and went home for the day.

Thirty
Mia

"Do you want another cup of wine?" Jade asked from the kitchen as I watched her refill her coffee mug.

"Sure." It was getting late and my mind wouldn't slow down about everything that had happened since Tuesday night. I had tried to sleep but it was pointless, which left me in this overly tired dog state that Jade was left to deal with.

I hadn't planned to come back to my apartment at last minute but after I talked to Jade and told her what had happened, she insisted that I get back here as soon as possible so we could talk about it. That was why I loved her, she was always there for me regardless of what the problem was.

Chase and I had been tense with each other all day yesterday and when I realized that it was going to be the same today, I left. I knew that he didn't really understand the things that had happened with Damian, I don't think anyone really did. But it was so frustrating to me that he wouldn't listen to me or take me serious about Damian being in his house.

We'd spent the day on Wednesday analyzing why Damian would come in and move my laundry around and at one point, Chase had actually laughed when I said- to mess with me! I felt like I was going crazy and it didn't help that it felt like Chase agreed with me. I just needed him to be on my side. To take me serious. To help me figure things out. I knew that it didn't make sense why IF Damian was there, he didn't just come find me and attack me. But I had heard the tone in his voice that night. I knew the game he wanted to play. And I knew that he was going to keep playing it until he could drive me away from everyone that could try to protect me. If he made me look crazy enough, people would walk away and he would have his chance. No one would notice if I was missing at that point because no one would care anymore.

I smiled up at Jade as she handed me the mug filled to the top with cold white wine. I wasn't sure that there was a wine that went well with Chinese take-out but neither of us bothered to complain as we ate and sipped our wine. It was too late to bother with cooking and we had spent so long talking and catching up that we hadn't noticed the time earlier. It was nice to hear about Jade's adventures through Haven Brook as she applied for different jobs and had a few run ins with the locals. It was a good distraction to keep my mind off of Chase and I was happy that she hadn't been sitting in the apartment by herself this week, hiding from Damian.

"You feeling any better?" Jade asked between bites of Kung Pao chicken.

"My head hurts and I feel like I've been hit by a train. Except that train is my life."

"I'm sorry. I really wish there was something I could do for you."

"Thanks. Me too." I took a bite of my food and scraped the chopsticks along the bottom as I fished out the last piece of shrimp from the container. I leaned forward and sat the empty carton on the coffee table as I steadied my other hand to keep from spilling the wine.

"It really sucks about you and Chase. I was really starting to like him."

"So was I. But technically I knew better than to let anything happen between us. It was really stupid to let my guard down the way I did." I pulled my legs up under me as I leaned back against the couch and took a sip.

"Why do you say that?"

"Because I'm not in any position to be dating. I'm technically still married." I threw my hand up in the air. "My actual husband is trying to find me so he can kill me and I'm off having an affair with my high school crush. I don't think that spells successful relationship."

Jade let out a soft laugh as she leaned forward and put her empty carton on the coffee table next to mine.

"I don't think that's how things are supposed to work," she said softly as she looked up at me, "but you shouldn't have to deny yourself what you really want, just because you married someone who won't let you go. You deserve happiness, Mia. You deserve love." She gently squeezed my leg and smiled.

"Thanks, Jade. I really appreciate having a friend like you." My hand reached down and squeezed hers.

"You mean sister." She winked as she stood up. "And this sister needs the bathroom. I'll be right back."

I giggled as she made her way to the bathroom and looked down at my phone. There were no messages from Chase, and no calls or messages from Damian which was odd. Then it occurred to me that I hadn't had any calls from him all day. I scrolled through the missed call log and found the last call from him was yesterday at 4:07. That was odd. My blood ran cold as I tried to think about why all of a sudden he would stop calling. Was he done playing the game and ready to find me? I was still staring at my phone when I heard Jade walk into the room, stopping next to the couch where I was sitting.

"Um, Mia?" Her voice was shaky.

"Yeah?" I looked up at her, concern on my face from her tone. She stared down at her phone as she covered her mouth with her other hand. My stomach was in a knot, knowing something bad had happened. Was it Chase? Was it Noah? Did Damian get to them?

"Damian..... he..." She let out a slow breath as I watched as her hand trembled. "He's dead." Her eyes looked down at mine as I let her words sink in.

"What?" I stood up and looked at her as if she had just told me the Earth was flat. If this was supposed to be a joke, it wasn't funny.

"Someone forwarded me the news story. He was killed in an accident last night. Just outside of Boston."

The room started spinning as I reached out and held onto Jade's arm. I couldn't hear the words she continued to say, everything was blocked out by this loud humming that took over and made my head feel like it was about to explode.

"It says that the car hit a tree at high impact which forced the car to be wrapped around the tree before it caught on fire. By the time rescue workers were able to put the fire out, it was too late for any survivors. They are still working the scene to recover what they can." Jade sat her phone down on the coffee table and looked at me as she held onto my shoulders.

"Mia, are you okay?"

"He's dead?"

"Yes."

"Like dead- dead?"

"Yes."

"So.... all of this... is over?" Hope filled my eyes as I blinked back tears. I didn't know if I was upset that he had died the way he did or if they were tears of relief that this was all over with now. It felt too good to be true.

"It's over. He can't hurt you anymore, Mia."

My hands covered my mouth as my body trembled and I dropped to my knees. Jade sat beside me and pulled me into a hug as I cried. So many things were going through my head as I tried to process all of them. It made sense now why he hadn't been calling me. How could he if he was dead?

I thought about calling Chase to tell him that Damian was dead but didn't feel like I had the energy for it. For now I just wanted to focus on myself and how I felt about everything before I started to pick up the pieces of my life.

Thirty One

Chase

Friday mornings should be happy and filled with excitement for the weekend. Mine was dreadful with a headache that continued to pound through the Tylenol that I had hoped would alleviate it. I had already been at the office for an hour and tried making myself productive with no luck.

Last night had been a waste as I barely made it home before crashing on the couch the moment I sat down. I didn't bother with dinner or looking over the reports as my body demanded to sleep. After getting some solid sleep last night I didn't feel as worried about the security system report I had printed out to look over at home but since I was caught up with nothing else to do, I printed another copy and looked over it at my desk.

An hour later and I had looked over it what had felt like 1000 times. The lines were starting to blur which meant I needed to step away and take a break. As I started to push the report off to the side I noticed a line at the very bottom of the second page that didn't have any markings on it, meaning I hadn't paid attention to it when I was highlighting and marking through things as I went through it.

I pulled it up closer to my face and looked at the time stamp on Tuesday- 1:35. My mind scrambled as I tried to think of where we were at that time. Were we leaving the house to go to the lake? I put the papers down for a minute while I closed my eyes and tried to retrace our steps. We had run errands in the morning and then came home to make sandwiches to take with us to lake. That was before noon because Mia suggested we do it mid-morning so we didn’t get too hungry and miss lunch. We got to the lake around 12:30 and ate lunch around 1 after we had fooled around. So how was there an entry at 1:35 if we were at the lake?

There had to be some sort of mistake. I quickly turned to my computer and logged into my account as I searched for that entry. I clicked on the 1:35 entry and read the details that popped up below it.

MANUAL OVERRIDE

What the hell? I ran a hand down my face as I stared at the words. My brain was trying to make sense of it but nothing was happening. I picked up my cell phone and called the security company as my foot tapped anxiously under the desk.

“Thank you for calling Force Field Protection, how may I help you?” A chirpy woman’s voice answered on the other line.

“Yes, I need some clarification about an entry on my account. I’m not sure that there hasn’t been an error.”

“Yes sir, I’d be happy to help you with that. May I have your account number and name?” Her robotic mannerisms made me more and more frustrated as I provided the information she asked for and responded to her questions. Finally she asked for the specific entry and had me hold while she pulled it up.

“Okay, I see that at 1:35 on Tuesday, you called in for assistance with turning off the alarm. It was a manual override on our end after we verified your security information.”

What. The. Fuck.

“Do you have a record of the call? Did it confirm my name?” I asked as I struggled to figure out who would have been able to call and change it.

“Yes, it shows that you called in and that you also requested to update the password on file for future manual overrides.” Her voice was hesitant as she reacted to my tone.

“I’m sorry, it’s been a long week and I haven’t had a chance to catch up on sleep. Can you remind me what the password was updated to?” I asked as calmly as I could even though I was far from calm.

“Damian.”

My heart dropped as I heard it. Mia was right. Damian had been in my house. He had played the security company and convinced them that he was me so he could get into my house and mess with her. My blood was boiling as anger shot through me. I wanted to find him and put his head through a wall. I didn’t realize I was still on the call until I heard her voice come through and interrupt my thoughts.

“Would you like to change it again, sir?”

“No, thank you.” I hung up before she could say anything more. I had what I needed and would deal with the password thing later. Right now my mind was focused on Mia. I had to see her and tell her. She wasn’t safe. I didn’t want to scare her by showing up unannounced so I sent her a quick text to let her know that I was on my way and that I needed to talk to her. I didn’t care whether she wanted to see me or not. I needed to make sure she was safe.

I nearly flew out of my office as Noah’s head whipped up and looked at me with surprise. I didn’t have time to explain it, I just needed to get to Mia.

“I’m going to Mia’s. Call in ten minutes, if I don’t answer- send the police.” He looked at me like I was crazy, which I probably was.

“I’m serious. Do it!” I banged my fist on his door a few times and took off down the hallway and out the door. I had to get to her before he could.

Thirty Two

Mia

Chase: I need to talk to you, heading your way.

I sat my phone down on the island and picked up my cup of coffee, savoring the rich flavor as it made its way down my throat. Last night was a long night and I looked like shit to prove it. If I was going to deal with Chase this early in the day, I was going to need some caffeine.

Jade had run out to the store to pick up the necessities that we were running low on. Wine. Ice cream. Coffee. Frozen pizza. Like I said, the necessities. She hadn't been gone long which would give me some time to talk to Chase by ourselves. I didn't know if he was at work or at home when he had text so I didn't know how long it was going to take him to get there. There was a knock on the door and I smiled as I sat my cup down. There was my answer.

I opened the door and my heart dropped as I stared at the person in front of me. Rough hands wrapped around my throat, pushing me back into the apartment as the door was kicked shut. I struggled to breathe as I clawed at the arms that held their grip on me as I tried to break free from their hold.

"Hello, Mia." His voice was hoarse, the smell of whiskey fresh on his breath. My feet no longer touched the floor as he lifted me up and threw me against the wall next to the fridge. His hands let go as I slumped down onto the floor, forcing my lungs to take in the air they needed. I looked up at him as he paced the area in front of me like a caged animal.

In all of the years I had been with Damian I had never seen this side of him. He was acting so primal and animalistic that it scared me. There was a large gash across his forehead that was still bloody along with burn marks under his chin and along his throat. He continued to pace in front of me as he kept wiping his at his nose. I stayed balled up against the wall as I watched the man I used to know stare at me like I was a trophy animal and he was going hunting.

"Is *this* what you wanted?" He asked as he spread his arms out in front of him and glared at me.

"To live some pathetic life on your own? To leave me? To make me look like a fool back home?" His voice grew louder and boomed throughout the room. I flinched at the sound.

"Do you know the things that I had to do to get here, Mia? Do you know the sacrifices that I had to make? How many hours I drove last night with NO sleep, just to get here to finish things off?"

I stayed silent as my chest heaved. My pulse rang in my ears as I tried to figure out what to do. I watched him continue to pace in front of me as he wiggled his nose and wiped at it, leaving a smear of blood above his lip.

"Of course you don't. You're so selfish. All you ever care about is yourself. But guess what? That's all about to end." He took a few steps forward as I heard a knock at the door. Panic filled me as I saw Damian's head turn toward the door before looking back at me.

"Expecting someone?" He raised an eyebrow as he walked to the door and flung it open. I watched with fear as I saw the look on Chase's face when Damian answered the door. He stepped back then ducked down as Damian swung at him and missed.

I got to my feet as quickly as I could, still struggling to catch my breath. I could hear Damian grunt as Chase swung and made contact with Damian's face, forcing him backward. Chase's eyes looked over me quickly before turning his attention back to Damian. I turned and ducked around the other side of the island as they scuffled toward me, swinging at each other along the way. I knew Chase was strong but I was worried about just how strong Damian was with whatever drugs appeared to be in his system. If he survived and walked away from a car accident a few nights ago, he was pretty much capable of anything.

I reached for my phone and started to dial 911 when Damian pulled out a gun from the back of his jeans and grabbed Chase in a headlock. My eyes went wide as I watched him push the gun against Chase's head while his other arm maintained its grip around Chase's neck.

"Put down the phone. NOW!" His voice boomed loudly as I tossed my phone on the island and raised my hands in surrender as I backed myself up against the kitchen sink.

"You don't want to push me, Mia, I'll put a fucking bullet in his head right now." He was constantly moving which made me nervous that he would accidentally pull the trigger. I looked at Chase as he looked at me and I saw worry lines on his face. It was in that moment that I knew this wasn't going to end well.

"I'm not pushing you, Damian." I took a step forward. "Why don't you just let him go? It's me that you're here for." Another step.

"Mia- don't," Chase said through gritted teeth as Damian's hold around his neck got tighter. My stomach churned as I watched Chase, helpless in Damian's hold.

"This has nothing to do with him. It's about me." I slowly rounded the corner of the island as Damian watched me. "You and me, Damian. Remember?"

His eyes went soft and for a moment I saw the man that I had once fallen in love with. There was a movement behind me and I realized that the door was still open from when Chase came in. I watched as Chase looked at me then looked to the far right before shifting his eyes back to the door. I had no clue what was going on as I slowly stepped to the side as Chase tried to direct me.

There was a loud sound that echoed through the apartment as I whipped my head around and found Noah in the doorway with a gun drawn. I looked around frantically as I searched for who had shot the gun- Damian or Noah. Within seconds Noah was standing in front of me with his gun still aimed at Damian who had released his grip on Chase as he stumbled to the ground.

"You okay man?" Noah called over to Chase who was bent over, trying to catch his breath.

"I'm good." He slowly stood upright and looked down at Damian before kicking the gun away from his hand.

My heart was racing as I watched Noah and Chase go over to Damian and check his pulse before Noah pulled out his cell phone and called 911. Chase came toward me with a look of concern on his face as he looked me over again. My throat was still sore from where Damian had grabbed me and I was pretty sure I would have a few bruises tomorrow from being thrown against the wall. I was lucky that Chase came in when he did, before it got worse. But I felt terrible that he ended up in the middle of it.

"I'm so sorry," I whispered as I began to cry. He rushed to my side and pulled me into his arms as I held onto his shirt, feeling the comfort from his touch.

"I didn't mean for you to get hurt." I stammered between sobs.

"Mia, I'm fine. I didn't get hurt." He leaned back and looked down at me. "Are you sure you're okay? Did he hurt you before I got here?"

"I'm okay." My hand reached up and touched the sore spots on my throat as his eyes followed. "I'm really thankful that you came in when you did. I don't know what he was going to do next. He was acting so strange, almost like he was on drugs." I shuddered as I recalled the way he stared at me as he paced back and forth in front of me.

"Me too." He leaned forward and kissed my forehead.

"What did you want to talk about?" I asked as I looked up at him, suddenly remembering his text about coming over.

"It's a long story but I wanted to apologize to you for not believing you when you said he had been in my house. I called the security company after I found a weird entry while we were at the lake." He sighed as he walked with me over to the couch and we sat down. It wouldn't be long until the place was storming with cops and paramedics and I wanted to make sure we had a chance to talk since it had sounded important.

"What did they say?"

"They had on record that I had called in to request help with the alarm and that they had manually overridden the system after verifying my information. Turned out that I had also updated my password to Damian." He chuckled as he looked over at me.

"I'm sorry that I didn't believe you."

"It doesn't make sense though." My mind tried to wrap around how he could have been at Chase's house in the afternoon on Tuesday and then back in Boston by Wednesday, which was when he had the accident. It was possible that he was never in Boston and someone else had wrecked his car but the wounds on his face seemed pretty consistent with an accident.

"Oh my God." My hand covered my mouth as goosebumps ran up my arms.

"What is it?"

"He was never here. That's why he was 'playing the game'- he wasn't here until this morning. He was stalling, making me think he was here when he wasn't." My head was spinning as I tried to piece together all of the pieces of the psychotic puzzle.

"Why do you say that?"

"Because he told me earlier that I didn't know the things he had to do to get here or that he had been driving all night last night with no sleep. And his face looked like he was in an actual accident. It all makes sense now."

“What accident? I’m so confused.” He leaned back against the couch as I turned my body toward him.

“Jade found out last night that Damian had been in a car accident just outside of Boston. The car had wrapped around a tree and caught fire so they didn’t think there were any survivors. Last night Jade and I thought Damian had died, but apparently he actually survived the accident and drove all the way to Haven Brook without stopping.”

“Then if he wasn’t in my house, then who was?”

“I have no idea. Damian was good at manipulating people. It could have been anyone.” I watched as the room began to swarm with cops and paramedics.

Noah talked to the first officers that came in and I could see him point to Damian as he talked before looking over at Chase and I.

“How did Noah know to come here?” I asked as I watched a female office approach us.

“I was coming to warn you about Damian but I didn’t get a chance to tell Noah so I told him I was coming here and to call me in ten minutes. If I didn’t answer, then he needed to call 911.” He stood up and walked off with the male cop that came to speak with him.

I sat on the couch and answered questions for what felt like hours as I watched the forensic team move around Damian’s body. Soon they had collected what they needed and loaded his body onto the gurney as they zipped up the body bag and wheeled him out. It was comforting to know that this chapter of my life was finally over. There were no questions or doubts in my mind, I finally had all of the answers that I needed and was ready to move on with my life.

Epilogue

1 Year Later

I looked up at the handwritten letter that was taped to the mirror in the bathroom, my daily reminder of where I truly came from. A year ago I was fighting for my life and trying to get away from the one man who had promised to always love me. Now I sat and watched as Jade slipped on her black stiletto heels and smoothed down her red floor length satin bridesmaid gown. She smiled warmly at me in the mirror as my fingers worked the last bobby pin into place. My nerves were starting to get the better of me so I sat back in the chair and read the words that had been calming me since I first read them 11 months ago.

Dearest Mia,

I hope this letter finds you and that you are doing well. I wanted to bring it to you in person but it didn't seem like the right thing to do. The right thing to do would be to forget about the letter and tell you in person, but my hands are shaking so bad trying to write this that I doubt my mouth would have been able to work properly if I tried to tell you in person.

You've been on my mind these past few months, ever since I saw you run out of the woods. I knew you were in trouble and the cop in me wanted to help you. But there was something different about you, something that I didn't know would impact me so deeply until I realized who you were.

And I'd like to say that the moment I saw those blue eyes look at me, I knew who you were. My mind knew what my heart couldn't accept. I'm sure you're wondering what I'm talking about, and I promise, I'll get to the point soon. You had mentioned that you grew up in Colorado, though you never said where. What you didn't know is that I had also grown up in Colorado. When we drove to the hotel I only said that Arlene and I were from Colorado, but I didn't tell you that I grew up in Eastern Point, which as you know, is very close to Haven Brook.

I spent a lot of time in Haven Brook as I was growing up and right after high school I met a girl named Bonnie. I fell madly in love with her and wanted to give her the moon and stars- whatever her beautiful heart wanted. And I tried. I tried constantly to give her what I thought would make her happy, but as you know, the list of things that made her happy was never ending.

Bonnie wanted to move to LA and pursue an acting career but I didn't have the money for us to go. She threatened to leave and even though it broke my heart, I told her she should do what she needed to do, so she could be happy. A few weeks later she told me that she was pregnant and had given up on the LA idea. I was so happy and ecstatic, I couldn't believe that I was going to be a father! I found a second job and started putting money in savings so I could buy us a bigger house. Bonnie found out about the savings and became irate that I would put money into savings for a child I didn't know, but I wouldn't do it to help her get to LA. I tried to reason with her but she left me. Called it quits and left.

I tried desperately to get in touch with her, to ask for another chance. I didn't want to miss out on being part of my child's life. A month had passed before Bonnie finally talked to me and it was to tell me that she had met a director who was going to help her get her acting career started. I asked her about being there so I could help with the baby and she told me that she had an abortion. She felt that if I wasn't supportive of her dream to be an actress, then she wasn't going to allow me my dream of being a father.

She left and I never heard another word from her.

My world had felt like it was collapsing around me. My mother had moved to Haven Brook to try to help me get on my feet again after Bonnie took all of the cash I had been saving for the house. Soon after that, I met Arlene and she was the one who saved me from myself. She convinced me that I had a life worth living and showed me how to love again. We moved to northern Colorado shortly after and I never looked back.

I ignored the letters from my mom as she talked about how Bonnie had come back with a stomach as big as a watermelon, and how Bonnie's little girl looked just like me when I was that age. My mother never gave up on the idea that you were mine and she's sent me updates throughout the years. When you graduated high school. When you moved to Boston. When you got married. She always found a way to stay updated with what was happening in your life.

When I heard you use your real name at the airport, I couldn't believe it. The woman my mother had been telling me about for 25 years was standing right beside me. My heart felt like it was going to give up on me that day and I thought- well at least you got to meet her before you died!

Never in a million years would I have ever imagined that you were mine. It's always felt too good to be true so I never wanted to allow myself to consider it when I would get the updates from my mom. If I allowed myself to believe it, and then it wasn't true, I didn't think I would survive it. My world felt like it had ended the day Bonnie said she had chosen to kill my baby than to allow me to be happy. That's not something that's easy to recover from.

I'm sorry that you grew up thinking that your father walked away and didn't want you. Please know that I have always wanted you. From the moment you were just a thought in my mind, I've always wanted you. I regret not believing my mom. I regret not coming to find you sooner. There are so many regrets, but never will I ever regret meeting Bonnie. Without her, I wouldn't have you.

I know that this doesn't make up for the 25 years of your life that I've missed but I would really love the opportunity to try to get to know you if you'd let me. If not, I understand and wish you the best.

All my best,

Joe

A single tear rolled down my cheek as I read the letter that always made me cry. To feel so much love from someone in a letter- it was mind boggling to me. A huge part of me wished that my mom would never have done what she did to Joe and that I would have been able to grow up knowing my father. How different would my life have been?

I stood up and smoothed down the white lace of my dress as I glanced at the bump that stretched it tight across my stomach. I tried to suck it in and giggled when I realized that it was still there. Gently I rubbed a hand over my swollen belly and closed my eyes as I thought about how lucky I was to be carrying his baby.

"You ready?" Jade's head popped in from behind the door as she reached her hand out for me. I pulled up the fabric behind me and carried it in one hand as I followed Jade down the hallway. The sun was getting ready to set and I was anxious to see Chase. My heart beat faster while I counted down the minutes before I would see him.

Outside I could hear as the music started, a soft sound that floated in through the open door. This was it. This was the moment I had been waiting for. I smiled as Joe walked over to me and held out his arm for me to take it. I wrapped my arm in his as he leaned over and kissed my cheek.

"You look absolutely beautiful. He's a very lucky man." He patted my hand gently as we slowly started walking toward the sliding glass door that led out to the patio. There were lights strung along the rail of the porch and all throughout the trees. Fresh rose petals were scattered along the path that led me to Chase and left a fragrant smell as I slowly walked through them. Everything looked beautiful and for a moment I couldn't believe that this was our backyard, it looked so formal and elegant, while keeping the simplicity of the backyard wedding that I had always dreamed of.

I smiled as Jade and Noah walked down the aisle in front of me, holding hands when they thought no one was looking. They had been dating for a few months but neither of them were ready to label it so we all pretended like we didn't know what was happening. We turned the corner and I could see Chase standing in front of the chairs that were filled with our family and friends. Liam was by his side, standing proud as he held the rings on the pillow. The mountain served as the backdrop behind them with shades of green and yellow illuminated by the setting sun.

Chase's family sat in the front rows while the family I never knew I had until a year ago, sat on the other side of the aisle. I smiled as Arlene watched us walk down the aisle and patted Jean, my grandma, as tears rolled down her cheeks. There was a happiness that overwhelmed me as I felt like my life finally felt complete. The music started to fade as I stood next to Chase. Joe's face lit up as he smiled up at us with tears in his eyes, our arms still wrapped together. I tried to force back the tears that threatened to ruin my makeup when they asked who gave me away and Joe proudly said, her father.

I took Chase's hands in mine as we looked deep into each other's eyes and repeated after the minister. Finally it was time for us to say our own vows and I felt the lump in my throat grow bigger as I listened to Chase speak as he wrapped his hands around my stomach.

"Mia, I have loved you since the day I met you. You are the most incredible person that I've ever met and your strength continues to surprise me. Your life has never been easy but you've always looked on the bright side of things and tried to make the best of everything. I'm so proud that someday you're going to teach our daughter how to do the same." He gently rubbed my tummy as a tear slid down my face.

"I promise to love you forever and to protect both of you, for the rest of my life. You will never have to want for anything because I will live all of my days making sure that you have everything your heart could ever desire. You make me the happiest man in the world and I'm so lucky that I get to call you my wife." He pulled me in and wrapped me in his arms as he leaned down and kissed me. Somewhere in the distance I could hear the words 'you may now.... continue to kiss the bride...' as laughter floated around us. My heart felt full as my husband and I started the beginning of our happily ever after.

****

Thank you so much for reading 'Til Death Do Us Part!

Ready for more? Find out what Noah and Jade are up to in

The Cradle Will Fall (Haven Brook Book 2)

https://www.amazon.com/Cradle-Will-Fall-Samantha-Baca/dp/B08GDK9JBC

Other Books By Samantha Baca

The Haven Brook Series:

'Til Death Do Us Part (Haven Brook Book 1)
https://books2read.com/u/m2RJNR

The Cradle Will Fall (Haven Brook Book 2)
https://books2read.com/u/b6O0QE

The Ties That Bind (Haven Brook Book 3)
https://books2read.com/u/mqgoz8

A Very Haven Christmas (Haven Brook Book 4- Novella)
https://books2read.com/u/mvqGjj

Three Strikes, You're Gone (Haven Brook Book 5)
https://books2read.com/u/mvqL2z

The Dark Shadows Series

Five Steps Ahead (Dark Shadows Book 1)
https://books2read.com/u/38Q0gO

Ten Seconds Too Late (Dark Shadows Book 2)
Coming 2022

Against The Clock (Dark Shadows Book 3)
Coming 2022

Out Of Time (Dark Shadows Book 4)
Coming 2023

The Stone Creek Series (Novellas)

Chocolate Covered Mistletoe (Stone Creek Book 1)
https://books2read.com/u/3LRk9N

Candy Coated Promises (Stone Creek Book 2)
https://books2read.com/u/mldP5Y

Pumpkin Spiced Possibilities (Stone Creek Book 3)
https://books2read.com/u/bojdwV

Stand-Alone Books

One Last Wish
https://books2read.com/u/mqg7D9

Finding Love In Apartment 2C (Novella)
https://books2read.com/u/bze9aZ

Cocky Counsel: A Hero Club Novel
https://books2read.com/u/31Kzkn

Holiday Books

Snow Place To Go
https://books2read.com/u/4A560N

A Christmas Wish
https://books2read.com/u/4EKXpE

Acknowledgments

First and foremost I would like to thank every single person who not only took the time to read this book, but who is also taking the time to read the acknowledgements. From the bottom of my heart, thank you and I appreciate you!

Writing a book was a childhood dream of mine that I was always certain would never come true. Thank you to my friends and family who pushed me and encouraged me over the years to get past my fears and self doubt so I could finally write my book. It wasn't always easy to believe in myself but you made it easier when you refused to give up on me.

I would like to thank my incredible sister, Sarah who not only excitedly offered to read the first draft, but who pushed me to keep working on the edits and to not give up. I appreciate all of the feedback you offered along the way, and that you read the book 3 times as I made significant changes with each draft. Your time and dedication to helping me reach my goals have never gone unnoticed. There are not enough ways to say thank you!

Thank you to my parents for encouraging me from a very young age to push myself harder and go after what I wanted in life. You've always seen things in me that I never saw in myself. Thank you for believing in me and being my biggest supporters. Mom, thank you for taking the time to read this and provide feedback. I love that you were so consumed by this book that it kept you up late at night because you couldn't stop reading it.

Thank you to Erin and Jordan for reading the first two drafts of the book and for giving me honest feedback about how to improve it and make it better. I loved that you were willing to give me advice from a literary perspective as well as from a reader's perspective.

I would like to thank Katie and Danielle for reading the final draft as beta readers and catching any plot holes that I had and for helping me think through things when I would message you with ideas that were stuck in my head. Your feedback was valuable and helped me tighten up the loose ends where needed.

A huge thank you to Debi for reading this as a beta reader as well as being a proofreader. I appreciate the effort you took to catch all of the small details that I missed and for your help with making sure the flow of the book stayed on track.

Last but not least, thank you to my wonderful husband who not only encouraged me to go after my dream the second I told him about it, but has encouraged me every single step of the way. The constant talking about the book and hashing out details to helping me with ways to make it even creepier, I really appreciate your support and feedback. Thanks for being the absolute best editor/proofreader/supporter that I could ever ask for.

To my sweet girls, I pray that one day you will believe in yourself and follow every dream you have. If I can show you anything in this world, I hope to show you that you can do anything you set your mind to. I'll always be your biggest supporter and your loudest cheerleader. If I can do this, I know you can do anything you set your mind to.

About the Author

Samantha lives in the southwest with her husband and two small children after abandoning her childhood dream of living in a cabin in Colorado when she found that she couldn't afford to live there and was deathly allergic to the woods. When she's not writing she's usually spouting off sarcastic remarks while drinking wine out of a coffee mug to look like a functional adult while chasing down her toddlers. She enjoys spending time with her family, watching reruns of FRIENDS, and the 24/7 flow of coffee that can be found in her veins. Be sure to follow her on social media for updates on what she's working on.

You can find her here:

Facebook: https://www.facebook.com/AuthorSamanthaBaca

Instagram: https://instagram.com/author_samantha_baca

Goodreads: http://www.goodreads.com/authorsamanthabaca

Facebook Reader Group: https://www.facebook.com/groups/2945710968775398/

Webpage: https://authorsamanthabaca.wordpress.com

Newsletter: http://eepurl.com/g0NcSj

Made in the USA
Middletown, DE
17 February 2022